EMPIRES IN RUIN

SAVAGE STARS BOOK 6

ANTHONY JAMES

THE CONTROL CORE

The air was chill and the light in the metal-clad viewing room was oppressive, as if the walls exuded their greyness and made everything seem dimmer than it was. An over-sized steel table had been pushed against one wall and the chairs had been removed. Given how much tech the Daklan had crammed into this underground facility, the only sign of it in this room was an ancient-looking commu-nicator over by the door.

Captain Carl Recker stared through the single window into an immense, square room, the alloy floor of which was two hundred metres below. Despite the chill and the gloominess, he felt a sharp-edged excitement, as if this part of the operation was on the brink of success.

In the centre of the huge room, a thirty-metre cube of near-black material was suspended in the air by gravity chains mounted in the ceiling above the viewing window. The cube's housing was dented and scraped. Considering what had befallen the *Aeklu*'s control core, the damage was surprisingly minimal.

Surrounding the control core, dozens of much smaller Obliterator processing units were contained within dedicated floor-mounted cooling blocks which maintained an inside temperature close to absolute zero, allowing the Obliterator cores to overclock – not strictly an accurate term, but one which even the tech teams still clung to - and run far beyond their design tolerances.

Torso-thick data cables linked everything, and teams of human and Daklan engineers crowded around a circular console directly below Recker, studying the output data.

"Soon," said Ilsre-Lunei in a voice that was harsh and rasping yet delivered with a contrasting melodious lilt. "It will happen soon."

Recker turned his gaze from the viewing window to the second occupant of the room. Ilsre-Lunei was female and, like most of the other Daklan females Recker had met, startlingly attractive in an alien way. Her skin was red, her eyes glowed the deepest of greens and her thick hair was dark as night and tied in an elaborate plait. Unlike the males, she was slender and not much taller than six feet.

"How do you know?" Recker asked, wondering if he'd get a straight answer this time.

Ilsre-Lunei grinned, showing perfect, humanlike teeth - humanlike except for the two upward-curving fangs which protruded even when her mouth was closed.

"Do you need to ask, Captain Recker?"

"I guess not."

The Daklan took pity on him. "When you work with the unknown long enough, you get a feel for it."

"It's been eight months," said Recker. "Eight months with those Obliterators running nonstop. I'd like to believe the breakthrough is coming."

Ilsre-Lunei narrowed her eyes. "Now," she said.

At that precise moment, the team of engineers below began clapping each other on the shoulders and one of the human members punched the air in celebration. Then, suddenly, they stopped like the enormity of the outcome was sinking in.

"Done?" asked Recker.

"Yes, Captain Carl Recker. It is done."

"What now?" asked Recker.

"Now we take the fight to our enemies."

"How long until we can use the data, I meant."

Ilsre-Lunei shrugged, somehow making even a dismissive gesture seem elegant. "As long as it takes."

"I thought you had a feeling for the unknown?"

The Daklan grinned, part in happiness and part predatorially. "You itch to be away from here. Pitting yourself against our opponents."

"They're coming for us, Ilsre-Lunei. The Laws of Ancidium. They've had time to modify their Extractors. If we don't stop them, we'll suffer losses beyond imagining."

"This I know," she said.

Ilsre-Lunei stepped back from the window and headed for the door. "Come."

Recker followed.

CHAPTER ONE

THE PLANET TRINUS-XN was a barren sphere of red rock, with a meagre atmosphere of nitrogen, carbon and oxygen, the latter in quantities too low to sustain life, even had the extremes of temperature not been so hostile to its formation. During the long day, the blistering heat of the WDE421-3T star turned the surface into a stark, burning hot oven, while at night, the cold was enough to create a beautiful layer of ice crystals upon every surface. In that darkness, the clear skies allowed a breath-taking glimpse of faraway stars drawn towards the supermassive black hole at the galaxy's centre.

Upon Trinus-XN, the Daklan had built a sprawling facility of monumental proportions - a facility they had named Ivisto. Alloy structures of all shapes and sizes, constructed off-world and transported here, covered hundreds of square kilometres, while the shipyards and landing fields occupied many hundreds more. Six massive ternium plants – two of which were sub-surface - provided endless power, while the nearby mining facilities and refineries allowed Ivisto to create its own alloys and machine them into every conceivable shape and size.

The only thing Ivisto lacked was its own food supply and, every few days, a trio of cargo vessels brought in a shipment of biological matter suitable for use in the base replicators.

The Ivisto base was, Recker believed, the single main reason the less populous Daklan had pulled ahead in the now-settled war with humanity and he wondered if, several decades ago, some bright spark within their military had looked into the future and seen the requirement for a massive shipyard capable of turning out twenty new warships every year. Had the war persisted, it would have been the deciding factor.

Certainly, the Daklan knew how to commit, which was more than could be said for the old guard within the HPA – an old guard which was no longer an effective force since Recker had cut the head off the snake when he fired a lightspeed missile into Fleet Admiral Solan's holiday home from twenty-five million kilometres in space.

The old bastard hadn't seen that one coming.

"What time is your FTL comm with Fleet Admiral Telar, sir?" said Commander Daisy Aston on the suit comms.

The words startled Recker out of his reverie, bringing him back to the present. He looked at the Frenziol-13 injector in his hand and stabbed it into his leg. Everyone on Ivisto took a quarter dose every three hours and a bigger dose before lights out - just in case the Lavorix dropped by to say hello - and the flesh on Recker's thigh burned constantly from the needles and because the Frenziol tended to accumulate in the place it was injected.

Fortunately, he had another thigh, a neck and a couple of ass cheeks – all of which were approved locations for injection – so maybe it was time to share the load.

"You know what time it is," he growled, his irritation at the needles making him sound angrier than he intended. Aston didn't deserve his temper and he forced a laugh. "Or are you just checking to see if I've learned anything more in the ten minutes since last time you asked?"

"This is a fast-moving situation, sir."

Recker turned briefly as he headed for the door. His room was built for a Daklan, which made it surprisingly big compared to the usual fare offered by the HPA. The furnishings weren't much of an improvement, consisting of a bed, a communicator and his own shower cubicle. It certainly wasn't any worse than he was accustomed to. "I'm heading there now. You still want to tag along for the ride?"

"Absolutely."

"Don't take long. I'll meet you at the airlock."

Recker exited his room into a long corridor, wide enough for two Daklan in combat suits to pass. The airlock was a short distance right, while to the left, other doors led to other rooms occupied by other officers.

He waited at the airlock, drumming his fingers and checking his gauss rifle. Less than two minutes later, Aston emerged from one of the airlifts in the corridor, forty metres away, wearing full combat gear and carrying her own gauss rifle. Moments later, she was standing in front of Recker and through the visor of her helmet, she grinned.

"I haven't checked on the construction progress for a few hours," she said in mock apology.

"A watched spaceship is never built," said Recker.

"You look worried, sir," said Aston, frowning and peering at him closely.

Recker didn't answer at once and he touched the access panel for the airlock. A light went green and then he pulled a horizontal lever in the middle of the door into its upright position. The door swung open soundlessly to reveal the three-metre-square airlock room. "It's been two months since we cracked the *Aeklu*'s control core. Each morning I wake up asking myself if today's the day the Laws of Ancidium will drop into Earth orbit and start firing their Extractors."

Aston tried to smile. "The construction work is coming along well. Last I heard, we're a month ahead of schedule on both ships."

"Those are long build schedules, Commander."

"I know. But they'll be ready soon."

Soon was a word Recker had heard too often of late. Everything was coming soon. Not now, not today, not yesterday, but sometime in that vague, undefined future known as *soon*.

"Come on," he said, hauling open the outer airlock door.

Bright light and the beating notes of a thousand propulsions flooded in, and Recker's suit HUD told him it was hot enough outside to boil an egg. He stepped over the raised lip of the doorway and onto the planet's desert-red stone which the Daklan had built directly onto.

A few metres out of the airlock and Recker turned briefly. Behind him, the building in which he was quartered was a three-storey, windowless, flat-fronted affair accessed by half a dozen ground-level doors. Similarly uninspiring buildings rose left and right, these ones housing many of the human technicians who'd been shipped in to work on the project which had taken up the entire output of the base.

To the left, one of the huge construction domes loomed, and it had always made Recker think of an alloy moon dropping below the horizon. Beyond the dome and higher yet, the eight-thousand-metre tenixite converter recovered by the Daklan only two years ago, seemed to reach for orbit in an unwelcome reminder of the Lavorix's technological might.

This was one of the quieter areas of Ivisto, with the only visible personnel being a few small groups of technicians, mostly heading for the elevated concrete shuttle pad a short distance away. A row of bulky Daklan gravity cars was parked in a line at the base of the ramp leading to the top of the pad, and several humans were talking animatedly nearby.

"Let's get to the shuttle," said Recker, pointing at the row of eight vessels on top of the landing pad.

He set off. Despite being stationed here for so long, Ivisto still felt utterly strange – a clash between technology and the barrenness of the universe. When he looked up, the sky was dark, while the ground was lit. All around, the mishmash of prefabricated buildings seemed like they had no place here. Yet somehow it all worked and Recker was comfortable.

"Have you spoken to Joe and Lois today?" said Aston.

Recker had never got used to hearing his parents called by their first names. "On time, like always. How's your brother?"

"Being a little shitbag." Aston smiled. "Like always." The smile fell away. "Everyone's scared, Carl. They don't say it and..." she faltered. "...and it sucks that we have to live with this hanging over our heads."

"I tell myself I can only do my best," said Recker. "It's going to be enough. And if it isn't..." He forced a smile of his own. "This is what Ivisto is here for, right? The big project to fix everything and make it right."

The concrete ramp leading to the top of the shuttle pad was fifty metres long and it was steep. By the time he reached the top, the muscles in Recker's legs were filled with the pleasant glow of exercise. The landing pad was 250 metres wide and the parked vessels were identical round-edged rectangles with squared-off noses, chain guns and armour. They didn't look much different to the models Recker had encountered in the past – in the times he'd have been exchanging gunfire with them.

"That's our shuttle," he said, pointing left.

A few mixed squads of human and Daklan soldiers patrolled the top of the shuttle pad, the latter appearing like giants in their combat suits. Recker glanced at one of the alien soldiers as he went past. The Daklan met his gaze and offered him a nod of acknowledgement.

"It's like the war never happened," said Aston.

"Maybe one day I'll understand it all," said Recker.

"Right this moment, I'm happy to accept the Daklan for what they are – strong, reliable allies."

He climbed up the steps leading to the side door in the shuttle's nose and thumped his hand on the access panel. The door opened and he squeezed into the smallest of airlock spaces along with Aston. Moments later, the airlock cycled and they entered the cockpit.

"Let's get going," said Recker, hardly noticing the rudimental console, nor the overly wide bucket seats. He wrapped fingers around the controls, while Aston brought up the sensors.

Like a car windscreen, the forward bulkhead became transparent and the feed wrapped 120-degrees around the cockpit. Nothing had changed outside, though visibility from the shuttle's greater elevation hinted at the extent of the base.

"We're clear on the flank and rear feeds," Aston confirmed. "And no passengers in the bay."

Recker checked in with the base mainframe and obtained flight clearance. Then, he brought the shuttle vertically into the air, leaving a gap in the parked row of transports.

"Comms Hub 3," said Aston.

"Yes. Our flight path goes straight past the main trenches."

At an altitude of five thousand metres, Recker turned the shuttle and aimed it towards the comms hub. The sky was crowded with silvery movement from the countless smaller vessels flying to and fro across Ivisto. A lower ranking officer would be required to activate the autopilot, but the Daklan gave senior officers more leeway.

Compared to the HPA's safety-first mentality, the aliens were decidedly hands-off - something Recker found liberating.

Engines grumbling, the shuttle accelerated across Ivisto. From this altitude, it was clear what an incredible quantity of resources had gone into the base, and not all invested by the Daklan. The aliens had laid the ground-work and much more, but in the ten months since the formal peace was signed, the HPA had done everything possible – financially and militarily – to assist with the expansion of Ivisto.

"There's the shipyard," said Aston.

Way across the tops of warehouses, domes and towers, the main shipyard was situated on a fifty-by-fifty-kilo-metre square of alloy-clad stone. To form the northern end of the square, the Daklan had been forced to excavate a high ridge, which they done – Recker believed – with the assistance of high explosives. Now, a five-hundred-metre vertical wall rose from the northern edge of the construction yard and this marked the perimeter of the base.

"The *Aeklu* and the *Verumol*," said Aston, shaking her head in awed wonder.

Recker felt the same emotions when he gazed at the two incredible hulls side-by-side in their construction trenches. They were so vast, they filled the shipyard and left no room for anything besides the stacks of ternium modules, the armour plates and the piles of control tech that needed to go inside to replace the Lavorix originals.

Aside from the hope and expectation, Recker also felt a clinging fear, which hung about his shoulders like a cloak of blood-sopping rags. The memory of what these two spaceships had once been was still strong.

"The *Aeklu* and the *Verumol*," he repeated quietly. "Disabled by the Dark Bomb but not destroyed."

"Near as damnit destroyed," said Aston.

It wasn't true and she knew it. Both Laws of Ancidium had been nose-first to the Dark Bomb at the time of detonation and their energy shields had – incredibly – soaked much of the half-billion-kilometre blast. The *Aeklu* had lost three thousand metres of its nose and its engines had been knocked offline, leaving it with no power for the life support or weapons. At the same time, the *Verumol* had lost nearer five thousand metres from its nose section and underside.

Recker wasn't strictly permitted, but he guided the shuttle closer to the two parallel warships, taking care he didn't interfere with the swarms of lifters and numerous other dedicated construction craft in the vicinity. The air in the cockpit became thick with vibration from the rows of immense gravity field generators which were holding the two captured warships above the ground, and a dull pain developed behind Recker's eyes.

A moment later, the base mainframe and then one of the senior ground operators gave him a friendly comms warning to let him know he should get out of the damned airspace. Recker smiled inwardly since he wasn't anywhere near the construction traffic. The ground operator cursed openly about sightseers and spaceholes, and cut the channel.

The two Laws of Ancidium were warships beyond imagination. At twenty-eight thousand metres and with a sixteen thousand metre beam, the reconstructed *Verumol* was the smaller of the two vessels. Its diamond shaped hull rose twelve thousand metres above the edges of the huge construction trench and a thousand or more repair craft worked to patch up its nose section. The rest of its armour was pitted and darkened to near black by the Dark Bomb explosion, but spit and polish was far down the priority list. Recker had always thought it was the older of the two spaceships, even if he preferred its design.

Adjacent, the *Aeklu* was larger by mass and volume. Rebuilt to its original thirty-two thousand metres, it rose almost twenty thousand from its trench, with a maximum beam of eighteen thousand.

The human and Daklan weapons engineers had been struggling to recreate the eight-thousand-metre barrel of the warship's main armament, which had been torn off in the blast. The Ivisto fabrication plant had manufactured a two thousand metre replacement – which was already installed – and the weapons teams were figuring out the means to fit rifled extensions that would increase the accuracy.

Aside from that, they'd got the turret motors and the magazine feed working, but nobody had even speculated on a test date. If the engineers couldn't be confident it was safe, maybe the gun would never fire again.

Like the *Verumol*, the *Aeklu* was also scarred and pocked from the explosion. The only data on the Dark Bomb blast came from the warship *Vengeance*'s sensors and so far, the scientists hadn't made much sense out of it. With no sign of a consensus, Recker didn't imagine the

HPA-Daklan alliance would be building Dark Bombs anytime soon.

"Have you seen enough, Commander?" he asked. Only a few thousand metres separated the former Laws of Ancidium in the shipyard and the two hulls were like alloy cliffs flanking the shuttle.

"Yes," said Aston. "Not much work left to do on the hulls."

"The interior refit will take another month from installation to testing," said Recker. "Then, if we defeat the Lavorix, both the *Aeklu* and the *Verumol* will be back in dock to iron out all the problems we can't waste time looking at now. That alone will likely see them grounded for a year or more."

"This is only a patch-up, I know," said Aston. "It makes me feel better to see it happening so quickly."

Recker brought the shuttle into a steep climb and it rose above the sides of the two warships. From this altitude, the sensors had a perfect view east through the clear skies, across the shipyard and then to the landing field beyond that.

Two desolators – the *Incendus* and the *Olsear* – were parked closest and their 2800-metre hulls, with front and rear Terrus cannons, blocked Recker's view of the terminator class *Vengeance*, which was at the farthest end of the landing field. It was a few days since he'd flown the warship and he was due back on patrol duties in thirty-six hours.

Denied a view of his spaceship, Recker took the most efficient route away from the construction yard airspace and got back on course for Comms Hub 3.

"You planning to wait around while I talk to Fleet Admiral Telar, Commander?"

"Hell no, sir. Adam and Jo are in the comms hub and I'm going to pester them. I asked Ken if he'd like a catch up, but as you're aware, he spends all his time with his new Daklan engine buddies in the shipyard."

"Discussing output charts and overstress rates."

"Scratching their asses and reminiscing about the good old days of valves and pistons, more like."

Recker laughed – Lieutenant Eastwood lived for new tech and he always got angry when accused of having an attachment to the obsolete. Naturally, the more he complained, the more he got.

Aston fished out a Frenziol injector, stared at it ruefully and then jabbed herself in the thigh. "I don't even get a buzz anymore."

"I'm glad – I long ago got sick of listening to everyone talk bullshit because they were on a Frenziol high," said Recker.

"I miss the constant feeling of contentment, even if it was artificial," Aston admitted. She pointed at the bulkhead screen. "There's Hub 3."

"I see it," said Recker.

The comms hub was a flat building, easily identifiable by the array of kilometre-high ternium amplifiers protruding from its roof. A recent breakthrough – resulting from a human and Daklan collaboration – had discovered a method of overstressing the ternium in those amplifiers at the same moment as a data packet went through. The result was that the transmission packets were hurled towards their destination at an enormously increased lightspeed multiplier.

A few tweaks at the receiving end and suddenly, FTL comms were passing between planets in minutes rather than hours. Whispers of real time transmissions were being heard amongst the theory teams, and that would be the most exciting development in comms technology for a hundred years.

The sight of the *Aeklu* and *Verumol*, combined with thoughts of technological advancements caused a wave of optimism to sweep through Recker. With the breakthrough on the *Aeklu*'s intact control core, the future wasn't as bleak as it might have been.

Holding onto his good mood, Recker brought the shuttle down to land on the pad outside the comms hub. He and Aston left the transport and hurried down the concrete ramp. A two-hundred-metre plaza in front of the hub was flanked by five-storey buildings on both sides, while a much larger dome was visible behind the left-hand structure. Larger yet, the eight-thousand metre tenixite converter was less than three kilometres from the hub and it towered over every other building. Seeing it made Recker shiver with a memory of what the converters could do when they were controlled by the wrong hands.

He averted his gaze and instead checked the road which entered the square from two directions adjacent to the bottom of the shuttle pad ramp. Gravity vehicles sped both ways, most of them carrying Daklan rather than human passengers.

Since the comms hub was a vital cog in base operations,

the Daklan had parked a pair of matte grey tanks in front of the building, one on each side of the entrance. Recker cast his eye over the vehicles – they were of a type he hadn't encountered until recently. At twenty-five metres in length, twelve wide and nine high, they were mean-looking and angular, with twin gauss main armaments, complemented by shoulder launchers and chain guns. Had Recker seen one of these heading towards his ground squad back when the HPA and Daklan were at war, he'd have known the game was up.

He and Aston made their way across the plaza, dodging moving vehicles and the other personnel, most of whom were on their way to or from the comms hub. At this end of Ivisto, the Daklan outnumbered humans many times over, though the aliens didn't so much as spare them a glance.

The tanks' gravity drives produced a low, yet penetrating hum, which, for the time it took Recker and Aston to walk between the vehicles, drowned out most of the other propulsion sounds from the shuttles above. They entered the five-storey hub through an ingenious rotating airlock which was designed to let dozens of people enter and exit at the same time without having to wait for the atmosphere to cycle.

A couple of Daklan entered the same compartment as Recker and Aston. The aliens didn't say anything and, in fact, didn't acknowledge the presence of the two humans. Recker didn't take it personally – the Daklan didn't go in for small talk. If they had nothing to say, they didn't feel obliged to come up with random crap just to fill the silence.

The lobby area was large and with a high ceiling.

Several passages led deeper into the building and many Daklan were in evidence, most of them female and all wearing spacesuits in a variety of colours. If you could forget the lack of windows and ignore the fact that the walls were unadorned alloy, this could almost have been just another comms hub on any one of fifty military bases. Almost.

"I'm going this way," said Aston, thumbing left.

Recker checked the time on his HUD - he was a few minutes early.

"I'll catch up with you later."

"I'll wait for you, sir." Aston grinned again. It was an impudent grin that no one could be offended by.

"Hanging on for the news, I'm sure."

"You're expecting news?" she asked, quick as a flash.

"Go," Recker waved her away.

With that, he headed towards his meeting. He'd been trying to hide it from Aston, but he suspected something big was imminent. After so long here on Ivisto, the start couldn't come soon enough. Recker quickened his pace.

CHAPTER TWO

THE MEETING ROOM was another boxy space in the already boxy comms hub. Like Recker's quarters, it was meant for burly Daklan, which made the quantity of space tolerable, though the unpadded seats would have been more palatable to 14th Century flagellating monks than those with untreated piles.

Luckily, Recker was in good health and the thick material of his combat suit made his perch bearable. He watched the viewscreen on the opposite wall and waited for the connection. At his side, a cup of evil Daklan brew steamed menacingly, daring him to partake of its contents. The rough translation for the drink's name was *crap*, yet the aliens couldn't get enough of it. He accepted the unspoken challenge and winced at the sharp taste. Truly the universe was a strange and wonderful place to accommodate such differences.

The dark viewscreen turned grey and static appeared, along with a burst of white noise from the ceiling speakers. A distorted image appeared, wobbled, and then stabilised.

"Carl," said Admiral Telar. The oak panelled walls in the background and framed picture of Telar's wife and three children indicated he was in his office on Earth.

"Sir," Recker greeted in return.

"How is Trinus-XN treating you?"

"Same as last time, sir."

The corner of Telar's mouth twitched upwards. "That's the formalities out of the way. Let's talk business."

"The evacuation of Lustre," said Recker, getting in quickly. "Is it complete?"

"It has reached the stage where I will expend no more resources attempting to persuade the stubborn. The last remaining soldiers have been withdrawn and the planet is without formal law enforcement. I have done what I can."

Recker could only imagine the logistics involved in evacuating seventeen billion people and finding them somewhere else to live. Doubtless Telar's few words hid endless tales of tragedy and loss, and for that the Lavorix were to blame.

"You can only give people so many chances." Recker briefly wondered if he was being unsympathetic, but then his expression hardened. The enemy wouldn't give quarter and everyone in the HPA was making sacrifices - it was the only way. "What's in the future, sir?"

"Something big."

Recker leaned forward. "Are the plans finalised, sir? Are we ready to act?"

"Soon, Carl."

That word again.

"How soon?"

"We'll talk about it in a moment." Telar pursed his lips and steepled long fingers, his expression inscrutable.

"You've got news," said Recker. "Something you don't like."

"It's news," Telar confirmed. "Whether it's good or bad, I haven't yet decided."

Recker's gaze didn't waver. "Tell me."

"You were present when we cracked the Lavorix comms and control encryption," said Telar. "And you know the processing core didn't contain the *Aeklu*'s transmission logs."

"Yes, sir – Ilsre-Lunei told me at the time the control core wasn't a data repository."

Telar's dark eyes gleamed. "And she was right. However, when the Dark Bomb shut down the power, the core was holding transient comms files which were on route to their storage arrays."

Recker straightened. "What was in those files?"

"Amongst the traffic, we found evidence the Lavorix are losing their war against the Kilvar. We believe they are planning a withdrawal."

"The Lavorix never struck me as the running type, sir. I was told their war was a holy one. Everything about the enemy makes me think they will not back down in a confrontation."

"A threat of annihilation does wonders for one's convictions, don't you think?" asked Telar. "Besides, you'll notice I said *withdrawal*, rather than full-scale retreat."

"The Lavorix home world is the Ancidium," said Recker.

"We don't know what the Ancidium is or where it is located, but it is logical to assume the Kilvar have not found it, otherwise it would have been destroyed."

Ever since he'd heard about the Ancidium, Recker had pondered what sort of place it might be. He had ideas in plenty and no way to confirm they were true. "The Ancidium may not be an easy target, sir."

"A target is a target, whether it's an easy one or not. With sufficient pressure applied, the Ancidium would fall."

Recker knew it too. "So we assume the Lavorix withdraw to the Ancidium. What then?"

"The Lavorix laid waste to Meklon territory, leaving behind many usable assets. Perhaps they will reclaim those assets and put them to use against the Kilvar."

"And if the Lavorix plan to resume their war, they will also require fuel in the form of life energy," said Recker, guessing which way the conversation was heading.

"Resources and fuel," nodded Telar. "They have a source of one and knowledge of the other."

"They'll turn their focus towards the HPA and the Daklan," said Recker.

"We've assumed – quite naturally, since our existence is under threat – that we are an important consideration to the Lavorix, when it is more likely we are no more than a distraction." Telar gave a fleeting smile. "Before we destroyed three of their capital ships, I doubt we were even a distraction."

"Just a source of life energy to be tapped once the Meklon were gone," said Recker bitterly.

"Tell me, Carl – how is the work on the *Aeklu* and

Verumol progressing? I would like your opinion on the anticipated results."

"We've got our best construction teams here, sir, as have the Daklan."

"Go on."

"Both of those ships could fly within the hour if it was important enough to give the order." Recker narrowed his eyes at the viewscreen.

"The order isn't coming yet," said Telar. "Go on."

"Our life support units don't have the capability to cover the interior of either the *Verumol* or the *Aeklu*. We'll have to accept partial coverage."

"Yes, that's something it'll take us at least two years to resolve. What else?"

"With the decryption of the *Aeklu*'s control systems, we can replicate the necessary commands to activate the weaponry and energy shields on both the *Aeklu* and the *Verumol*."

"Almost everything apart from the Extractor will function once the reconstruction work is finished," said Telar. "We have dozens of Obliterator cores working on the *Aeklu*'s data arrays."

"And since those data arrays are still inside the vessel's hull, that work will stop the moment the spaceship is required for action."

Telar nodded. "It is vital we decrypt the Lavorix star charts. Without those, we are at their mercy, passively awaiting an attack on our planets."

"I'm confused, sir," said Recker. "One moment you're talking like you'll order the *Aeklu* and *Verumol* out of their trenches, the next you're concerned about star charts – star charts we can't extract once the spaceships are ordered to active duty."

"You're hearing the words, Carl, but the message has flown by."

Recker kept his expression neutral, while he thought hard. "We don't need to be passive. We can use the Lavorix's own comms system as a lure to draw them into an attack at a place of our choosing. They won't know we'll be fighting them with their own warships, giving us a chance to kick the crap out of their fleet."

Now Telar smiled. "That's what I'm planning," he said. "In collaboration, of course – our Daklan allies have much to say on the subject."

"Are the plans finalised?" asked Recker.

"Not yet. We're still outgunned – at least according to our projections based on known data – and we don't yet want to commit to an all-or-nothing confrontation that might wipe out our fleet."

"The *Aeklu* and the *Verumol*, along with support craft will be a challenge for anything, sir." The irony of describing Daklan annihilators and HPA battleships as *support craft* wasn't lost on Recker. He continued. "We don't need to send our entire fleet."

"Our primary objective is to knock out the Laws of Ancidium," said Telar. "I don't need to spell out the problem with that." His image flickered on the screen and then steadied.

"The Lavorix control three Laws of Ancidium and we control only two," said Recker. "On top of that, the Lavorix crews are experienced and their ships are likely to be in full working order."

"That is why we must set our trap carefully."

"What kind of trap?"

"Something which will level the playing field."

Telar liked to string out his revelations, which could, at times, be frustrating. Having no choice other than to go with it, Recker invited the disclosure. "We've been working on some new tech."

"Not new tech, Carl! Tech which was already in our control! A weapon!"

Light dawned. "We built another Tri-Cannon?"

"Not the side guns, but we have another shield breaker." Telar thumped his fist on the table and that alone was enough to betray how much of a triumph he felt this was. "A shield breaker we will conceal on a planet and which we will use against our enemies!"

Telar wasn't usually demonstrative in his excitement and it started rubbing off on Recker. "I don't see why the plan shouldn't work, sir. It'll be tough – especially against the Extractors – but if we strike hard, we'll teach those Lavorix bastards that it isn't only the Kilvar they have to fear."

"You'll be flying the *Aeklu*, Carl," said Telar. "You're the one I most trust to get a result."

The confirmation of something Recker had expected nevertheless came as a surprise.

"Thank you, sir, it's an honour." Adrenaline pumped into his body and he bared his teeth. "I'll give the enemy hell."

"You're damn right you will. I spoke to the *Aeklu*'s chief construction officer earlier today and ordered him to accelerate the installation of our control tech. Once the mission gets the all-clear, everything on the bridge will be familiar to you. I'll issue you the command codes we extracted from the control core. Without those codes, the *Aeklu*'s backend systems will lock out our hardware after a few minutes."

"Yes, sir, I know." Recker's pocket communicator buzzed and he looked at it surreptitiously. "The command codes arrived."

"Good. Upload them to your suit computer."

"I'll do that, sir. Who have the Daklan chosen to command the *Verumol*?"

"Captain Razdin-Tiel," said Telar. The stream became heavily pixelated, as if the FTL comm was on the verge of dropping out. After a second, it cleared up.

"I don't recall the name," said Recker.

"He was involved in the Daklan attack on Lustre. Damn, that seems like a lifetime ago," said Telar without humour. "Captain Razdin-Tiel has had a long and fruitful career. Unfortunately, most of that career was spent destroying HPA spaceships." Telar's face showed he didn't hold a grudge.

"I should meet him."

"I'll leave you to make the arrangements. Captain Razdin-Tiel will be with you for the mission. The command hierarchy is not yet agreed, though I expect we will settle on an equal partnership."

"Whatever comes, I'll deal with it."

"I don't doubt it for a moment, Carl."

"I'll have my choice of crew and soldiers for the *Aeklu*, sir."

Telar gave a mock sigh. "A concession I will happily

grant. However, the *Aeklu* will require a crew of eight, rather than five."

"I'm sure you'll pick the best officers to fill the gaps, sir."

"I have already chosen, and your additional crew members, plus backups, are currently in transit from Earth. They should arrive within forty-eight hours, by which point the final equipment will be installed onto the *Aeklu*'s bridge and the tie-ins completed. You will begin full-scale preparations at that moment."

"Yes, sir. How long do I have?" Recker pressed.

"There's never enough time, Carl," said Telar evasively. "You know that as well as I do."

Again, the FTL comms link went shaky and Recker waited for it to stabilise. This time, it went dead, leaving him staring at a blank screen. The meeting had been winding down, but sometimes Telar stored up a juicy morsel for last-moment delivery. With a shrug, Recker stretched across to the desktop communicator and requested a new channel. An error appeared on the hardware and when he saw it, Recker was frozen, unable to believe what he was seeing.

Null response #0

It was the same code he'd seen time and again on both the *Indarox* interstellar and the Empiron-1 deep space construction station – a code he'd come to hate.

Not here. Not now.

Before he could raise the alarm, Recker was gripped by the agony of an Extractor attack.

CHAPTER THREE

WHEN RECKER REGAINED CONSCIOUSNESS, his first thoughts weren't of pain but of anger. The Lavorix had somehow managed to attack Ivisto with such speed that the early warning alarms hadn't triggered. Those alarms were sounding now, in the corridor outside and no doubt across the entire base.

Snarling, Recker grabbed the edge of the table with both hands and hauled himself upright. His head thudded and his vision went out of focus. Unsteady fingers withdrew a Frenziol injector from his leg pocket and Recker stabbed himself with feeling. Drugs entered his veins and, when he dropped his suit helmet into place, the HUD warned him his heart rate was climbing.

Too much Frenziol.

Recker dragged his thoughts into a semblance of order. The Lavorix had come to Trinus-XN, which meant the outlook for the HPA and Daklan was likely dire.

He leaned across the table and checked the desktop communicator. It was still showing a null response, which meant the enemy had disabled it for the foreseeable. Recker tested the comms unit in his suit and it linked straight away to a man who knew a thing or two about fighting in the most terrible of circumstances.

"Sir, all hell's breaking loose here," said Sergeant Vance.

"Where are you Sergeant?"

Vance talked at his usual pace and in his usual tone. This was just another day at the office. "Barracks 12, sir. The platoon is with me. I can hear explosions outside but we're still getting on our feet here."

"I need intel, Sergeant. Tool up and await orders."

"We're staying put?"

"Yes – keep your heads down until I learn more about the situation."

"This isn't a wipe out attack, sir," said Vance. "If it was, the Lavorix would have dropped incendiaries."

Recker was starting to piece things together. "I think they came believing it would be a simple attack and kill mission, Sergeant. It must have come as a surprise for them to find the *Aeklu* and the *Verumol* in those construction trenches."

"They've changed their mission," said Vance.

"That's what I think, Sergeant. They'll attempt a recapture of their warships."

"Barracks 12 is four thousand metres from the edge of the construction yard, sir. After that, it's a long run to the *Aeklu*, and the *Verumol* is further still."

"Like I said, hold steady. I need more information before I send you out of cover."

"We'll listen for the word, sir."

Recker closed the channel. A dozen or more connection request lights were flashing on his comms unit. He located the one he was looking for and linked.

"Commander Aston, a shitstorm has come to Trinus-XN."

"The enemy want their ships back, sir."

"That's the same conclusion I've reached. We'll have to stop them."

"It's going to be tough."

"I've had enough of these Lavorix assholes, Commander. The *Aeklu* and the *Verumol* are ours now and I'm damned if I'm giving them up."

"We had a fleet in orbit and we saw those two desolators on the landing strip."

"And the *Vengeance*, Commander. Eighty klicks away and out of reach." Recker gritted his teeth. "I hate being blind," he said. "We had enough firepower in the air to give the Lavorix something to think about. If we're lucky, they're holding the enemy at bay. Maybe they'll even drive off whichever capital ship dropped out of lightspeed on top of us."

At that moment, Recker felt and heard a booming explosion somewhere outside the comms hub. The alloy walls shook with the magnitude of the blast and a second followed close behind. For a second, the lights went out before they came on again.

"Should I stop and check inside one of the comms

rooms?" said Aston. "They have links to the orbital sensors from here."

Recker wanted to say yes, but interfering with the comms teams wouldn't help anyone. They had enough to deal with.

"Let the personnel do their work, Commander. We'll pick up the details when we can."

"Do you have a plan yet, sir?" said Aston.

"I'm working on it. Speak to Ken, Adam and Jo. Find out where they are and tell them to be ready."

"The Lavorix haven't laid waste to Ivisto yet – that means they're considering their options."

"I know – this is our opportunity to act. The Lavorix don't piss about, so whatever they decide, it'll happen soon." Recker headed for the door. "I'll meet you in the entrance lobby."

He closed out of the channel and touched the door access panel, half-expecting the enemy to have locked down the base security as well. The door opened without hesitation and Recker exited the room. Out in the corridor, the alarm was louder and the sound had a sharp edge which made him glad he was wearing his helmet.

A few Daklan were visible, heading in different directions. They weren't running – in fact, they didn't look at all perturbed by events. There again, the aliens didn't usually get emotional, even when the bullets were flying.

Recker walked instead of sprinting, only because he needed the time to think. A new comms request came in from the base commander – a Daklan officer called Daxtil-Tilok who had a rank which didn't directly translate into an HPA equivalent. On the single occasion Recker had met Daxtil-Tilok, he'd been impressed by the Daklan's aura of competence and he felt sure the base defence was in good hands. It would need to be.

Accepting the channel request, Recker informed the Daklan of his belief that the Lavorix planned to steal back the Laws of Ancidium. The base commander agreed and added his own take on the situation.

"Ivisto is home to two million personnel, Captain Recker. It is possible the enemy have arrived in sufficient numbers to sweep and eradicate, but I doubt they are here for an extended campaign."

"They'll focus their efforts on the shipyard and destroy everything else," said Recker.

"I believe that is the most likely outcome."

"I'll leave you to your job, Daxtil-Tilok."

The Daklan wasn't finished. "You are in Comms Hub 3 on the construction yard outskirts," he said. "You will do what needs to be done."

"Yes."

Without a further word, Daxtil-Tilok cut the channel, leaving Recker cursing the situation. He mentally pictured the base map. The command and control areas were central, and most of the personnel worked in the research and manufacturing areas south of that. While the construction yard was the largest area of Ivisto, much of the work there was automated. A couple of well-placed incendiaries would kill most of the personnel, leaving the *Aeklu* and *Verumol* untouched.

Recker had an idea and he requested a channel to Captain Razdin-Tiel, who was to be in command of the *Verumol*.

"Greetings, Captain Recker." The Daklan had a voice like fingernails across a sheet of coarse sandpaper.

"I thought I'd introduce myself," said Recker, stepping over one of the hub personnel who hadn't yet regained consciousness from the Extractor attack and was slumped across his path.

"Greetings. We will not be undone by this," said Razdin-Tiel.

"Not if I have any say. The enemy want their spaceships back. Since they didn't set off the base alarms before firing the Extractor, they must be at long range. If they want to put troops on the ground, they'll have to send in transports."

"To do so they must neutralise both our fleet and our ground launchers," said Razdin-Tiel. "Whatever happens, our casualties will be enormous."

"If we lose the *Aeklu* and the *Verumol*, our war may as well be over," said Recker.

"I agree. I have commandeered some trusted soldiers and will attempt to reach the *Verumol* – it has Daklan equipment already installed and I believe it will fly."

"I see we think alike," said Recker. "I'm planning to board the *Aeklu* – if we're lucky we'll both make it. If we're even luckier, our warships will hang together during lift-off and their weapons systems will fire as intended."

"We will make our own luck, Captain Recker. Anger burns within me and it requires an outlet. I wish to bite the heads off a thousand Lavorix and spit bile into their blood-jetting arteries."

The Daklan talked a good fight and Recker had no doubt his skills and experience matched the talk.

"Have you got a comms link to the defence fleet, Captain Razdin-Tiel?"

"No – the main ground comms are disabled as you've already gathered. This is only a small problem for our warships, since they can link directly to our comms units, but so far I have heard nothing. I cannot offer anything useful from my position on the ground, so would not expect my brothers in arms to waste time speaking with me. Admiral Ivinstol commands fleet operations – I will not interfere."

"Some intel might help us reach the *Aeklu* and *Verumol*."

"Yes – I will request details when the moment is right."

Recker had no idea when the moment might be right, though he understood Razdin-Tiel's reluctance to stick his oar into the middle of an ongoing battle. Doubtless the comms crews on every warship were already inundated with countless requests for information, so it was vital that Admiral Ivinstol had a clear comms path to every operational warship.

Commander Aston was waiting with Lieutenants Burner and Larson at the entrance lobby, and they were all armed with gauss rifles. The hub was primarily operated by Daklan, and Recker's crew looked small amongst the huge aliens who strode across the floor.

"None of them are leaving," said Aston, indicating the hub personnel. "And no sign of panic."

"Have you spoken to anyone in the know?"

"There's nobody in the know, sir - the cause of the failure is still undetermined."

In the past, the Lavorix had used a combination of physical devices and their ranged core override to control HPA and Daklan hardware. It was highly unlikely that enemy soldiers had infiltrated all four of the comms hubs without the alarm being raised, which meant they'd fired a core override. Recker knew from experience what a pain in the ass the weapon could be – a pain in the ass that was only recently beaten into second place by the Extractors.

The moment he thought the word *Extractor*, he was hit by the weapon again. Recker's lips drew back involuntarily and his legs felt weak. Nearby, Aston's closed her eyes tightly and her expression was one of absolute concentration. Meanwhile, Burner swore and the usually clean-mouthed Larson uttered a few oaths that would have turned a veteran trooper's ears red.

"Hell no," Aston said, struggling against the weapon's effects.

Recker fought back too, with the assistance of the Frenziol-13 he'd recently injected. The pain of the Extractor was no better and no worse than it always was, and a far corner of his mind recognized this as a positive. It was better to suffer transient agony and live than to drop dead and have the energy from his cells channelled into a battery somewhere on a Lavorix capital ship.

The Daklan weren't quite so resistant to the effects. Several keeled over, while others lowered themselves to the ground, panting and with their eyes aimed at the floor. Not one called for assistance and Recker was impressed by their stoicism.

When the worst of it passed, he checked around in case any of the nearby personnel required immediate medical intervention - not that he was knowledgeable enough to offer anything beyond a Frenziol-13 injection.

"Do I get a prize if I guess what the plan is, sir?" said Aston. Her face was screwed up from the aftereffects, but she had a firm grip on her rifle.

"There's a plan?" asked Burner, his unruly mop of curly hair sticking to the cold sweat on his forehead.

"I thought you'd have guessed it by now, Commander," said Recker, ignoring Burner's question.

"We're going to board the *Vengeance* and then shoot down a few Lavorix warships," said Aston confidently.

"Not this time – we'll be flying something bigger."

Aston's eyes widened. "The *Aeklu* isn't meant to fly, let alone engage the enemy."

"The Lavorix are here for that ship, Commander. What better way to stop them than by flying it out of the construction trench ourselves?"

"It's an eight-klick run from the main portside entrance to the bridge," she said.

"Didn't you hear? They got the original topside airlifts working again. That cuts the running to an easy five hundred metres."

"Whatever you say, sir. The *Aeklu* it is."

A third explosion came, this one louder and nearer than the earlier two combined. The walls and floors shook harder than before and Recker turned his eyes to the ceiling, half-expecting it to come down on top of him.

"Plasma missile on the comms hub," he said. "Damnit!"

"We should get out of here," said Larson.

Recker had a feeling the world outside wasn't going to

be a much friendlier place. Still, if he was going to die, it might as well happen while he was trying to accomplish something instead of laying low in the alloy ruins.

Weakness from the Extractor lingered and seemed to coexist with the Frenziol's promises of invulnerability. Commanding his muscles into action, Recker ran for the airlock.

CHAPTER FOUR

OUTSIDE, Trinus-XN's transition from day to night was well underway. In the short period Recker had been in the comms hub, night's darkness had come knocking. The day wasn't completely over, but it was in the dying throes and the shadows were long.

Here, beyond the muffling walls of the comms hub, the dense, percussive booms of explosions came in beating waves from every direction and flashes of white lit up the skies. Far fewer personnel were in the plaza now, and those who were visible stumbled for the illusory cover of nearby buildings. It was telling that none headed for the comms hub – it didn't require a tactical genius to understand the structure was a primary target for the enemy.

The two tanks had moved from the hub doorway and were parked on opposite sides of the plaza, next to the flanking buildings. Against ground troops, a tank was a formidable weapon, but not so much against enemy warships. Recker knew those tanks were vulnerable and he didn't envy their crews.

Overhead, a four-thousand-metre Daklan annihilator flew across at such a low altitude that Recker could make out the underside Graler turrets on its thick plating. The warship was travelling at speed and it spilled missiles and countermeasures into the sky. A moment after it passed, the rumble of its engines hit Recker like a solid wall and he heard the distinctive thump of missile propulsions.

"That's the *Langinstol*," he said, belatedly remembering the battleship's name. "They're acting as a mobile defence system."

As he spoke the words, he watched a half-dozen streaks of Graler projectiles converge on incoming missiles. A split-second later, the Daklan tanks ejected missiles from their shoulder launchers and their chain guns roared. Countermeasures hit their targets and shards of pulverised alloy crashed into one of the dome buildings a few hundred metres to the left of the shuttle platform. Pieces from a second destroyed enemy missile landed much closer, hitting the ground directly between the tanks and flattening with the impact.

"Those were aimed at the comms hub," said Aston.

"Some of the perimeter multi-launchers are assigned specifically to defend the comms hubs," said Larson. "One of the Daklan officers told me."

"Come on, we're taking a shuttle," said Recker, preparing to set off across the plaza.

Before he'd taken a step, movement caught his eye. Directly ahead, one of the desolators from the landing field lifted off, climbing with such ferocity that it dwindled to a grey speck in no more than a handful of seconds. As it gained altitude, the heavy cruiser unleashed its own countermeasures. Recker braced and the sonic booms hit him like a kick in the chest. A twin thump-whine of immense gauss coils discharging came next and he knew the desolator was firing its Terrus cannons at enemy warships high above the planet.

Once again, the annihilator's countermeasures targeted incoming missiles and this time, a warhead made it through. A flash lit up the surrounding walls and the thunder of a plasma explosion filled the plaza. Instinctively, Recker turned, but he was too close to the comms hub. Wherever the missile had struck, he couldn't see it from here.

Though Recker had only exited the comms hub a few seconds ago, it felt like he'd been inactive for many minutes. A rush of fear swept through him and, at that moment, he knew what it felt like to be an animal trapped in the headlights, frozen in place and waiting for death.

Aston felt it too. "We can't head out into that, sir," she said.

Faltering, Recker was on the brink of ordering a return to the comms hub. Much of the building was underground and maybe they could take shelter there until the worst of the assault was over. He couldn't give in to the weakness. The Lavorix wouldn't retreat from this and he doubted the combined Daklan and HPA fleets had the firepower to knock out even a single one of the enemy capital ships.

As if to drive the message home, several fast-moving objects dropped through the darkness ahead, their orange propulsions vivid against the night. Four were engulfed by plasma explosions, while the fifth escaped and disappeared behind the dark outline of the dome. Recker guessed what it was.

"A troop transport," he said. "The Lavorix need a presence on the ground to storm the *Aeklu* and the *Verumol*."

"If they're throwing dropships at Ivisto, maybe they aren't so confident they can crush our fleet," said Larson.

The thought offered Recker some hope. He knew the Lavorix were experienced in war, but so were the HPA and the Daklan. Recker wasn't ashamed to admit that the Daklan warships were better than their human equivalents and, just maybe, the allied fleet was putting up more resistance than the enemy were expecting.

"Come on!" he urged.

"I don't think a shuttle is the safest place to be, sir," said Burner.

"Would you prefer to walk, Lieutenant?"

Recker was acutely aware that flying across Ivisto in a shuttle was risky, but he didn't believe those risks were much greater than those faced by any other personnel on the base. The Lavorix had plenty of high priority targets to focus on before they started wasting ammunition on the thousands of smaller vessels.

The doubts which had gripped Recker only seconds before faded and he sprinted towards the shuttle pad with the others following.

"Did anyone get in touch with Lieutenant Eastwood?" asked Recker as he ran between two gravity cars. In the cabin of one, the Daklan driver was in her seat, eyes closed like she'd stopped to take a nap.

Recker suspected the alien was dead, but he couldn't

afford the time to stop and check. He continued towards the shuttle pad, looking briefly over his shoulder at Comms Hub 3. The structure had suffered far more damage than he'd realised - the visible upper levels were buckled and thick smoke poured from the alloy. The most recent plasma missile strike had impacted near the base of the antenna and several of the support beams had been severed by the force of the explosion. Another direct hit and the thousand-metre structure would come crashing down.

Not intending to be around when or if it happened, Recker charged up the shuttle pad ramp. His nose caught the scent of burning metal and, from his elevated position, he saw the low-lying glow of fires to the south. Another seven or eight Lavorix missiles broke through the shield of countermeasures and each one created a white-glowing sphere of detonation in the command area of Ivisto.

At the top of the landing pad, Recker dashed for the door of the nearest shuttle. A smack of his palm on the panel gave access to the airlock.

Recker hesitated briefly on the threshold and scanned the visible skies. The *Langinstol* was low to the north and banking in a tight circle over the construction yard, while another annihilator – either the *Vantrian* or the *Ildinir* - was far to the south, along with a mixed group of HPA and Daklan heavies, protecting the most heavily-populated areas of the base. Each warship directed unending, concentrated firepower towards the unseen Lavorix attackers.

And then Recker saw it. An ovoid of blue raced across the sky from east to west, so high and travelling so fast that his eyes could hardly trace its progress. He knew what was coming and uttered a curt warning to his crew.

"Extractor."

The enemy fired the weapon again and Recker's grip on the handle at the side of the shuttle's door weakened. His knees buckled and he toppled from the steps. His brain juggled its efforts to remain conscious with his body's need to arrest its fall and Recker tried to twist in the air so that he wouldn't land on his head or neck. His shoulder hit something and he caught a glimpse of Aston.

Before he hit the ground, Recker blacked out.

Someone groaned.

"Shit," said a voice. Maybe it was his own, though he couldn't be certain.

The pain hit Recker and he felt as if each individual nerve ending had been wired up to an electrical supply. He had nausea as well, either resulting from the pain or just another effect of the Extractor attack. For a few seconds he lay unmoving, too drained to do otherwise. Slowly – not nearly as quickly as he'd have liked – the pain became more of a background distraction than the all-encompassing agony it had been at the start.

He opened his eyes and discovered he was facing the sky. Objects and lights moved across his vision and the effort of focusing was too great. With his return to aware-ness, Recker noticed he was lying on top of an object – an object which was hurting his spine.

"Get off me, sir," said Aston weakly.

"I'm comfortable," Recker said. It wasn't a time for jokes, so he had no idea why he came out with the response.

"Move," Aston said, pushing him away.

Larson was first to her feet and she offered Recker a hand up, which he gratefully accepted. Once he was upright, he hauled Aston from the ground.

"Thanks for breaking my fall," he said.

"No problem." Aston stooped to collect her rifle and grabbed Recker's at the same time.

"Here."

Recker took the gun without looking, since his eyes were aimed upwards. He didn't know how long he'd been unconscious, but that last Extractor discharge had been harder to handle than all bar the very first one he'd suffered on Oracon-1. It hadn't just been him and his crew affected – the personnel in the defence fleet had evidently been knocked out as well, and the Lavorix had taken advantage, albeit in a surprisingly limited fashion.

One of the allied spaceships – either a desolator or an HPA heavy cruiser – was aflame, far to the south. The warship was turning sluggishly and its countermeasures came in sporadic bursts. Two of the other vessels had also taken damage and plasma clung to the *Langinstol*'s upper plating.

Recker was desperate to find out what was going on, and even more desperate to play a role in it, but his short-term priority was to reach the shuttle's cockpit. Warily, he checked for signs of a Lavorix energy shield anywhere overhead. Wherever the enemy craft had gone, it wasn't here and the optimist in Recker suggested that the attacking Law of Ancidium had only dared a single, rapid flyover because its shield was taking too much punishment.

"The enemy could have landed another dozen transports while we were out cold," said Aston.

"I know," said Recker. "And they could have knocked out all of these visible warships protecting Ivisto at the same time. They didn't, and to me that means the Lavorix are under more pressure than they expected."

"Without the Extractor's insta-kill to rely on, they're not so tough," said Aston.

They both knew the Laws of Ancidium were more than just mobile Extractor guns, but it was good to think the Lavorix couldn't simply murder everyone on Ivisto with the press of button. Their energy shields could soak a lot of damage – Recker had seen first-hand how much – but he'd also seen that their power reserves were finite. Hit those shields hard enough and for long enough and eventually they'd collapse.

By this moment, Lieutenant Burner was awake and on his feet, though he looked like crap. He didn't complain.

"Come on," Recker urged.

For the second time, he climbed the shuttle's boarding steps and this time he made it into the interior, with his crew right behind. They dashed into the cockpit and Recker dropped into the pilot's seat. The nausea threatened to return following the burst of action, but he wouldn't allow it. Taking deep breaths, he scanned the console in front of him.

"The shuttle's comms are offline," he said.

"While it's in range of the base, its hardware is programmed to route through the comms hubs," said Burner from the second seat. "I could override it in a few seconds on an HPA shuttle. It might take me a couple of minutes to figure it out on this Daklan craft."

"Don't bother. We've got our suit comms – we'll rely on them for the moment. Check it out later if the chance arises."

"Yes, sir," Burner replied. "Bringing the sensors up."

Recker's hands were on the controls, but he wasn't ready to lift off quite yet. "I need to find out what our situation is." He opened a new channel, this one to Sergeant Vance. "Speak to me, Sergeant."

Vance sounded gruffer than usual. "We're staying low like you ordered, sir. We were under pressure from a bunch of the barracks officers, telling us where to muster. The last Extractor took away some of the heat. I guess those officers have enough on their plates without having to deal with stragglers."

"What about the Daklan members of the platoon?" asked Recker, suddenly fearful.

"They're awake, sir. Sergeant Shadar reckons that last Extractor was only a little worse than the one before it."

"I believe the enemy keep adjusting the weapon, Sergeant. I don't know how long it'll be before we're falling dead instead of just unconscious."

"We're the guinea pigs, sir. If the Lavorix kill us here on Trinus-XN, they'll send that knowledge to their other ships."

"One way or another, they'll figure things out," said Recker. "We've got to stop them recapturing the *Aeklu* and *Verumol*."

"Is the order still for us to keep our noses out of trouble, sir?"

Vance didn't usually ask for confirmation and that meant he was desperate to do something other than hide in a barracks block waiting for the incendiaries to land.

"Orders have changed." said Recker. "You're in Barracks 12?"

"Yes, sir."

"I'm in a shuttle with most of my crew. We're coming to pick you up and after that we're heading to the *Aeklu*."

The relief was evident in Vance's response. "Private Raimi's plucking his eyebrows, sir. I'll make sure he's finished in time."

"You do that, Sergeant."

Recker closed the channel and addressed his crew. "According to the base map, we're five klicks from Barracks 12. We'll fly low – keep your fingers crossed the Lavorix don't notice us."

"I'll find out if there's any useful information out there," said Burner, flexing his fingers in anticipation.

"And find out where Ken's hiding," said Recker. "We're going to need him."

"I'll deal with that, sir," said Larson on the officer channel. The cockpit only had three stations, so she'd harnessed herself into one of the passenger bay seats.

"Thanks."

The shuttle's bulkhead screen illuminated and Burner adjusted the focus of the sensors at the same time as he operated the comms. He could perform both tasks simultaneously on a fully-fledged warship, so doing the same on a small craft like this was no challenge.

"The *Langinstol* is still in the air," said Recker. "That other annihilator is definitely the *Ildinir*."

"Doesn't look like it's taken too much damage," said Aston.

While the two Daklan battleships were apparently fully operational, the heavy cruiser which Recker had seen burning when he was on the shuttle pad, was losing altitude. It came down at a shallow angle and was barely more than two thousand metres above the tops of the structures below.

"The pilot has some control," said Recker. "Enough to avoid landing on the base."

Watching the final moments of a warship was something Recker usually found poignant – at least when it was a friendly ship or an enemy who'd fought well. Right now, he couldn't allow his gaze to linger and he diverted his attention to the shuttle's console.

"Up we go," he said, lifting the vessel vertically into the air.

Immediately the shuttle was off the ground, Recker felt the imagined weight of Lavorix eyes upon him. A stationary craft was easily ignored, but a moving one invited all kinds of explosive interest. Once more, he reminded himself that the risks were acceptable and that the Lavorix had their hands full with a well-armed and well-trained fleet of allied warships.

Five klicks, he thought. *Not far.*

Recker's plan was to pilot the vessel along the streets of Ivisto and hope the enemy were looking elsewhere. He fed in the power and the shuttle accelerated.

CHAPTER FIVE

FLYING along the plaza's eastern exit road, Recker held the shuttle midway between the eight-storey flanking buildings. Below, many of the personnel gravity cars were parked at the sides, while others were stationary in the middle of the road.

Bodies of Daklan personnel – thousands of them - lay everywhere, some sprawling from the cabins of their vehicles and others in the road. A few of the aliens had regained consciousness and these ones sought refuge in the buildings nearby.

Several of the larger vehicles – trucks and a lone tank - had veered into the smaller vehicles parked at the edge of the road, while others had come to a standstill. One flatbed transport was crossways over several lanes, making it difficult for anything coming behind to get through. The road was on the brink of becoming completely blocked.

"The Daklan took that last Extractor attack badly as well," said Aston.

"At least they aren't dead, Commander," said Recker, hoping that the unmoving aliens were simply unconscious.

"How long before the base commander gets hold of the situation?" asked Burner. "Everything looks screwed up at the moment."

"I spoke to Daxtil-Tilok already," said Recker. "He sounded like he was up for the fight."

"You've met him before?" asked Burner.

"Yes – first impressions were good, but there's not much he can do if three-quarters of his troops are out cold."

Recker didn't invite any more questions and glanced at the base map he'd called up on one of his screens. The shuttle appeared as an orange dot overlaid onto a satellite image of Ivisto. A short way ahead, he planned to turn south along one of the wider streets. Maybe the shuttle would be a little more visible taking this route, but Recker wanted to reach Barracks 12 as soon as possible.

"There goes that heavy cruiser," said Aston.

The still-burning hull of the warship vanished from sight behind the buildings on the starboard feed. Its rate of fall had increased and Recker guessed the pilot had lost the last vestiges of control. If the spaceship landed outside the base, the shockwave damage would hopefully be limited to the perimeter structures.

"I'm picking up some bits and pieces on the tier two command and control channels, sir," said Burner.

"What sort of bits and pieces?"

"We are dealing with a single Law of Ancidium, name unknown and capabilities unconfirmed, but with mass and dimensions similar to those of the *Aeklu*. The enemy capital ship was accompanied by twenty other vessels of varying sizes and capabilities."

"How many confirmed kills of enemy ships?"

"Unknown, sir – *more than zero* is the only estimate doing the rounds. We've lost more than seven of the defence fleet."

"They took us by surprise," said Recker. "The Lavorix would have got off the first salvoes."

"It seems as if the Lavorix were surprised by the ferocity of our response," said Burner. "The bulk of their fleet is staying out of range, while our own warships have been ordered to stay close to the planet."

Recker nodded. "It's going to turn messy."

"I wonder if the Lavorix knew about the *Aeklu* and *Verumol* being here," said Burner.

"The more I think about it, the more I believe they located Ivisto without knowing their captured ships were here," said Recker. "Shit luck for us and we're going to have a real job turning this around. Where's the capital ship?"

"They're currently in an erratic, high-speed orbit of Trinus-XN, sir, and accompanied by four of the larger attacking vessels."

"That last Extractor shot was bad," said Recker. "Worse than the ones before it."

"You're not the only one to notice," said Burner.

"The Lavorix have had plenty of chances to tune the Extractor before now," said Aston. "And they still can't get it right."

"Alterations to the weapon might not be straightfor-ward, Commander."

"That last one hurt a lot," said Larson. "I don't know how many more alterations I can handle."

"Should we take another shot of boosters?" asked Burner. "I already feel like I could throw up after the last injection."

"You can't vomit when you're on the Frenziol," said Aston. "You might feel like you're about to spill your insides, but it won't happen. Take too many shots and your heart will give out."

"I think everyone knows all there is to know about Frenziol since high command ordered us to inject the stuff a half dozen times a day," said Burner.

"Hold the injections until we hear otherwise," said Recker. He'd been told unofficially that most fit and healthy humans within a certain age range could safely take four booster shots in rapid succession before the risk of heart failure became unacceptably high – whatever *unacceptably high* meant. For the Daklan, the safe dose was only three shots, which wasn't so good for the aliens given that they were also more vulnerable to the Extractors.

"The cruiser just impacted," said Aston. "Our instrumentation picked up a primary and secondary shockwave."

"Not enough to cause any major surface destruction," said Burner. "Makes a change."

From this low altitude position, Recker saw nothing, though he was sure a few buildings would have crumpled nearer to the crash site. The turning south came and he aimed the shuttle along a multi-lane road. Here, the flanking structures were more various in shapes and sizes, including low domes, high domes, towers and sloping-roofed storage facilities.

Again, the normal base transport vehicles had been abandoned. More bodies – dead or unconscious – lay everywhere and the Daklan had parked dozens of mobile gauss repeaters along the middle lanes. In the distance, a long row of tanks sped across an intersection.

"Cock-guns," said Aston, pointing at the multi-barrelled mini-Gralers.

"Not when they're on our side," said Recker. "When they're on our side, we call them Churners."

"Does this mean the Daklan are recovering?" asked Burner.

"Churners can operate without a crew, Lieutenant. They can be remote activated, given a destination and sent on their way. Those ones are probably being coordinated by the ground control mainframe," said Recker.

"Can they take out a warship-launched plasma missile?" asked Burner doubtfully.

"I don't know, Lieutenant. I'm sure we'll find out before this is over."

Recker didn't know how to describe his relationship with *luck* or even if luck existed such that he could have any sort of relationship with it. Certainly, he was acutely aware that some events appeared more than coincidental and, at that moment, he received further reinforcement of his view.

Suddenly, the Churners turned their guns towards the sky. A row of red lights appeared on Recker's console and an alarm chimed. The meaning was clear – the targeting computers of several different Churners wanted him to get the hell out of the way. Then, a warning message from the ground controller appeared on his central screen, giving him five seconds to clear the airspace.

"Shit," said Recker.

Giving the engines extra power, he banked the transport and increased altitude. Having faced these shuttles in combat before, Recker wasn't shocked by the craft's agility and it raced over the top of one of the storage buildings. Even before he was clear of the road, the Churners further south had begun shooting and their slug tracers ripped through the air.

Gripped by a feeling that all hell was about to break loose, Recker didn't reduce velocity and he kept the shuttle skimming low above the building's roof. A glance at the bulkhead screen was enough to make him curse again.

Three huge Lavorix warships came across the horizon at tremendous velocity, their heat trails leaving orange smears across the feed. With physics-defying deceleration, they came to a halt directly above Ivisto's landing strip, no more than a thousand metres above the tops of the *Aeklu* and *Verumol*. Each had taken missile strikes from the ground batteries and those missiles continued crashing into their armour, creating angry flashes of sun-bright plasma.

"Battleships," said Aston. "Big enough to take a beating."

Each of the three enemy craft was larger than the *Langinstol* - which was the closest allied spaceship. The captain of the annihilator reacted with incredible speed and he rammed his spaceship into one of the Lavorix craft.

At the same time, missiles ejected from the Daklan ship's launch clusters and they detonated against the second of the enemy craft. The enemy fired missiles too, though the sudden acceleration of the annihilator and the close range combined to ensure that many flew past their target.

"Looks like a crapstorm is heading our way," said Burner. "Someone put up an umbrella."

From the east, the second annihilator, *Ildinir*, fired dozens of its own missiles before it, too, accelerated towards the shipyard. An incomprehensibly vast explosion tore a six-hundred metre hole in the first of the Lavorix battleships and then a swarm of orbit-launched missiles from the allied fleet rained down on its topside plating.

"I bet those Lavorix bastards thought they were going to surprise the Daklan," said Burner in admiration.

The Daklan were savage opponents and they didn't hold back. The fast-approaching *Ildinir* executed a last-moment rotation that caused its flank to smash into the nose of one of the enemy craft. At the same time, the colossal thrust from the *Langinstol*'s engines pushed the first Lavorix ship south-west, away from the landing strip.

"We're in the path," said Burner.

Recker didn't want to be caught beneath two raging battleships, but their approach trajectory meant he'd either have to do a complete reversal of course or he'd have to fly as quickly as possible in his current direction and hope for the best. He chose the latter and the shuttle gathered speed.

"They're launching dropships," said Aston.

"I see them," said Recker.

Despite the punishment they were suffering, each of

the three Lavorix battleships was ejecting smaller vessels from their underside chutes. Lieutenant Burner didn't need his duty spelling out and he got on the comms to make sure the base commanders were aware of the danger.

By this moment, the two low-altitude heavy cruisers – the HPA ship *Pulveriser* and the Daklan desolator *Incendus* – were giving the enemy battleships the full treatment. The desolator's Terrus cannons sent hardened alloy projectiles thundering into the plating of the Lavorix craft, while a series of monumental blasts on the nose section of the first battleship indicated it had been struck by multiple Hellburner missiles.

Although Recker had seen more than his fair share of combat, the hairs on his neck and forearms rose in awe at the technological onslaught taking place above Ivisto. The locked annihilator and Lavorix battleship fought their way towards the shuttle, like bulls with their horns locked. Smaller missiles, fired from the ground, punched into the descending transports and the Churners directed a continuous stream of projectiles at the launch clusters of the enemy warships to knock out the warheads as they emerged.

Missiles from all directions poured into the attacking spaceships. The Lavorix fought back with their own gauss guns and warheads. With his eyes on the *Langinstol*, Recker almost missed the *Incendus* coming down fast in front of the shuttle. The Daklan heavy was hardly damaged, so he guessed it had been hit by a core override and he banked right to avoid it.

"Come on, get it purged," Recker muttered angrily.

The purge wasn't something the crew could speed up

– a combination of Obliterator cores and fast data transfer were the only way to clear the override and it took anything from ten seconds to a minute.

Down came the *Incendus*, passing within two hundred metres of the shuttle. The desolator crunched underside first into the tops of a tall building ahead and then its rounded nose crumpled one of the huge dome buildings. The warship had plenty of momentum and it ripped a 1500-metre-wide channel across Ivisto. Luckily – if luck played any part in it – the desolator's trajectory took it into the edge of the shipyard, rather than deeper into the inhabited areas of the base. Regardless, the casualties were going to be enormous.

Before the *Incendus* came to a halt, the *Langinstol* and the Lavorix battleship passed by overhead, the resonance from their competing ternium drives threatening to knock the shuttle to the ground. With an iron grip on the control sticks, Recker held his craft aloft while his mouth cursed as if his life depended on it.

The Lavorix battleship broke free of the *Langinstol* and began to accelerate south-east, with its hull wreathed in plasma. Another wave of missiles from the ground batteries crashed into its visible flank with devastating effect and massive slabs of its armour were ripped tumbling away to the base beneath.

"It's coming down," said Recker.

The Lavorix battleship wasn't completely done. Although most of its flank and topside armaments were out of action, the underside launchers were intact. Missiles burst from their clusters, flying in every direction and exploding against buildings and vehicles below. One detonated on the roof of the structure beneath the shuttle and the vessel was caught in the blast's periphery. Again, Recker struggled with the controls, while thanking the Daklan for building their transports so damned tough.

Emerging with little more than hull scarring, the shuttle flew on.

"Barracks 12, dead ahead," said Aston.

Such had been Recker's concentration that he hadn't realised how close he was to the pickup location. His gaze swept across the buildings in front and he found his destination. Barracks 12 was one of four rectangular structures surrounding a central square and all of them were full of missile holes. Flames and dark smoke were everywhere, and one structure had sagged in the heat.

As he looked at the scene, Recker couldn't imagine that anyone was left alive inside the ruins.

CHAPTER SIX

THE CENTRAL SQUARE was cluttered with over-turned gravity cars, though some of the larger armoured transports were unmoved by the blast waves. Lieutenant Burner had already spoken to Sergeant Vance on the approach, so Recker knew the platoon was safe in the passenger bay of one such vehicle. What level of instinct had prompted Shadar or Vance to order the soldiers out of the building, Recker didn't know. One thing was certain – he was glad they hadn't perished in the blaze.

Recker set the shuttle down in one of the few clear spaces. He gave the comms signal and the soldiers emerged from a low-profile transport about sixty metres away. They sprinted for the shuttle and Recker watched Corporal Hendrix, the heavy medical box on her back identifying her amongst the others. His mind was filled with regrets and he cursed the war anew for driving a wedge between them.

"Anyone else with you, Sergeant Vance?" he asked on the comms.

"Just us, sir. Barracks 9 through 12 got an evacuation order the moment the Lavorix arrived, so those other buildings should be empty."

They escaped one death and surely found another.

A new comms link formed and this time it was Lieutenant Larson. She informed Recker that Lieutenant Eastwood had taken cover in one of the construction yard's underground monitoring stations, a few hundred metres from the *Aeklu*'s docking trench.

"Can he make it to the *Aeklu*?" asked Recker.

"Not without risk, sir. He asks if you're ordering him to make a run for it."

"Not yet. Tell him to stay safe."

Larson dropped the channel and Recker continued watching the feeds. The buildings around the square cut the visibility arc, concealing much of the fighting which raged over the base. Flashes lit the sky continuously, and shapes sped by in the darkness. Lieutenant Burner didn't let up in his efforts to obtain details on the situation, though he found little more than snippets and even those morsels described events which Recker had already witnessed. It was frustrating and his temper was fraying.

"If we're to reach *Aeklu* in one piece, I'm going to need more than table scraps," he said angrily.

"The base commanders are still joining the dots and I don't think anybody has the full picture, sir," said Burner.

"Is the *Aeklu* still our best bet?" said Aston. "We could Fracture the support warships. That'll slow them down."

"Believe me, nothing would give me greater pleasure

than to fly the *Vengeance* again, Commander," said Recker. "However, my primary concern is the *Aeklu*. We can't risk the enemy stealing it back and they only need to get a few hundred soldiers and crew inside to make it impossible for us to recapture it before they lift off."

"The Lavorix won't know how to operate the tech we installed. They won't even have access to the consoles," Aston protested.

"I know, but they'll have hardware that'll give them access. Sooner or later, they'll figure out a way to get off the ground."

"We don't know what's happening on the landing field, sir," said Burner. "It may be we're in control."

Recker valued the input of his crew and he acknowledged their suggestions. "We'll do what's right when we get there," he said.

"Is that our cue to shut up talking?" asked Burner.

Smiling thinly, Recker didn't answer. He watched the last member of his platoon clamber into the shuttle. He didn't wait any longer and pushed the button on his console to close the hull door.

"Hold on tight, folks," he said on the open channel. "We're getting out of here."

Recker felt a sudden unease. Having learned to trust his inner alarms, he requested full power from the engines and the shuttle leapt off the ground with everything shaking and rattling.

As it climbed above the sides of the ruined barracks, Recker looked to find out what had got his intuition stirred up. Of the three Lavorix battleships, the one which the

Langinstol had rammed was in pieces on the southern edge of landing field.

"I can see the *Vengeance*," said Burner at once. "Nothing landed on it, but it was close."

The second and third enemy warships were under heavy bombardment and it was a miracle they were holding together given the extensive cratering which left hardly any part of their hulls untouched.

"We're giving them hell," said Aston.

"The *Langinstol* and the *Ildinir* have taken a beating as well," said Recker, pushing the control sticks forward. The shuttle accelerated for the construction yard, while the clamouring alarm bells in his mind chimed louder.

A pattern of much larger explosions appeared on the flank of the closest Lavorix battleship and Recker was sure they were caused by Hellburners launched from the *Pulveriser* or one of the other HPA cruisers in high orbit. The damage was too much for the enemy spaceship and its engines shut down while it was travelling at a low velocity. Mentally, Recker predicted its downward trajectory.

"It's going to hit the southern edge of the base."

"There's going to be nothing left, even if we win," said Aston.

"There's talk on the command and control channels of Lavorix on the ground," said Burner. "Multiple reports and multiple locations, east and west of the construction yard."

"Was there ever a doubt?" asked Recker bitterly.

"On the plus side, the Lavorix aren't likely to fire the Extractor again," said Burner. "Not unless they can focus it into a narrow area."

"Which means an incendiary attack on the southern area of Ivisto," said Recker, realising what his brain had been worrying about. "Shit."

"Our warships will shoot down the cannisters, right?" said Burner.

"Not if one of these two battleships deploy them, Lieutenant. They're too low for us to stop them."

Burner jerked bolt upright in his seat, and Recker knew he'd been right.

"Two cannisters just landed near the southern perimeter," said Burner.

Recker didn't care which of the two Lavorix battleships had deployed the weapons and he cursed them both equally. He turned the shuttle directly north and it sped across the rooftops. Missiles and Churner fire still raked the sky and he stayed clear of the streets in which the ground vehicles were positioned.

The last of the Lavorix warships broke up in a violent expulsion of heat and ternium particles. Debris rained down on the central areas of the base and Recker was relieved to find that none of the pieces were heading his way.

"Here come the flames," said Aston.

On the rear feed, twin circles of red, orange and blue fires swept outwards from the incendiary detonation points. The burning wall came with incredible speed and Recker had no way to judge how far it would reach. He assumed the Lavorix wouldn't want to incinerate their own ground forces, but in the past they'd shown little consideration for their own side.

"Going up," said Recker.

The shuttle was already under full acceleration and it wouldn't go any faster. It suddenly felt sluggish and gained altitude steadily, rather than with the urgency Recker demanded.

"Come on, come on," said Burner.

Recker's eyes darted to the base map. The shuttle was only two kilometres from the southern end of the construction yard and the Lavorix were north-east and north-west. That meant the enemy could potentially be forty or fifty kilometres away, putting them a long way from the incendiaries.

The shuttle sped across the southern edge of the construction yard at a ten-kilometre altitude. From this height, the sensors offered a much better vantage of the base, though it made Recker feel like he was going to be taken out by an enemy missile at any moment.

Ahead, the *Aeklu* and *Verumol* were immense shapes on the forward feed, while behind, the expansion of the incendiaries slowed suddenly as their fuel became exhausted.

"Five klicks short of the construction yard," judged Aston. She shook her head as the likely extent of the casualties sunk in. "We could have lost a million or more personnel."

"We've lost more than just personnel, sir," said Burner. "The command and control buildings were hit by the incendiaries and about seventy percent of the high-level comms receptors have turned from green to grey."

"Those buildings are prefab, but the subterranean levels beneath them aren't," said Recker. "Daxtil-Tilok and his team are five hundred metres below ground."

"Right. I'll check out what's happening."

While Burner hunched himself over the comms console, Recker turned his gaze to the feeds. The southern half of the base – including the most heavily-populated areas – was like a sea of flames that lit up the horizon. Incendiaries didn't burn for long, but they burned hot, and Recker had no doubt that few people would have survived.

In a war filled with atrocities, this was another to add to the total and he blanked it from his mind. The Lavorix were here to recapture the Laws of Ancidium and Recker wasn't in the mood to let them get away with it.

"Let's check what's down there," he said, sending the shuttle nose first towards the construction yard.

A sudden clattering of gauss slugs against the hull made Recker bank instinctively. His eyes found the source of the attack - tracer lines of white came from a place on the western edge of the yard. Burner focused one of the sensor arrays on it and enhanced the image.

"Mobile repeater, sir," he yelled over the metallic hail beating against the hull. "Between two of those warehouses."

"It's outside our nose gun's current firing arc," shouted Aston.

"I'm not intending to trade blows with it," said Recker. "We're getting out of here."

The shuttle was at altitude and the ground repeater was in a good position, which meant the incoming fire persisted far longer than Recker wanted. He focused on one of the storage buildings on the southern edge of the base and flew straight for it, all the while reminding himself the Daklan bolted their tech together properly.

"Shit! Missiles!" said Aston.

Recker glanced at the two fast-moving red dots which had appeared on the rudimental tactical display. Then, he saw the missiles on the bulkhead screen - twin orange streaks hurtled across the sky, coming from the east, several kilometres beyond the *Verumol*. The shuttle wasn't manoeuvrable enough to avoid them and Recker didn't want to test out its armour. It didn't look as if he had much choice, since the cover offered by the building was too far away to reach in time.

From one of the southern streets about two thousand metres east, more projectile tracers appeared, sweeping west as they tracked a target. The red dots vanished from the tactical and Recker flew the shuttle behind the storage building and brought it to a halt fifty metres above the ground in a normal-looking street with a few parked gravity vehicles and no sign of dead bodies.

He turned to look at Aston.

"All praise the Churners," she said.

Recker nodded his agreement, but didn't want to dwell on their escape. "It doesn't seem like the direct approach to the *Aeklu*'s going to work," he said.

"I'm checking over the sensor recordings," said Burner. "Let's see if I can find any evidence of Lavorix foot soldiers."

"Commander Aston, you do that instead," said Recker. "Lieutenant Burner, what happened to those comms?"

"It's not good news, sir. The Daklan fitted Ivisto with physical cabling in case something happened to the comms hubs. The command and control section is set to use them automatically in case of a failure in the main hubs. Unfortunately, they didn't bury all those cables underground, so a bunch of them were burned out by the incendiaries. They're busy rerouting, but a suit comms unit won't penetrate five hundred metres of rock. For the moment, there's no one at the top giving orders."

Recker met the other man's eyes. "We're in the shit here, Lieutenant Burner. I need you to unearth whatever intel is available on the Lavorix in and around the construction yard. Most importantly, find out if we have any troops coming this way."

"I'll get hold of a senior officer, sir, just don't expect a direct channel to Daxtil-Tilok."

"Don't even try – the Daklan have competent officers at every level of their hierarchy. You might even find a few amongst the HPA. Find someone and squeeze until you get answers."

"Yes, sir."

"There're signs of troop activity on the landing strip, sir," said Aston, tapping her fingertip on the recorded feed.

Recker looked over at the screen and spotted out-of-focus movement a few hundred metres in from the western edge of the yard. The sensor array hadn't been aimed directly that way, so it was difficult to be sure if the movement was a tightly clustered group of soldiers or a vehicle.

"Can't even see if those are Lavorix," he said.

"No, sir. There's other movement here," said Aston. "These grey lines might be repeater fire caught on the sensor lens periphery. And look here..."

This time, she'd spotted an object dropping from the sky and disappearing behind one of the western buildings.

"Another transport," said Recker.

"Maybe."

The lack of reliable information was starting to anger Recker and he struck the pilot's console with his fist.

"There's an alley between these two buildings ahead of us, sir," Aston pointed out. "If you fly us into it, we could take another look at the construction yard without being visible to the missile launcher."

"Good idea, Commander."

The street above which the shuttle hovered continued for a few kilometres, but a left-hand turn a little way along led back to the construction yard. Recker accelerated towards it and warily guided the shuttle into this new road. It was hardly an *alley* like Aston had described it, being wide enough for the largest of gravity crawlers.

"Let's see what's out there," said Aston.

"Time is passing, Commander," said Recker. He was become edgy – how much was down to the Frenziol he didn't know, but he didn't want it to dictate his actions.

His eyes went to the sensor feed. This street just about lined up with *Aeklu's* portside flank and the colossal warship was oriented south to north, blocking the view of anything happening in the gap between the two Laws of Ancidium, and also preventing sight of anything on the eastern side of the construction yard.

"Repeater fire over there," said Recker.

The darting lances of hot slugs were hard to miss and they came from the west towards one of the clusters of personnel huts positioned near the *Aeklu's* midsection. Several other repeaters attacked the same buildings from different locations in the west.

"No sign of return fire," said Aston. She cursed beneath her breath when she spotted something else on the feed. "I think this used to be a tank, sir," she said, focusing the sensors on a smoking alloy wreck several kilometres away and not far from the yard's western edge.

"How many tanks are assigned to guard the construction yard?" wondered Recker, trying to pull the figure from his mind. Neither the Daklan nor the HPA had anticipated a ground assault, so most of the defences were patrolling the skies. He thought maybe twelve or fifteen tanks were on permanent guard duty in the yard. Where they were, he didn't know.

"Sir, I've got Lieutenant Bridget Hale on the comms for you," said Burner.

"Who?" asked Recker, trying to remember if he'd heard the name before.

"She's the officer in charge of the western construction yard security, sir."

"Good work, Lieutenant Burner. Bring me into the channel."

"Captain Recker?" said Lieutenant Hale at once. She sounded calm and competent and Recker felt immediately reassured. What was less reassuring was the sound of repeater fire in the background.

"Lieutenant Hale, reliable information is a commodity in short supply. What can you tell me?"

"We've lost contact with our CO, sir. He was located in the main command and control section south of here."

"That area was hit by an incendiary, Lieutenant," said Recker. "They might restore their comms links soon or they might not. Tell me your situation."

"We're in trouble, sir. Our spotter shuttle counted fifteen transports landing within two thousand metres of the construction yard perimeter. That's on top of the four which landed right next to the *Aeklu*. Our tanks took care of those ones."

"Where are you now?"

"We're in the personnel huts west of the *Aeklu*, sir. The enemy are keeping us pinned down with mobile repeaters."

"I can see it from here, Lieutenant," said Recker. "Where are the tanks? They should be enough to tear the crap out of any ground forces and whatever mobile repeaters they brought with them."

"They were needed on the eastern edge of the yard, sir. Lieutenant Ixivar's over there and he's neck deep."

"Can you hold out?"

"Not against explosives. Where's our air cover, sir?"

"I'll get you some, Lieutenant. One way or another, I'll get you that support."

"Thank you, sir."

Recker closed the channel and resisted the urge to punch his console for a second time. The allied fleet still had four warships guarding the air, which suggested that widespread comms failure was the only reason the Lavorix were able to act so brazenly.

Just to piss him off even more, a Lavorix repeater kilometres away to the west found an angle to fire at the shuttle. The clatter of impacts started up, so loud it was hard for Recker to think.

"Kill the bastards!" he roared.

Aston didn't need to be asked twice and she aimed the

nose gun along the path of the incoming fire. An extended burst from the shuttle's high calibre repeater added to the harsh din in the cabin. Five seconds later, everything went quiet again.

"Done," said Aston.

"I will not be a spectator any longer," said Recker. He flew the shuttle backwards along the alley towards the east-west road. "Lieutenant Burner, this time I want you to speak to the comms team on one of those warships and make them aware of the situation down here."

"Yes, sir."

"What's our plan, sir?" said Aston. The look in her eye suggested she had a good idea what was coming.

Recker turned the shuttle into the road, facing east. He pushed the controls forward and the vessel acceler-ated, low above the gravity cars and transport trucks.

"If our troops need air support, that's what they'll get. We're heading for the *Vengeance*."

Just saying the warship's name gave Recker comfort and he watched the road below speed by as the shuttle flew towards its new destination.

CHAPTER SEVEN

THE SHUTTLE WASN'T HALFWAY to the landing strip when the *Langinstol* and the *Ildinir* passed directly overhead, side-by-side and at a five-kilometre altitude, trailing flames and smaller pieces of debris. All the while, they ejected missiles and countermeasures into the planet's orbit and Recker wondered how long the two battleships would be able to maintain their continuous fire.

"I got through to the *Langinstol* and they're on their way to support our ground forces, sir," said Burner.

"Good work, Lieutenant."

"We should take a look," said Aston, only half-seriously.

Unable to resist, Recker brought the shuttle a little higher, so that the portside and rear feeds had visibility over the Lavorix positions.

"Give them hell, boys," said Aston wistfully.

The warships did exactly that. While they couldn't fire indiscriminately for risk of killing HPA or Daklan troops, the two annihilators halted directly over the western fringe of the yard. Burner focused the sensors on that area, giving the shuttle's crew a clear view of the Graler fire being directed into the streets below. The gauss fire continued for many seconds and then one of the huge warehouses erupted into a cloud of roiling fire when half a dozen plasma missiles punched through its flat roof and exploded within. Eight or ten additional blasts followed and Recker was reminded how bad it was for ground troops in the age of all-powerful warships.

Not that he gave a shit when it came to the Lavorix.

With the western Lavorix forces either wiped out or their numbers heavily diminished, the annihilators broke formation. The *Langinstol* gained altitude so quickly that in the blinking of an eye, it became no more than an orange speck. Meanwhile, the *Ildinir*'s pilot didn't waste time rotating the warship and he accelerated eastwards over the tops of the *Aeklu* and *Verumol*.

"They're heading east to help Lieutenant Ixivar," said Burner.

"Did you hear anything from the *Langinstol*'s comms team about the overall situation?" asked Recker.

"It's a stalemate, sir," said Burner, his head cocked to indicate he was listening to one of the comms officers on the battleship. "Our fleet has destroyed three-quarters of the Lavorix support vessels, but are unable to break the shield protecting the enemy capital ship using conventional missiles." Burner jerked suddenly upright.

"What is it?" asked Recker.

"The Daklan lightspeed missiles are able to bypass the shield, sir!"

"Are you sure?" Recker asked sharply. "Each one of those annihilators is carrying enough lightspeed missiles to put a ten-klick hole in the side of the enemy ship. Why haven't they?"

Burner talked with the Daklan comms officer for another few seconds. "The lightspeed missiles are designed to re-enter local space a fraction of a second before impact, otherwise they'd fail to detonate. Re-entry is designed to happen at the last possible moment, but since they're travelling at 299,000 kilometres per second when it happens, their guidance systems err on the side of caution in case the missiles overshoot."

"So they're exiting lightspeed outside the enemy shield and then blowing up against it?"

"Yes, sir. Given the speeds and distances – the Daklan comms officer promises me a longer explanation when this is all over – there's a degree of inaccuracy in the missile re-entry, and a couple emerged from lightspeed within the enemy shield."

"I bet the Lavorix shit their four-legged pants when that happened," said Aston.

"When the missiles exploded, the enemy capital ship entered a short-range lightspeed transit," said Burner. "And then it came back. The Lavorix are acting cagey now, but they show no sign of retreating."

"Do we have enough missiles?" asked Recker. His mind was on the conversation while his hands piloted the shuttle. The long street ended at an intersection ahead. After that was a quick left-right onto the landing strip.

"No, sir - the Daklan fired most of them shortly after the initial success. Now they're trying to figure out a way to reprogram their guidance systems so they'll re-enter local space a fraction of a second later. Unfortunately, with the comms having gone to shit and likely most of the weapons engineers being incinerated, the reprogramming might not happen soon."

Recker grunted humourlessly. "So the Lavorix mothership is wary because of the lightspeed missiles, but we're unable to reconfigure those missiles mid-engagement."

"The Daklan don't like a stalemate and the Lavorix don't like a stalemate," said Aston.

"We all know it, Commander," said Recker. "Something's going to give."

He tried desperately to guess the next moves in this conflict. Recker's previous encounters with the Laws of Ancidium had taught him that the Lavorix couldn't tolerate their capital ships suffering any kind of damage. As soon as that shiny armour suffered a nick, a scrape, or an impact from a 424-million-ton ternium-accelerated projectile, they'd back off rather than sticking around to see what other tricks their opponent might have ready.

Recker had also learned that the Lavorix weren't cowards. Their capital ships might withdraw quickly enough, but they wouldn't retreat – once they'd evaluated the situation, they'd come back for a second try. And a third and a fourth after that.

"The *Aeklu* and the *Verumol* are too important to the Lavorix," said Recker. "This attack force isn't leaving anytime soon."

"What if they're waiting for some other Laws of Ancidium to show up?" asked Burner.

Recker guessed at the answer. "If that were the case,

the Lavorix wouldn't be pushing so hard here at Ivisto. Either they don't have reinforcements coming anytime soon or they're fearful of what we might do with the *Aeklu* and *Verumol* if they give us the opportunity."

"The Extractors failed on both of those captured ships, didn't they?" said Burner. It was common knowledge

"That's not something the Lavorix will know," said Aston. She chewed her bottom lip. "Though it's possible they could pull the information from our comms system if they've infiltrated the data arrays in any of the main hubs."

"We're piling up the guesses, folks," said Recker, guiding the shuttle through the final right-hand turn. High-sided buildings rose on each side and the landing strip was visible ahead. "And we all know what happens then."

"One more guess, sir," said Burner. "If the Lavorix ground attackers are dead, there's nothing stopping the mothership from using its Extractor again."

"Thanks, for the prediction, Lieutenant."

Instead of flying straight onto the landing field, Recker slowed the shuttle at the last moment, so that his crew could scan for threats.

"There's the *Ildinir*, sir," said Aston, pointing at the feed.

A twin row of warehouses separated the landing strip from the construction yard and the annihilator was positioned directly over them, eight kilometres north.

From the size of the fires and the quantity of debris, Recker could tell that the battleship's crew hadn't restrained themselves. As he watched, the *Ildinir* pelted several further structures with plasma warheads. The warship didn't wait around and it climbed vertically away from the destruction, rotating smoothly in the air as it gained altitude.

Content that any nearby Lavorix forces had been eliminated, Recker flew the shuttle onto the landing strip. This was the first opportunity he'd been granted to observe the wreckage of the crashed enemy battleship and it was no less impressive than he'd expected. Two vast sections of the hull – just about recognizable as having once formed a spaceship – lay west to east along the landing strip. Craters and torn armour told of the damage the enemy craft had suffered and the heat was nowhere near dissipated.

Other, smaller but not small, pieces of the warship were scattered more widely and Recker piloted the shuttle around them while keeping his eye on the *Vengeance*, twenty kilometres away near the far corner. Wreckage had landed near the warship, but the worst of it was farther north.

"Maybe we should fly back to the *Aeklu* in this shuttle, now that the *Langinstol* and *Ildinir* have cleared the way," said Aston. "It'll be a lot quicker than boarding the *Vengeance*."

"I already thought about that, Commander," said Recker. "All it takes is a single Lavorix missile launcher, hidden under cover somewhere, and this shuttle will be destroyed. We're going to spend that extra few minutes and we're going to return with the big guns."

"And if we happen to get a shot at a few of those enemy support craft at the same time, so much the better."

Recker glanced over and Aston's expression was

studiously neutral. "The *Vengeance* is our best bet, Commander."

"I agree, sir. It's my duty to advise you of the alternatives."

He smiled and nodded. "Thank you." With that out of the way, Recker gave his next command. "Lieutenant Burner, I'd like to speak with Captain Razdin-Tiel. He's been assigned to fly the *Verumol* and was planning to board that warship if he was able."

"There's no sign of a comms receptor for him, sir," said Burner, shortly after. "Who does he report to?"

"Admiral Ivinstol."

Burner went quiet for a few seconds. "The Admiral's channel is either unavailable or is being hidden to limit the inbound comms requests."

"Leave it for the moment," said Recker. "We're getting better results talking to the warship crews, so keep on at them."

"Yes, sir."

Recker switched to the squad channel. "Sergeant Vance, Sergeant Shadar, in about sixty seconds I'm setting us down on top of the *Vengeance*. We're exiting this shuttle at the double and entering the warship through the topside hatch."

"Yes, sir," said Vance.

"Has Lieutenant Larson been keeping you updated?" asked Recker.

"Yes, sir, she has."

Recker closed out of the channel and concentrated on the forward feed. The shuttle passed a lump of burning alloy, a few million tons in mass, and then sped into an open area of the landing strip. Not far ahead, the *Vengeance*'s menacing low-profile shape grew until it filled the bulkhead screen. New scars and old covered its armour and Recker itched to be onboard.

At the last moment, he brought the shuttle into a climb, which gave a better view of the *Vengeance*'s V-shaped hull. Recker's eyes sought the location of the topside hatch and he found it after a few seconds.

"There," he said, turning the shuttle in the air. "Let's set down and get out of here."

With a thump, he landed the transport and then held his breath for a few seconds in case it began sliding along the gentle slope of the *Vengeance*'s hull. The shuttle held and Recker took his hands off the controls.

"Move!" he ordered on the comms.

Recker jumped from his seat, grabbing his rifle from the floor where he'd left it. Three strides and he was out of the cockpit and into the passenger bay, where the soldiers were already clustered near the exit door.

"Ready, sir?" asked Vance.

"Do it."

Vance opened the side door and jumped outside, along with Sergeant Shadar and Private Gantry. Recker and his crew were the only ones who could open the *Vengeance*'s hatch and the other soldiers made space for them to pass.

The night-time air had fallen well below zero and the HUD in Recker's suit flashed a reminder that he shouldn't take his helmet off. He jumped onto the hard exterior of the *Vengeance* and hurried down the slight incline to where the hatch was located, fifteen metres away.

The slope of the armour wasn't so much that Recker needed to watch his feet and he looked around him. North, puddles of red and orange covered the downed wreck of the Lavorix battleship, while to the west, the incomprehensible mass of the *Verumol* blocked sight of anything beyond. South, the horizon possessed a sullen glow from the aftermath of the recent firestorm which had killed so many of the base personnel. Only to the east was the pure darkness of night retained and Recker stared for a moment into those endless depths.

Vance was nearby. "Sir, the hatch."

Another few steps and Recker was at the access panel. He was about to stoop to open the hatch when he was gripped by a feeling of dread. Movement in his periphery made him turn towards the south, where he saw the blue ovoid of the enemy mothership's shield. The Lavorix vessel was travelling fast and on a low trajectory that would see it land directly on the base.

"What the hell?" said Recker.

Rather than crashing, the Lavorix warship levelled out at an altitude of less than a thousand metres. It didn't slow and its energy shield tore through the ruins of Ivisto like a plough ripping up frozen ground.

"Oh shit," said Private Ken Raimi.

Onwards came the enemy ship, its shield creating a huge furrow of broken and uprooted buildings. The filthy light of the shield wasn't enough to hide the outline of the warship within and Recker was granted a first sight of his opponent.

Like the other Laws of Ancidium, this warship was so massive that it defied both the eye and the brain to believe such a construction could exist. Recker guessed it was longer than thirty thousand metres, with a rounded cuboid for its main section and a tapered nose. Underneath, he saw what appeared to be two enormous, full-length landing skids, attached to the main structure of the warship by many huge beams. The obscuring effects of the shield blocked his view of the external weaponry, though Recker was sure the enemy craft had plenty of everything.

Even as it approached, the Lavorix craft launched a tremendous quantity of missiles into the sky, while its hundreds of gauss repeaters created a lightshow of clean, sharp lines which raked into the heavens.

"What's it doing, sir?" asked Private Weiland Steigers.

The answer came to Recker like a punch in the temple. "It's trying to block our access to the *Aeklu* and *Verumol*," he said. "The Lavorix are going to use that energy shield as protection while they pile their troops into the spaceships. Then, they're going to fly out of here and there won't be a damned thing we can do about it."

"Damn," said Private Eric Drawl.

Recker couldn't have put it better himself.

CHAPTER EIGHT

LIKE RECKER HAD FEARED, the enemy spaceship flew in a direct line towards the construction yard. The *Langinstol*, the *Ildinir* and the HPA heavy cruiser *Pulveriser* bombarded its shield with missiles, while the orbital fleet rained down hundreds more. The Law of Ancidium responded in kind and the *Ildinir*'s countermeasures were overwhelmed by a punishing wave of Lavorix missiles.

The visor on Recker's helmet darkened automatically. It wasn't enough and he shielded his eyes to see how this spectacle would end.

Struck multiple times, the annihilator broke off, its hull showing terrible damage. The battleship's propulsion betrayed no loss of efficiency and the Daklan craft hurtled towards the eastern horizon, still firing missiles and countermeasures.

For long moments, Recker found himself mesmerised by this display of unrestrained technological savagery. The allied fleet didn't withdraw - the *Langinstol* stayed in proximity and was joined by the *Pulveriser* and the *Incendus*. All three hovered north of the construction yard and, though each one had taken a beating, they didn't let up in their attacks.

Then, missiles sped in a blur from east, so low across the landing field that they barely cleared the wreckage of the Lavorix battleship, before smashing into the energy shield.

"The *Ildinir* didn't go far," said Recker in admiration of the crew's bravery.

"Sir, the hatch," said Vance, more forcefully this time.

Recker crouched and touched his fingers to the access panel. The hatch slid open, revealing a ladder. At the bottom, was an airlift that went almost to the bridge. He lifted his head again, in time to see the Lavorix spaceship halt directly above and between the *Aeklu* and the *Verumol*.

With no idea what the enemy shields were capable of, Recker wasn't surprised to find that the two docked Laws of Ancidium weren't knocked aside when the barrier hit them. Instead, each was partially encompassed within the ovoid. Where the blue energy touched their hulls it formed a perfect join. Then, the shield expanded along all three axes until the *Aeklu* and *Verumol* were both completely inside.

"Maybe it's weaker now that it's bigger," said Private Drawl hopefully.

"Let's hope so, Private," said Recker. He gestured towards the hatch. "In," he ordered, reaching for the top rung of the ladder.

A pulse of energy swept across the landing strip and it was the first time Recker had felt the Extractor as a physical force. It struck him hard and his limbs became frozen. Already committed to the ladder, he toppled towards the opening. The last emotion he felt in the moment before he lost consciousness and before the pain became too much to bear, was anger at his enemy and at his own body for succumbing once again to the Extractor.

Time passed, though Recker was oblivious. He heard a noise somewhere nearby and his mind assembled the components of the sound into words.

"Time to get up, sir."

"Wakey," said a second voice.

"What?" Recker mumbled. In his chest, he felt a painful thudding, like his heart had gone into overdrive. He must have fallen into the entrance shaft, yet somehow, he hadn't broken his neck.

His eyes didn't want to open and he was dimly aware that someone was shaking him. He remembered the anger and his eyes snapped open. Everywhere around him was dark, though he saw shapes recognizable as humans and Daklan.

"What happened?" It was the first question that jumped into his mind.

"You fell and Corporal Hendrix caught you, sir. I've never seen anyone move so fast." This time, Recker's brain identified the owner of the voice. It was Private Ossie Carrington.

"Where are we?" he asked.

"The *Vengeance*'s airlift, sir," said Private Titus

Enfield cheerfully. "Unvak's carrying you over his shoulder."

"You have been injected with an additional dose of Frenziol," said the Daklan.

The airlift stopped at the bottom of its shaft and the door opened, letting in more light. In moments, the soldiers – no more than half of the platoon - had exited and Recker spotted Commander Aston cradled between the arms of Lumis. She was awake, but her eyes were half closed.

"Put me down," said Recker. The thumping in his chest hadn't gone away and his breathing was fast and shallow, but he was feeling stronger by the second. He sensed distant pain and guessed the Frenziol was keeping it at bay.

"As you wish," said Unvak, leaning forward and dropping Recker onto his feet.

"Thanks." Recker's legs wobbled, though not enough for him to fall. His confusion was rapidly fading and his mind patched in the missing pieces of information.

"Is someone bringing the rest of my crew?" he asked.

They're probably arguing over who gets to carry Lieutenant Larson.

Sergeant Shadar was a little way further along the corridor. "The lift has returned to collect them."

"I'm going to the bridge," said Recker. "Commander Aston?"

"Shitting shitbags," she said with feeling.

"I'll take that as a yes."

Recker's first two paces were accomplished with the support of the cold passage wall. Then, his balance improved and, shortly, he was running as quickly as the cramped interior of the warship allowed. Aston had shaken off the worst of the effects and she kept pace. When Recker glanced over his shoulder, she gave him a defiant grin.

"I heard what Private Carrington said."

"Yeah?"

"I bet Corporal Hendrix would appreciate the thanks."

"Later," Recker said. He didn't need to think about it right now.

Aston knew when it was time to shut up and she changed the subject. "How come the platoon handled the Extractor better than we did?" she asked.

"Sergeant Vance and Sergeant Shadar are seasoned officers, Commander. If I had to guess, I'd say the moment they heard the Lavorix had arrived, they all took two extra booster shots instead of just one."

"Crafty bastards. I say that in full admiration."

"Whoever the order came from, they've given us a chance."

"A chance at what, sir?"

"I don't know," said Recker. He ran past the turning that led to the tiny mess room. "I've been thinking about what Lieutenant Burner heard about the lightspeed missiles." He arrived at the steps leading up to the bridge and he sprang up them two at a time.

"Are you going to tell me?"

"I always do, Commander," said Recker, striking his palm onto the bridge access panel.

The door opened and the bridge was exactly how it

always was – metals an eternity old, moulded into technology capable of destroying planets. Recker dropped into his seat and Aston sat in the one adjacent.

"Pre-flight checks while we wait for Adam and Jo," he ordered.

"You're going to keep quiet about your idea for as long as possible, aren't you?"

Recker laughed, though it made his head hurt. "I'm sorry, Commander, that's not my intention. I'm turning things over in my mind – that's all it is."

The *Vengeance* had been on regular, active patrols during the last few months, and its online systems were in a state of readiness. Recker checked in with Burner and Larson on the comms and learned they were both awake and heading for the bridge. He also learned a new curse word from Larson, who, as one of the more refined members of the crew, did not usually dabble in the vernacular.

Recker closed out of the channel and watched the bulkhead screens illuminate. A few seconds later, the external feeds appeared.

"Sensors up," said Aston.

"What have we got?" asked Recker, his eyes jumping from screen to screen.

"I need to adjust the lens direction," said Aston. "One moment."

The bridge door opened, allowing Burner and Larson to enter. The latter was no longer uttering the same imprecations as earlier and she took her seat at once.

"Commander Aston, I've got the sensors," she said.

"All yours, Lieutenant."

"Damn, I need a coffee," said Burner, dumping himself into his own seat.

"Forget the coffee – Lieutenant Eastwood is somewhere in the middle of all that crap," said Recker. "Find out if he's alive and find out what the defence force is planning."

"Yes, sir."

Judging by the sensor feeds, the defence force was planning to hit the Lavorix capital ship with high explosives until either its shield ran out of power, or their magazines ran dry. Recker knew how strong that shield was, but if he'd been asked to lay a bet, his money would have been on ten thousand plasma warheads as the eventual winner.

The Lavorix would know that too and, though he hadn't been given much time to think about it, Recker suspected the enemy had taken a gamble. The big question was how much they'd risk before they ran for the hills.

"Time to spill the beans, sir," said Aston.

"You've already guessed what I'm thinking, Commander. I can see it in your face."

"There's a plan?" asked Burner.

"The Captain has taken inspiration from the Daklan lightspeed missiles, Lieutenant."

Recker nodded and spelled it out. "We're going to perform a mode 3 transit through the enemy shield and put an Executor hole right where they don't want one."

"Couldn't we wait the six minutes for the standard warmup procedure to complete, sir?" asked Larson.

"Two problems with that suggestion, Lieutenant – time and distance. In six minutes, the enemy may have accomplished their mission, and secondly, the control software for the standard drive warmup won't permit an on-off propulsion switchover in such a short time. We'd need to fly a sufficient distance away from the enemy ship at sub-light speeds before we could attempt the lightspeed jump into their shield."

"So we mode 3 in and then they blow the crap out of us," said Burner.

"Maybe," said Recker. "Or maybe they hit their own mode 3 button and disappear into the sunset."

Burner wasn't done yet. "Our sensors will be offline after the transit, sir – we'll be blind for several seconds. We may not even get an Executor shot unless we fire it without help from the sensors."

"That's why we're aiming for the bottom of the construction trench beneath the *Aeklu*. There's plenty of room and we'll be out of the enemy sensor view."

"The gravity fields holding up the *Aeklu* will attempt to hold the *Vengeance* as well, sir," said Larson.

"Our propulsion has plenty of grunt – we'll pull clear."

"Slowly."

"It won't be so slow with the engines in overstress," said Aston.

Larson didn't look convinced, but she didn't argue further. "As long as we get our chance."

"We'll get that chance, Lieutenant," Recker assured her.

Burner had thought of another problem. "Lieutenant Eastwood's comms receptor is grey, sir. I think he's some-where inside that energy shield."

"We're all facing the same crap here, Lieutenant," said Recker.

"I know, sir. This is bigger than one man." Burner's voice was flat.

"It *is* bigger than one man, damnit!" snapped Recker. "Do you think I want to kill my officers? This is what we have to do, Lieutenant!"

"Ken wouldn't want it any other way," said Aston softly.

Burner's shoulders slumped. "I know." He raised his head, though his eyes were looking into empty space. "This crap never seems to end."

"It *will* end," said Recker. "And when it's over, we'll be able to look in the mirror knowing we faced the worst of the universe and didn't back down."

"Yes, sir," said Burner. "I don't know where the anger came from."

"I'm feeling it myself," admitted Recker.

"When the war's over, I'll recommend you for the *Valorous Ingestion of Caffeine* award, Lieutenant Burner," said Larson.

Burner blinked in surprise. "Is she allowed to take the piss, sir?"

"I'll leave that for you to decide, Lieutenant." Recker gave a thin smile. "No more talk unless it's about our situation." He glanced at the instrumentation and all the readouts were in their expected ranges. "We're ready to lift off and once we hit mode 3, we'll be committed."

"What are you aiming to knock out with the Executor, sir?" said Aston. "I assume we're going to target our single shot carefully, but we don't know where the Lavorix have installed their individual hardware modules."

"I know," said Recker. "The *Aeklu* and the *Verumol* had their Extractors in different locations, but they both had their shield generator modules on the lower midsection."

"The *Aeklu* and *Verumol* are completely different warships, sir. They weren't designed the same and they don't even look the same," said Aston. "The *Aeklu*'s shield generator was ten klicks back from the nose and seven deep from the underside plating. The *Verumol*'s was twelve from the nose and four deep. The Executor only has a two-klick blast diameter, plus another thousand metres rupturing effect from the shockwave, give or take. We're guessing and even if we guess right, the Executor may not have the penetration."

"I know," Recker repeated.

Aston shrugged and gave another grin. "What choice do we have, huh?"

"Exactly."

"Can I have my medal now, sir?" asked Burner, all traces of his anger gone. "I'd like to pin it to my chest before I die."

"You're not going to die, Lieutenant."

"Damn right you're not," said Aston.

The time had come. "Let's focus," said Recker. "Ivisto isn't coming back from this, so let's make sure the enemy pay a heavy price for what they've done."

He accessed the engine control software. Normally, Lieutenant Eastwood handled this and Recker took a little longer to locate the correct options. Engine mode 3 could be activated by a simple press of a button on the control bars, or it could be manually programmed to run for a set amount of time or distance. Using the data from the *Vengeance*'s sensors, Recker tapped in the details.

"Done," he said. "When I activate mode 3, it'll fly us straight into the middle of that energy shield, directly below the *Aeklu*."

"This is going to work, isn't it?" said Burner.

"We'll soon find out. Make sure the other members of our fleet are aware of what we're attempting."

"None of the Daklan or HPA warships are in a position to help us, sir. They're too close to the planet to perform an in-out transition, and they've got their hands full with the enemy support craft."

"We're not waiting," said Recker. "If it works, we'll have proven the method and the rest of our fleet – not just the warships here at Trinus-XN – will benefit from it."

"Yes, sir."

Recker's eyes were locked on the sensor feeds. The Lavorix capital ship was still ejecting vast quantities of missiles, while spraying gauss countermeasures in hundreds of directions. It wasn't enough to negate the allied attack and the enemy craft was under such heavy bombardment that the entire visible shield was hidden by continuous bursts of plasma.

Recker didn't know how long the enemy power source could hold up under such punishment and maybe the Lavorix would knock out the HPA and Daklan fleet before it happened. Either way, he felt sure the enemy would be deploying troops as rapidly as possible. The best hope was that their access to the *Aeklu* and *Verumol* would be slowed by the newly installed HPA and Daklan security hardware.

"Here we go," said Recker.

The control bars glided along their runners and the *Vengeance*'s propulsion grumbled like it always did outside of its overstressed state. A booming note of displaced air rolled across the landing strip as the warship climbed vertically into the air.

"The details I programmed in assume a launch altitude of one klick," he said.

In moments, the warship's altimeter showed exactly one thousand metres and Recker held it there, with the nose pointing downwards and directly at the star-bright ovoid of plasma and energy. He switched the propulsion into mode 2 and the grumbling was replaced by a low howl of metallic perfection. Recker moved his thumb onto the mode 3 activation button.

Taking a deep breath, he sent the *Vengeance* into lightspeed.

CHAPTER NINE

SO SHORT WAS the journey that Recker's brain didn't even register it happening, and the Frenziol coursing through his veins suppressed the usual compounded nausea that came from a rapid in-out transition. The sensors feeds were blank and Recker waited to find out if they'd come online before the Lavorix detected the *Vengeance* and blew it to pieces. A quick check of his status panel told him the warship's velocity was at zero and its engine had switched back to mode 1.

The seconds dragged out and Recker scraped his teeth together. "Where are those sensors?" he asked.

"Coming online!" yelled Larson.

All at once, the arrays came up. They required adjustment and Recker struggled to make sense of the *Vengeance*'s surroundings. Below, everything was dark, the same as it was above. Portside, he saw varying hues of grey, while the starboard sensors registered dark blues and lighter greys.

Burner and Larson made rapid alterations to the focus and direction of the lenses and suddenly everything snapped into place.

"We're beneath the *Aeklu*," said Recker. "It worked."

The trench holding the massive spaceship was several kilometres deep and the *Vengeance* was right in the middle of it and facing north. Overhead, the adjusted sensor feeds allowed Recker an excellent view of a twenty-missile launch cluster on the *Aeklu*'s underside, along with the two eight-barrel gauss repeaters flanking it. One day, maybe he'd turn those weapons against their makers.

Recker shifted his attention to the other feeds. On the alloy-clad ground below, he saw hundreds of the immense gravity field generators that were supporting the *Aeklu*'s weight, and their presence explained the dullest of vibrations he could sense running through the *Vengeance*.

About four thousand metres above, on both port and starboard sides, the long gaps between the *Aeklu*'s flanks and the edges of the trench appeared too small for the *Vengeance* to fit through. Recker was going to give it a try whatever happened.

Once the *Vengeance* was detected, he expected it to be subjected to an intense and sustained attack, so Recker knew it was vital to get the Executor shot off quickly and in the right place. Therefore, he spent a moment peering through the starboard gap, hunting for visible clues on the hull of the active Lavorix warship. The angle wasn't perfect, but it was good enough for him to discern the massive gauss repeaters on the huge craft's underside, along with the swarms of much smaller vessels flying through the intervening space.

"A mixture of our shuttles and their shuttles," he said. "Plenty of both."

From what Recker could see, the Lavorix were potentially deploying tens of thousands of troops. It made sense, given they only had this one chance to take back the Laws of Ancidium.

"I can't identify a definite target area on the enemy ship from here," he said. "It's time to act."

Recker rotated the *Vengeance* so that it was facing east towards the *Verumol*. Then, he slid the control bars away from him and watched the propulsion output gauge climb, while the velocity gauge remained stuck on zero. Clenching his jaw tightly, he increased the power further. The grumbling note of the engines became a roar of chained fury and still the *Vengeance* didn't move.

"That's a tight gap between the *Aeklu* and the trench, sir," said Aston.

Recker knew what she was getting at. To escape the gravity chains, he'd need to switch the *Vengeance*'s propulsion into overstress, at which point it might suddenly rip free and accelerate into the side walls of the construction trench. The warship would survive the impact, but Recker didn't want to risk an unforeseen hardware failure.

For a split-second, he considered launching missiles at the closest gravity field generators. Recker dismissed the idea - the generators shared their load and he might be required to destroy twenty or more before the hold on the *Vengeance* lessened, and that would destroy any hope of surprising the Lavorix.

"Mode 2 it is," he said.

The moment he switched over the propulsion, he felt

the warship straining eagerly, even with the output at less than twenty percent of its new maximum. Recker lifted the nose and, metre-by-metre, the *Vengeance's* over-stressed ternium propulsion overcame the insistent force of the gravity field. It was a challenge for Recker – the field generators pulled constantly at the warship, attempting to bring it back to its original position.

Gradually, the warship crept towards the gap and the sight of Lavorix transports flying unmolested towards the ground taunted Recker.

"Enough!" he said. "We're getting out of here."

The field generators didn't slacken their grip and it seemed to Recker as if they were wilfully combating his efforts. In anger, he increased thrust another ten percent towards maximum and the *Vengeance* gathered speed. A further five percent was enough for the warship to break the shackles and it accelerated rapidly towards the opening – an opening which seemed to shrink as it came closer, rather than widen.

"Going to be tight," said Burner.

With barely twenty metres to spare top and bottom, the *Vengeance* sped through the opening. The moment it broke from the gravity field, the warship surged to a terrifying velocity that brought the solid flank of the *Verumol* closer in the blinking of an eye. Reacting fast, Recker banked the *Vengeance* as hard as he could. It wasn't enough and the warship's starboard plating struck one of the *Verumol's* gauss cannons.

The impact was enough to knock the *Vengeance* off course and Recker grappled with the controls. He railed at himself for screwing up – he was wasting time correcting his error, instead of blowing the crap out of his enemies.

Coming around in a tight arc, the *Vengeance*'s nose ended up facing north and Recker's brain absorbed the details all around. West lay the *Aeklu*, with its slab sides and the protruding four-thousand-metre-high cuboid that ran the full length of its hull. East, the *Verumol*'s sloping sides were studded with gauss turrets in different shapes and sizes, those guns now idle.

It wasn't the captured warships which Recker was most interested in. Overhead, the thirty-five-thousand-metre Lavorix capital ship formed what seemed almost like a roof, confining the *Vengeance* to a limited space within a combat arena of the enemy's making. Two angled plates – with no seams showing anywhere – formed the massive spaceship's underside and Recker spotted dozens upon dozens of missile clusters, along with ten-barrel gauss repeaters and several huge domes which he thought might house particle beam generators.

North and south, the energy shield formed the last walls of Recker's prison. Seen from within, the barrier was translucent in a way which reminded him of frosted glass or the frozen surface of a pure lake.

Against the might of this opponent, the *Vengeance* was no more than an insignificant speck and Recker fought against the cold dread seeping into his bones at the fire-power on show. This unknown Law of Ancidium was packing more conventional weapons than either the *Aeklu* or the *Verumol*, as if it had been purpose-designed to wipe out entire fleets.

Recker couldn't allow himself to think what would

happen when those underside armaments locked onto the *Vengeance* and started firing.

We've been through worse situations and lived.

The thought gave him some resolve. His eyes scanned for a place to fire the Executor, without knowing exactly what he was looking for. Deep down, Recker accepted he was relying on luck and intuition rather than skill and experience. It was a truth he didn't like and the taste of it was bitter.

Unbowed by the thoughts, Recker piloted the *Vengeance* beneath the enemy ship. All around, Lavorix transports were ejected from square launch hatches in the mothership's armour and they fell towards the construction yard like a stinking rain of alien crap. Recker ignored them – their time would come if his plan worked out – and he kept his narrowed his eyes on the forward feed.

"Multiple ground launchers have locked onto us, sir," said Aston. "We've got one mesh deflector charge."

"Hold onto it," said Recker.

"Setting mesh deflector to manual activation."

About six thousand metres starboard, Recker spotted an ugly puncturing of the capital ship's armour. He looked closer at what turned out to be a still-smoking armour breach a few hundred metres across.

"Lightspeed missile strike," he said. The Daklan warheads packed a tremendous punch, and he could imagine why the Lavorix wouldn't want to risk their hull becoming riddled with such craters. Recker turned his gaze forward again and something caught his attention. "I think I've found something..." he said.

Five thousand metres ahead, a rectangular area of the

enemy warship's underside plating was surrounded by missile clusters and turrets. No armaments were fitted on the rectangle, as if the Lavorix had installed an enormous hardware module through a now sealed opening in the plating.

"That's the place," Recker said under his breath. "Commander Aston, target the area I've highlighted on the feed."

"Got it, sir," she said. "And those ground launchers just let rip."

"They're designed for use against tanks and armoured vehicles, not warships," said Larson. "They're too small to hurt us."

"Given enough time, they'll do some damage, Lieutenant."

"Maglors set to track and destroy," said Aston.

The *Vengeance*'s countermeasures fired at once, their pulsing beat coming up through the floor. At the same moment, Recker spotted the nearby underside gauss repeaters on the enemy capital ship rotate with incredible speed. Within a moment, dozens were pointing directly at the *Vengeance* and their barrels started turning.

"Commander Aston, fire the Executor."

"Executor discharged."

The dark explosion of the weapon tore into the Lavorix mothership, creating a two-thousand-metre ragged opening that went deep into the interior. At the same time, the force of the energy ruptured the surrounding alloys, forming rough waves of buckled metal, along with thousands of stress fractures which snaked away from the opening. Debris tumbled out, like guts from the slit belly of a slaughtered beast.

The thumping expulsion of Executor backlash swept through the bridge and, though Recker was braced for it, he knew it would hurt. Once again, the Frenziol came to his aid and the edges of the kick-in-the-balls pain and nausea were blunted enough that he could manage them without losing his focus on the outside world.

"The energy shield is still operational, sir," said Aston. "And the enemy ship hasn't moved."

It was a bad outcome and Recker fought to contain his fury. So much was happening that he couldn't allow his emotions to rule and he held down his anger. The enemy ship was damaged and there was still a chance it would take to the skies. Meanwhile, the *Vengeance* was trapped within the shield, at least until the mode 3 five-minute cooldown expired.

A couple of ground-launched missiles evaded the Maglors and crashed into the *Vengeance*, their explosions stark on the underside feeds. At the same time, dozens of gauss repeaters from the capital ship sent an unimaginable cascade of projectiles into the warship's armour. The distant drone of the impacts wormed its way straight into Recker's head and he tried to shut out the noise.

"Take them down, Commander," he said, accelerating towards the Executor opening.

Aston didn't need to have it spelled out. Fast as lightning, she selected targets and sent missiles at them. Two Lavorix transports – each a hundred metres in length and with a payload of six-limbed alien scumbags – were turned into molten scrap by missile impacts. Farther below, several ground launchers were given the same treatment and white plasma flashes marked the places of their destruction.

Many of the capital ship's ten-barrel gauss repeaters were torn apart by warheads, though the quantity of inbound fire didn't lessen noticeably. Hoping to cut down the number of turrets and missile clusters with a firing angle, Recker piloted the *Vengeance* towards the enemy hull. The overstressed engines hurled the warship across the intervening space and within a moment, only a hundred metres separated the vessels. To Recker, it felt as if he was flying amongst a forest of gauss turrets and all of them were turned his way.

Falling back on his experience, Recker's breathing deepened and his eyes took in the details from the sensor feeds and from his console. Though only a few seconds had passed since the Executor discharge, it already seemed apparent the Lavorix capital ship was going nowhere, and that was the worst possible outcome.

Another realisation came. More than enough time had passed for the enemy to target and fire their missile clusters or a particle beam, yet they'd only brought their missile countermeasures to bear.

Maybe their missiles can't target from so close. Or maybe they can't hit anything inside the shield perimeter.

Whatever the truth, the *Vengeance* was still in one piece and the Lavorix were still attempting to access the *Aeklu* and the *Verumol*. Recker glanced at the Executor timer - it had more than four minutes left until it was recharged.

"Those ground launchers have fired again, sir," said Burner.

Red dots appeared on the tactical and the *Vengeance*'s Maglors fired at the inbound warheads. The enemy missiles weren't sophisticated and they flew in a straight line, which made them easy targets for the gauss turrets. A short, thudding discharge from the *Vengeance*'s underside turrets knocked out all bar one of the enemy warheads and that last one produced a pitifully small blast on the armour.

"Underside missile clusters one and two fired. Holding uppers one to four – we're too close to the enemy warship," said Aston.

The *Vengeance* wasn't fitted with as many launch clusters as a larger spaceship, but the missiles it carried were an advanced Meklon design and carried a large payload. Twenty-four warheads from the underside clusters streaked after their targets. Numerous transports and ground launchers were destroyed by the missiles, while the Maglor slugs pulverised several more.

Five hundred metres ahead, the edge of the Executor hole loomed, its edges rimmed with expansion heat and splayed outwards like jagged alloy teeth. Sensing he was on borrowed time, Recker piloted the *Vengeance* directly for the opening. All the while, gauss projectiles tore into his warship's armour, turning the outer few metres into a mess of heat-softened craters.

"In we go," he said, dragging back on the controls.

The opening was easily large enough and the *Vengeance* entered the interior of the Lavorix warship without scraping the sides. Immediately, the droning of gauss projectile impacts stopped and the cessation was an immense relief.

Having seen what damage the Executor could do to its target, Recker wasn't surprised to find the insides of the Lavorix spaceship so badly mangled. Sheared structural joints and thick sheets of internal plating hung down, and lights flickered irregularly in places, casting shadows and exaggerating the lines and edges. In the deepest part of the crater, the presence of a darker material made Recker think the Executor had damaged one of the spaceship's ternium modules. For all the damage, the shield generator module hadn't gone offline.

Hiding within the enemy's hull granted Recker the smallest of respites and he had a good idea how to make use of it. Steady hands on the controls brought the *Vengeance*'s nose upwards, so that it pointed directly into the innards of the Lavorix spaceship.

"What happens if we activate the Fracture while we're within the energy shield?" asked Burner.

"Interesting question for another time, Lieutenant," said Recker. Despite himself, he answered anyway. "We'd turn this bastard to dust and do likewise to the *Aeklu* and the *Verumol*."

What the outcome would be for Trinus-XN and the *Vengeance*, Recker didn't know. If the Lavorix were on the brink of recapturing the Laws of Ancidium, maybe the destruction of everything would be the best possible outcome. He pushed the idea to the back of his mind.

Once he'd finished positioning the *Vengeance*, Recker made the briefest check of the sensor feeds. Below and through the opening, much of the construction yard was visible and Larson had highlighted numerous targets. The tactical was tracking ninety-five Lavorix transports and ground vehicles and several of the former had parked on top of the *Aeklu*. It wouldn't be long before the enemy gained access to those spaceships.

Aston wasn't giving them an easy ride and she fired individual missiles from the rear tubes as quickly as she could select a target and send the launch command to the battle computer. While that happened, the Maglors spewed high-velocity death at the enemy, smashing their vehicles and pounding them into unrecognizable lumps of metal.

"Commander Aston, launch from our forward clusters," said Recker.

"Shit, wait!" said Aston.

Recker turned sharply towards her. "What is it, Commander?"

Aston talked fast. "You told me about that nuke you fired into the *Galactar* way back on Oracon-1, sir. When the crew and I were already knocked out by the Extractor."

"Yes, I remember," said Recker impatiently, his eye on the tactical. The ground launchers in the construction yard fired another salvo. Two of the missiles avoided the Maglor slugs and detonated against the *Vengeance*'s rear plating.

"The *Galactar* entered lightspeed, taking the nuke with it."

"Shit," said Recker, echoing Aston's curse from a moment ago. "If we drive this enemy away while we're in its hull, we'll go with it."

"And when it exits lightspeed, we'll have nowhere to go, sir."

"So we either go outside and offer the Lavorix an opportunity to target us with their external weapons, or we stay in here," said Recker.

He was taken by a great certainty that if he fired enough missiles into the Lavorix ship's interior, it would go to mode 3, leaving the deployed troops to finish capturing the *Aeklu* and *Verumol*. From what Recker had seen, those troops stood an excellent chance of completing their mission, unless they were interrupted in the next few minutes.

Caught between a rock and a hard place, Recker made his choice.

"Fire the missiles, Commander."

CHAPTER TEN

AS HE SAID THE WORDS, Recker gave the *Vengeance* maximum reverse thrust and the spaceship emerged from the hull breach at the same time as twenty-four high-yield warheads exploded in the comparative confines of the Executor crater.

Heat and expanding air buffeted the *Vengeance* and, for a moment, the warship was completely engulfed in plasma.

Still accelerating, the *Vengeance* raced stern-first towards the construction yard, its Maglors delivering pain without cease to the Lavorix transports and ground launchers. Falling wreckage from the missile blasts above came as well, and they crashed into the softened plating of Recker's ship.

"Go!" shouted Larson at the enemy.

The mothership didn't leave and its gauss cannons took less than two seconds to reacquire their targets. Their hail of slugs drummed once more into the *Vengeance*, the noise interfering with speech and thought. Hoping he was correct to think the Lavorix missiles couldn't target within the energy shield, Recker brought the *Vengeance* to a halt a thousand metres beneath the enemy ship and rotated it quickly into a new position.

Walls and consoles groaned with the strain, but when Recker was done, the loaded portside missile clusters were pointed at the Executor hole. He accelerated vertically towards the opening.

"Wait until we're too close for these gauss turrets to knock out our missiles, then fire again, Commander. Hit them where it hurts."

The *Vengeance* sped into the crater, the insides of which were now all colours of hot. Torrents of liquid alloy poured down, glistening with reflected oranges, reds and whites.

"Portside clusters one and two fired," said Aston.

An additional twenty-four warheads plunged into the damaged interior of the Lavorix ship, and the new explosions blinded the sensors. Though Recker had kept his spaceship as close to the entrance as possible, the plasma blasts wrapped the *Vengeance* and spilled out into the surrounding space.

Knowing he was playing a dangerous game, Recker flew the *Vengeance* straight out of the Executor hole again. His intention was to hurt the enemy enough that they'd mode 3 out of the combat arena, but not while the *Vengeance* was within their hull.

More alerts went off and distant thuds indicated that

another huge quantity of molten debris had been torn out of the mothership. The sensors attenuated and Recker saw dark shapes in the brightness. A massive piece of something heavy caught the *Vengeance* on its nose and then slid away. Down it fell, crashing into the alloy surface of the construction yard.

The drumming of the gauss guns began again and a salvo of ground launched missiles struck the *Vengeance* in several places. To add insult to injury, a few of the transports were also firing their nose guns. Without the ground missiles and the mothership's chain guns, those shuttles might as well have been pissing in the wind, but added to everything else, it was damage to his ship Recker could have done without.

"The enemy vessel is still not moving, sir," said Burner.

"I can see that, Lieutenant."

This was the time when Lieutenant Eastwood would have proved his worth by scanning the enemy ship for power fluctuations. Output spikes or drop-offs could provide clues about an enemy's intentions. Neither Burner nor Larson had the expertise, while Aston and Recker couldn't divert themselves from their tasks.

"Ready the starboard clusters," said Recker as he rotated the *Vengeance* again.

"Starboard clusters ready."

Intending to repeat his earlier manoeuvre, Recker accelerated for the opening. The missile detonations had turned the Executor crater into something much more significant, and the hole had been increased to twice its original volume. Yet more debris fell and the *Vengeance* was struck time and again.

The starboard missiles remained in their launch tubes. Having seen enough, the Lavorix activated a mode 3 transit and the Law of Ancidium vanished from the construction yard, leaving behind thousands of troops and dozens of transports. The instrumentation on Recker's console registered a violent displacement of air and an expulsion of energy, neither of which were sufficiently powerful to affect the 2.7-billion-ton *Vengeance*.

"They hit mode 3," said Aston, blinking in surprise, like she'd thought it would never happen. Slowly, she withdrew her finger from the missile launch button.

"The mothership has gone, but we've still got a job to do, folks," said Recker loudly. Part of him was just as surprised as Aston.

The generous speckling of red dots on the tactical reminded him exactly how many Lavorix had deployed in the construction yard and he scanned the sensors for the highest priority targets.

"There," he said, spotting a transport which had landed on top of the *Aeklu*. Its cargo of troops was disembarking and making a run for the unfinished turret, like they knew of an entrance hatch somewhere close by.

Recker turned the *Vengeance* so that its nose was pointing north and he accelerated towards his intended position midway between the *Aeklu* and the *Verumol*.

"Prioritise and destroy," said Aston with relish.

She selected targets rapidly and the priority list appeared on the tactical. The Maglors clanked and

Lavorix died. In a few seconds, Recker had the *Vengeance* in place, with the flanks of his warship facing the two Laws of Ancidium. This allowed the maximum quantity of firepower to be directed at the enemy and he held stationary while Aston eliminated the enemy troops and vehicles.

"We're not killing them fast enough," said Recker.

"We've got backup coming, sir," said Burner.

A huge shape dropped from the sky and came to a halt five kilometres from the *Vengeance*. The *Langinstol* looked like crap, but its weapons and propulsion appeared to be working fine. Equipped with far more guns than the *Vengeance*, the annihilator chewed through the Lavorix with relentless ease.

"Here comes another," said Larson.

The *Pulveriser* appeared and then came the *Ildinir*. Neither was shipyard fresh but again, they had enough active weapons to give the Lavorix a fatal headache.

"Let's take a look at what's happening below," said Recker.

He guided the *Vengeance* nearer to ground level and positioned it so that one of the forward arrays obtained a clear view into the space beneath the *Aeklu*. Sure enough, a pair of Lavorix transports had taken refuge there and Aston hit them with a burst of Maglor fire. Banking away, Recker flew close to the *Verumol* and again, the sensors located enemy transports. Maybe there was an underside entrance hatch – he wasn't sure – but a few thousand Maglor slugs ensured this incursion didn't achieve its intended goals.

"Would you look at that?" said Larson in wonder.

A company of Lavorix soldiers had taken refuge

behind one of the many personnel cabins, a few hundred metres below the *Vengeance*. Brazenly, the alien soldiers fired handheld weapons and shoulder launchers at the *Ildinir*.

"Any of ours in that cabin?" asked Recker.

"I can't locate any comms receptors, sir," Burner confirmed.

"Good," said Aston. "Let's try this on manual." Taking control of a portside Maglor and without compunction, she delivered a spray of gauss slugs into the single-storey cabin. Its walls crumpled and the building was knocked across the ground, leaving a greasy red smear on the landing strip.

Recker wasn't normally the bloodthirsty kind, but the wholesale slaughter of these Lavorix seemed righteous. Unfortunately, he had other work to finish.

"I'm going to land on top of the *Aeklu*," he said. "If the enemy ship comes back, I want to be on the bridge of a vessel capable of trading blows. That, and I won't rest easy until I'm certain the Lavorix troops didn't find a way inside."

"I've communicated your intent to the other members of the fleet," said Burner.

"How many of the fleet remain?" asked Recker.

"Twelve, sir. They finished off the Lavorix support vessels while the mothership was on the ground."

The losses were heavy and, given the enemy firepower, Recker couldn't decide if the allied fleet had got off lightly or not. Having seen the armaments on the capital ship, he suspected the outcome could have been far different.

The Lavorix won't give up.

The thought added impetus to Recker's actions and he flew the *Vengeance* at high velocity over the topmost edge of the *Aeklu*.

"Has someone passed on the order to Sergeants Vance and Shadar?" he asked.

"Yes, sir," said Larson. "I've told them to muster at the forward boarding ramp."

"Thank you," said Recker, glad his crew were on the ball.

Even though the enemy mothership was gone, the pressure he felt hadn't subsided. Turning the ship so the forward boarding ramp was closest to the topside entrance, Recker dumped the *Vengeance* down on top of the *Aeklu* hard enough to produce a series of groaning complaints from the landing legs.

"Let's go," he said.

Pausing only to grab his gun, Recker dashed from the bridge and his crew followed. The sprint for the airlock passed in a blur and soon they arrived where the soldiers were waiting.

"Open the ramp!" yelled Recker.

"Ramp opening," called Vance.

Clamps banged and motors whined. Cold air rushed into the *Vengeance* and Recker breathed it in. The soldiers ahead got moving and he followed, adrenaline and Frenziol mixing to produce a heady feeling of battle lust and desperation.

Stepping onto the hard surface of the *Aeklu*'s topside armour and seeing the scale of its construction from so close was enough to make Recker giddy. Two thousand metres away, the turret of the warship's main armament – just the turret – was larger than two HPA battleships side-by-side, while the lesser guns and the missile clusters were monumental in size when viewed from foot level.

Adding to the spectacle, the *Ildinir*, the *Langinstol* and the *Pulveriser* flew across the construction yard, their guns and propulsions producing a physical wall of sound which threatened to trigger Recker's primal flight instinct. He clenched his jaw and turned east, wondering if he could see the *Verumol* from here. Although the *Aeklu* was the taller of the two vessels, the faraway edge of its plating intruded upon his sight and denied him the view.

Recker shook his head clear. The platoon members were similarly dazed by their surroundings and he barked an order to snap them out of it.

"Move!" he shouted, pointing west.

The entrance was no more than a hundred metres away, at the base of a gauss repeater turret. Recker broke into a run, craning his neck to check the external damage on the *Vengeance*. All he could see was the underside and a part of the nose which had escaped the worst of the gauss impacts.

A freezing wind swept across the warship's hull, producing a dreary, hollow sound as it blew into Recker's helmet microphone. He located the entrance – it wasn't a hatch in the conventional sense, since it was twenty metres square – and hurried over to the flush access panel. The nearby repeater towered over everyone, each of its eight barrels large enough to accommodate a – doubtless reluctant – Daklan and capable of discharging four hundred rounds a second. The *Aeklu* had hundreds like it.

Recker brought his attention back to the panel. The old Lavorix access system had been ripped out and the HPA security hardware replacing it was familiar. Recker stood adjacent to the panel and waited for his platoon to gather. One of the first to arrive was Corporal Hendrix and when Recker looked, her eyes skated away.

"Thanks for earlier," he said on a private channel.

"No worries."

Recker crouched and activated the panel. He felt a clunk of metal underfoot and the entrance slab dropped twenty metres into the hull. Another clunk and an eight-metre platform emerged from the side of the shaft, five metres below the surface, and a set of alloy steps slid into view. It was somehow amazing to think that the Lavorix had conjured up such an ingenious method.

The only thing missing was a handrail.

Approaching the steps, Recker took a deep breath. Each tread was a metre wide, but very shallow and he considered turning so that he could descend backwards.

Movement in the sky east caught his attention and he spun towards it. A transport had come from nowhere and it flew across the plating at a slight angle which suggested the vessel was damaged or its pilot an incompetent.

"Shit, it's going to hit us," said Private Drawl.

The shuttle didn't collide with the squad, though its landing was far from perfect. Its legs hit the *Aeklu*'s plating and, still moving, the vessel scraped its way to a juddering halt fifty metres away.

"What the hell?" asked Recker, irritated by a combination of the shuttle's arrival and the treacherous steps he was about to climb. "Sergeant Vance, find out who's in that shuttle and chew their ear."

"Yes, sir."

Vance hadn't made it more than a handful of steps when the transport's side door opened and a figure jumped heavily to the ground.

"Lieutenant Eastwood reporting for duty, sir. I thought you might need some assistance."

"Damn right we do, Lieutenant. And when this is all over, maybe I'll teach you how to fly a shuttle."

Feeling suddenly much better about the situation, Recker descended the steps without giving them any more thought. The Lavorix had installed an airlift all the way through the armour and it was accessed from the platform. A thump of his palm on the security panel called the car from the depths below. Instead of watching the closed door, Recker offered his hand to Aston as she followed him down. Then came Larson, Burner and last member of his crew, Eastwood.

"Good to see you again, Lieutenant," said Recker, clapping the other man on the shoulder.

Eastwood's face was even more lined than usual, though he otherwise appeared in good health. "I didn't think I was going to make it, sir. Not after that last Extractor and not after all those Lavorix troops started dropping from the sky."

"A story for later," said Recker. An image of an ice-cold beer appeared in his head from out of nowhere and he felt pangs of longing. "We'll make time – I promise."

The lift arrived and the door opened to reveal a car large enough to accommodate the entire platoon. Recker hurried inside while the soldiers descended the steps. Having gone through so much crap, first in the Daklan war and now in this war against the Lavorix, nobody wanted to die falling off the *Aeklu*'s steps, and the platoon took extra care. Fully understanding, Recker kept his mouth closed and allowed them the time they needed.

"That's everyone in," Vance announced.

Recker was at the panel near the door and he selected the lowest level. He felt the surge of acceleration as the airlift's gravity field propelled the car towards its destination. Despite the technicians being ahead of schedule, he knew there was plenty to do and he hoped they'd pulled off a few miracles to make the spaceship flight capable.

The lift stopped and the door opened onto darkness. It wasn't a good sign.

"Where's the light switch?" asked Private Raimi.

Turning on his helmet torch, Recker stepped into the corridor and listened. Creaks of flexing metal came from everywhere, the ebb and flow of the sounds making him think of an ancient wooden ship sailing the wide oceans of planet Earth. He didn't know if the *Aeklu* had always been like this, or if the detonation of the Dark Bomb and the shipyard's imperfect reconstruction had affected its structural rigidity in a way which couldn't have been predicted.

Underlying everything was the angry note of its propulsion. To Recker's ear, it sounded lumpy and coarse, yet he knew exactly what the *Aeklu* was capable of. The warship's ternium drive output exceeded the combined output of every vessel in the HPA fleet.

The admiration Recker felt was tempered by his

knowledge of how the Lavorix had used the *Aeklu* to murder and destroy. He was sure the Meklon were not the first species made extinct by this massive spaceship and the other five Laws of Ancidium, though he was determined they'd be the last.

"It stinks of Lavorix," said Private Carrington, emerging from the lift and making a few exaggerated sniffing noises.

The *Aeklu* did have a distinctive smell and, though Recker knew it was impossible, it was as though the alloys had become impregnated with the scents of its former masters. He drew in the odours through his helmet filter and wrinkled his nose. A staleness permeated the *Aeklu*, as if it were constructed ten thousand years ago and had overseen the lives and deaths of five hundred generations of Lavorix as they hunted through the universe for life energy to charge the Ancidium for war.

"I don't like it," said Drawl. He tapped his gauss rifle against one of the walls. "Feels like we're only borrowing this ship from its real owners."

"The Lavorix are going to have to come through you if they want it back, right, Private?" said Recker.

"Hell yes, sir. I'll put a bullet through every alien bastard – present company excepted – who even thinks about setting foot onboard."

"That's what I like to hear," said Recker.

"Which way to the bridge, sir?" asked Corporal Nelle Montero.

The pause outside the lift hadn't been more than a few seconds and Recker was glad of it since he'd forgotten the way. Now Montero had asked the question.

"I'm checking the map, Corporal." Recker told everyone the truth. "This is the first time I've been inside the *Aeklu*," he said.

"I thought the HPA would have..." said Raimi.

"It was less than two hours ago that I was given the command," said Recker.

"Damn," said Private Hunter Gantry. "So how did you know the way in?"

"Plans and schematics, Private," said Recker.

"What are our precise goals here on the *Aeklu*?" asked the broad figure of Sergeant Shadar.

"This is a reactive mission, Sergeant. It's possible a bunch of Lavorix soldiers made it inside, so we're going to secure the bridge." Recker took a deep breath. "We drove away that new Law of Ancidium but lost most of our fleet in the process. If they come back, we'll be in the shit."

"The enemy will not permit the *Aeklu* or the *Verumol* to fall into the wrong hands," said the Daklan.

Despite Shadar's comparatively lowly rank, he possessed a high degree of insight into many things, and in this, the Daklan reflected Recker's own thoughts.

"Whatever happens, the enemy won't let us have these spaceships," Recker agreed. "And whatever happens, we can't let them be recaptured."

"The fight will continue until one side or the other loses," said Shadar.

Deep down, Recker had known this would be the case from the first moment he heard about the enemy capital ship's arrival in the WDE421-3T system. The Laws of Ancidium were too potent to let go and too much of a threat for the Lavorix to leave in the hands of the HPA and the Daklan.

"Come on," said Recker, indicating in the direction of the warship's nose.

He set off, his mind working overtime as it tried to predict the coming minutes and hours.

CHAPTER ELEVEN

THE INTERIOR of the *Aeklu* wasn't much different to any other warship Recker had commanded. While the passage along which he led his platoon was wide enough for three soldiers to pass, and with a ceiling high enough for the Daklan, many of the side corridors were single file only.

They came to no doors and saw no sign of technology. No glowing panels were fixed to the walls and there were no console stations to monitor the underlying health of the hardware modules. In this, the *Aeklu* was the same as every warship in the HPA fleet, though on a monstrously larger scale.

From his discussions with the shipyard workers and the plans they'd drawn up of the interior, Recker had learned that the *Aeklu* was more or less solid ternium, with room to transport far fewer Lavorix than one might have imagined given the overall size of the vessel.

This solidity gave the spaceship an estimated mass of

2.5 trillion tons – a figure enormously greater than anything produced by the HPA, anything planned by the HPA and anything which the HPA military would likely have ever conceived of building. Yet here it was, sitting in a construction yard in defiance of all logic which said such a warship could never be created.

And still, after ten months of extensive investigation and exploration, nobody knew where several of the main hardware modules were located, even though the reconstruction involved tying in the HPA control systems. How they planned to get everything talking, Recker had no idea and he could only hope the technicians had figured things out.

"I've patched into the internal comms," said Burner. "The lights may be out, but at least the comms are working. Some of the comms, anyway. I'll run a full audit once we reach the bridge."

"Is anyone else patched in?" asked Recker, wondering uncharitably if all the technicians had run for cover when the enemy arrived.

"I can't find any receptors, sir," said Burner. "However, my suit comms won't allow me to locate private connections to the network."

"Aren't they supposed to be refitting this ship with HPA kit?" asked Private Steigers. "I haven't seen any sign of the work."

"The new control hardware goes on the bridge. The tie-in work happens throughout the interior," said Recker. He spoke the words confidently, to hide his concern. Maybe the shipyard's progress wasn't so advanced as he'd been led to believe.

They came to a flight of steps which led to the bridge doors and Recker heard retreating footsteps from the top. Instantly, the soldiers were ready.

"That wasn't Lavorix," Recker growled. "This is Captain Recker!" he shouted through his helmet's chin speaker. "Show yourself!"

"Captain Recker?" came the uncertain reply. "I'm Lois Roy – one of the lead technicians assigned to the *Aeklu*."

"We're coming up," said Recker, not in the mood to parley from the bottom of the steps.

"Okay. Good," said Roy.

Recker ascended twenty steps to a four-metre landing space. Ahead, twin protective blast doors had partially retracted into their recesses. A wall panel dangled from a hole in the wall and a silvery cable disappeared into the opening. Someone had plugged a handheld device into the panel and left it on the floor nearby. The tablet's screen was on, suggesting it had been abandoned in a hurry.

One of the shipyard technicians poked a head cautiously around the edge of the doorway and then emerged.

"Captain Recker." It was Roy by her voice. She was younger than he expected, or maybe he was just getting old.

"You're aware what's happening outside?" asked Recker.

"Yes, sir. We didn't receive orders to leave, so we stayed put." She glanced over her shoulder. "I think maybe some of the other guys took their chances out in the construction yard."

Recker cut to the chase. "I'm about to fly this warship out of its trench, LT Roy. What works and what doesn't?"

"I don't know how to make the answer straightforward, sir."

"Try." Recker brushed past and onto the *Aeklu's* bridge, where two other technicians were busy studying readouts from handheld diagnostic equipment.

He absorbed the details – the bridge was a rectangular area, about ten metres by six, which made it rather more compact than Recker had imagined. A feeling of age and emptiness clung to the place and it made his head swim.

So much death.

Clearing his head, he looked around. The shipyard had installed a total of ten standard warship control consoles and four others were lined up against the left-hand wall, awaiting connection to cables which protruded from holes in the floor. A multitude of screens covered the forward bulkhead, every one of them blank.

The last of the old Lavorix hardware had been removed days ago, though Recker saw a few sheets of alloy housing on the floor near the right hand wall, which looked suspiciously like they'd been cut up with a good old-fashioned angle grinder.

"It's been flight capable for weeks, sir – that was the priority fix," said Roy, hurrying after Recker as he walked towards the command console. "All the other stuff..." she waved vaguely at the consoles and the holes in the floor, "...that's what takes the time."

Recker turned and gestured at his crew, indicating they should find their stations. "So what you're telling me - without telling me - is that you don't know what works and what doesn't." Recker arrived at the command console, which was front and middle of the bridge. He leaned over the seat and studied the console screens. The lines of data on each one indicated the console was in diagnostic mode.

"Yes, sir," said Roy. "Getting something like the *Aeklu* working isn't the same as plugging in a cable and…"

"I know," said Recker, not unsympathetically. He'd been around warships long enough to have learned plenty about the construction process. "You have installation and tie-in plans that ensure nothing is overlooked and after that comes the configuration and testing."

"Yes, sir," said Roy, evidently relieved that she wasn't about to be reprimanded for simply doing her job.

Recker turned her way and noticed the tiredness in her features that even the Frenziol couldn't hide. She'd probably been working twelve hour shifts for months.

"The enemy capital ship has left Trinus-XN," he said. "One way or another, they'll be back and the *Aeklu* is one of only two ships capable of facing them."

Roy shuffled her feet. "What you see on the bridge is the last of the physical work. We've had a few teams working on configuration, but the testing hasn't started."

"There's been no testing whatsoever?"

"No, sir."

"Well, damn. I thought configuration and testing went hand in hand?"

"Not on the *Aeklu*, sir. We were instructed to put off the testing until last." Roy attempted a smile. "Every technician has at least ten years of experience, sir."

Recker wanted to swear, but it wouldn't have done much good. He tried to see the positives. "A skilled technician should get the configuration right first time, every time."

"Yes, sir." Roy's face told the story.

"Let's pretend the testing is finished, Lead Technician Roy."

"There's three of us here on the bridge, sir, and another five teams scattered around the *Aeklu*. I can order them to move straight onto testing."

Recker took the command seat and switched the console into an operational state. He linked his suit computer to the HPA hardware and fed in the command codes Telar had provided earlier. Those codes were sent to the Lavorix backend systems and that, in theory, was enough to allow him control over the warship. He looked once more at the waiting LT Roy.

"This ship is coming out of its trench as soon as my crew and I are ready. I'd guess you have less than ten minutes."

"That won't be enough, sir."

"I know. If you can fix the bridge door so that it closes, I'd appreciate it."

"What about these other four consoles?" asked Roy, pointing towards the equipment awaiting installation. "I was about to summon one of the lifter bots and have it drop them into position."

"You're out of time," said Recker. "Besides, I don't have enough crew to fill the existing stations." Aston had taken the adjacent station and he turned to make sure the others were seated. They were.

Roy didn't leave and Recker guessed she was waiting for him to spell everything out for her. He obliged, though his patience was rapidly running out. "Speak to the other teams and let them know I don't want them pissing about switching the hardware into different states while I'm flying the damned spaceship. After that, fix the door and keep out of the way."

"Yes, sir, I'll do that." Roy hastened off and Recker forgot about her at once.

"Are you online, Commander?" he asked.

"Everything seems to be tied in, sir," Aston replied. "I've got links to the weapons systems."

"Any failures?"

"Amber lights on several gauss repeaters, amber lights on several of the missile clusters, amber lights on all of the particle beams, incendiaries available for deployment, tenixite converter available to fire a depletion burst, but showing a red on anything other than the lowest setting."

"The Lavorix used up most of the *Aeklu*'s supplies of ternium ore before we captured the ship," said Recker. "The bay holds a few million tons and it was in the plans to bring some more onboard, but that was last on the list. What about the topside gun?"

"The big one," said Aston. "The backend weapons system name it the Toll, and there's a red light on it." She smiled. "But the targeting and activation facilities are available anyway."

"Expect to see a lot more inconsistencies like that one, Commander."

"Just what we need in battle." Aston shrugged and continued her pre-flight routines.

"The shipyard checked out the magazine for that main armament," said Eastwood. "We're carrying eleven projectiles and they're ternium-accelerated like the ones on the Tri-Cannon. Except these ones have a mass of 1.96 billion tons."

Everything about the Laws of Ancidium was on a colossal scale and Recker could only nod at the figures and be grateful he was no longer on the receiving end of those slugs. He put the gun from his mind for the moment – the flight preparations couldn't wait.

"Lieutenant Burner, we're waiting for those sensors," said Recker.

"Yes, sir, they'll be online in a moment. Someone got a few wires crossed and the menu for the topside arrays accesses the data analysis tools instead. It's taking a few moments to unravel."

"How about you, Lieutenant Eastwood?" said Recker. "Did you and your engine buddies figure out all the technical data?"

"Yes, sir, my engine buddies and I did exactly that. As you know, the *Aeklu* has a Gateway that taps into the same ternium ore reserves as the tenixite converter, but I suspect we don't have enough for even a single activation. Aside from that, we have a shedload of thrust even with the propulsion running unstressed. Switch over to a stressed state and the output climbs eight hundred percent and gives us the ability to hit mode 3 several times in rapid succession."

"As you said, I know the tech specs, Lieutenant. It's the green lights I'm interested in."

"Everything is good to go, sir, including the energy shield. Did you hear the latest discovery about how that works?"

"No. Tell me," said Recker. His own checks were finished, leaving him to contemplate the control bars protruding from the sloped front of his console.

"I'm sure you guessed that the propulsion modules sustain the shield during normal operations. However, it turns out that during a sustained bombardment, the tenixite converter kicks in and supplies an extra boost to stop the shield collapsing."

"That's why the *Aeklu*'s tenixite stores are so nearly depleted," said Recker in understanding.

"Yes, sir, and it's the reason why it survived the Dark Bomb. I was given access to the shield data logs and at the time of the blast, they show an output spike way off the scale. The tenixite stores originally held ten billion tons of ore." Eastwood let that one sink in.

"The *Aeklu* had to convert nearly ten billion tons of tenixite into energy to sustain its shield during the blast?" asked Recker in disbelief.

"Not quite ten billion, sir. This spaceship must have been away from base for a long time already and I estimate its stores were down to four billion tons when the Dark Bomb went off."

"It was due a refuel and still it managed to resist the biggest explosion ever recorded," said Recker.

"So how come we drove off the *Galactar* by shooting it with the Tri-Cannon?" asked Burner.

"I don't have an answer to that," said Eastwood. "Each Law of Ancidium is different and it's possible they don't all have the ability to convert tenixite into energy, or can only do so in a limited way."

"We have weapons and we have propulsion," said Recker. "Now we need those sensors."

"Sensors online!" said Burner.

The bulkhead screens lit up with feeds from the *Aeklu's* numerous arrays and the world outside was not pretty. Parts of Ivisto still burned, and the furrow created by the Lavorix capital ship's approach was an immense open wound neither the HPA nor the Daklan would ever attempt to heal.

Nearby, the construction yard was littered with flaming wreckage of Lavorix transports and ground launchers, while countless smaller shapes of allied vehicles swept in, mainly from the west.

"The *Langinstol, Ildinir* and *Pulveriser* are close by, sir," said Larson. "The desolator *Incendus* is back in the air and is stationary overhead."

"Any news from Captain Razdin-Tiel?" asked Recker. "If the enemy ship comes back, I'd prefer we had the *Verumol* with us."

"Negative, sir, he's still off-grid," said Burner.

It sounded increasingly as if the Daklan's efforts to reach the *Verumol* had resulted in his death and Recker had no idea if the aliens had a backup officer, or who that officer might be.

"We're lifting off," said Recker. He rested his hands on the familiar HPA control bars. "Coordinate with the *Langinstol* and the other warships."

"Yes, sir."

Recker requested power from the *Aeklu's* propulsion and the grumbling background note increased in volume. He half-expected the entire warship to begin vibrating in tune, but instead, everything settled and the ever-present creaking and groaning vanished completely, as if the warship had never been meant to sit idle.

"We're still held by the trench gravity chains, sir," Eastwood warned.

"Damnit, how stupid of me," said Recker. "Someone figure out how to switch them off."

"I don't know how to do that, but I'll link in with the construction yard control mainframe, sir," said Larson. "Maybe it'll accept your command codes."

Recker swore at the unwanted delay and considered the simpler method of using brute force to tear free. He mentally gave Larson one minute to accomplish the task by finesse.

"Sir, I'm getting some crazy readings from the tenixite converter," said Eastwood.

"I thought you said our tanks were dry," said Recker, detecting the fear in the other man's voice.

"I'm not talking about our storage bay. I mean that tower out there, sir!"

Recker shifted his gaze to the portside feeds, where the eight-kilometre tenixite converter cylinder was visible, towering above every other structure on the base except the *Aeklu* and the *Verumol*.

"What readings?" Recker had already guessed. He took one hand off the controls and aimed his fingertip at one of the reconfigured buttons on the panel.

"Massive readings. I think it's about to drop a full-strength depletion burst on Trinus-XN, sir."

Recker had no idea if the planet held enough ternium

ore to allow the tenixite converter to fire. He suspected there'd be plenty.

"How?" asked Burner in shock.

Making no effort to answer, Recker touched his finger on the activation button for the *Aeklu*'s shield. Instantly, an ovoid of translucent energy sprang into being around the warship, which the sensors penetrated without impediment. A gauge appeared on one of Recker's screens and glowing digits informed him of the shield's status: 100%.

"Energy spike gone. Discharge," said Eastwood.

Outside the *Aeklu*'s shield, everything went black.

CHAPTER TWELVE

THE *AEKLU'S* shield gauge plummeted and Recker didn't want to see how far it would drop.

"Tell those four warships out there to stay within our shield!" he shouted.

He hauled on the control bars. A roar of propulsion came through the walls and the warship accelerated ferociously. As far as he was aware, the ovoid of the *Aeklu's* shield was not interrupted by the surface of the construction yard and he wondered if the matter inside the shield would be dragged upwards or if it would pass clean through into the destruction outside.

Nothing came up with the shield and Recker knew that he'd effectively killed everyone who was left down there. The guilt would come later, but for now his only concern was keeping the *Aeklu* intact so that it could be used against its creators.

"The *Langinstol*, the *Incendus* and the *Pulveriser* are with us, sir," said Burner.

"What about the *Ildinir?*" asked Recker. Too late, he saw that the annihilator was no longer on the sensors – they must have flown outside of the shield's perimeter while the *Aeklu* was on the ground.

The bad news piled up. "The enemy capital ship came back, sir," said Larson. "It's attacking what's left of our fleet."

"Now we know what triggered the depletion burst," said Aston.

"Get me a target lock on that ship," yelled Recker.

"It's the *Hexidine*, sir," said Larson. "The name just came up on my screen."

Recker had his hands full with the *Aeklu*. The technicians hadn't loaded his preference data and the controls felt stiff in his hands, while the arrangement of programmable options on his screen and top panel had been left at the factory defaults. It was something Recker knew he'd adapt to, but this was not the best time to find out how long that would take.

"Our ships are having a hard time keeping up, sir," said Burner.

"We haven't even set our propulsion into overstress," said Eastwood in wonder.

Having experienced the *Galactar*'s incredible ability to be wherever it wasn't wanted, Recker was not surprised that the *Aeklu* could significantly outperform a Daklan annihilator. Hoping his obligation to protect the other members of the allied fleet wasn't going to see his own ship destroyed at the same time, he held the acceleration at a level the three accompanying warships could match. The darkness outside was still absolute and the sensors received no input whatsoever, while the shield gauge continued falling.

"Thirty percent left on our shield," said Recker.

"The fall rate is declining, sir," said Eastwood. "I think we're coming out of the blast."

"We've still got the *Vengeance* on our roof," said Burner.

At twenty percent, the shield gauge stabilised for a moment and then began climbing. Watching the rate of increase, Recker could understand why the Laws of Ancidium were such challenging opponents. The *Aeklu*'s shield had just held off a depletion burst and in a short time it would be back to one hundred percent. In combination with mode 3 manoeuvrability, it was no wonder these warships had brought down the Meklon empire.

Yet the Lavorix are losing their war. What opponents the Kilvar must be.

"Sensors clear!" called Burner. "Shit, there's not much of Trinus-XN left."

Recker tried not to be distracted by the sight on the underside feeds, but it was hard not to stare. The depletion burst had gouged out a hemisphere which was likely sixty percent or more of the planet's mass and this matter had been turned into a fine dust that didn't seem more than the tiniest fraction of the original quantity, as if the weapon had somehow completely unmade part of the universe.

The section of Trinus-XN which had escaped the initial obliteration reminded Recker of a volcano, only on a vastly larger scale. With its cold outer crust and burning inner core exposed by the depletion burst, the planet was doomed and he had no idea if its remnants would hold together or if the weapon's effects would continue at a slower pace until nothing was left other than dust.

"Sensor lock on the *Hexidine!*" shouted Larson. "It's stationary at one million klicks."

A huge red circle representing the enemy ship appeared on the tactical with four green dots nearby. Four became three. The last count Recker had been told was that twelve members of the Trinus-XN fleet remained. With the three inside the *Aeklu*'s shield, that meant only six were left, plus the *Vengeance*.

Larson finished her adjustments to the forward arrays and Recker got a view of the engagement. Those few allied warships which remained had suffered considerable damage and he doubted they'd survive much longer than a few seconds.

"Our warships lack the firepower to hurt the enemy, sir," said Aston.

"Get me a weapons lock, Commander Aston."

"Only the depletion burst and topside cannon will lock from this range, sir, and we don't have enough tenixite for anything other than a low-level discharge. Since our shield survived a full-strength blast on Trinus-XN, I'd suggest we hold the depletion burst."

Recker was desperate, but not so much that he wanted to risk the main armament this early in the confrontation. "Lieutenant Eastwood, program in a mode 3 jump with an end point right next to those Lavorix bastards."

"No need sir – just select a target on the tactical and then activate mode 3 from the control bars."

The method was beautifully simple and Recker took

advantage. His finger touched the enemy ship on the tactical and a series of additional options appeared, one of which was to approach it using a short-range lightspeed transit.

"Ready on the weapons, Commander," he said.

Feeling his anger rising, Recker activated mode 3. He experienced the stacked nausea and he refused to let it cloud his brain. The Lavorix had evidently overcome the usual delay in the sensors coming online and each of the arrays began gathering data almost immediately.

"The *Hexidine*," said Recker.

Ten thousand kilometres to starboard - though the magnification of the sensors made it appear close enough to touch - the *Hexidine* continued its attack on the last members of the Ivisto defence fleet, its shield flashing up in scant patches that indicated its battle with the allied ships was almost done.

Recker saw that the hull of this Lavorix ship was scraped and scarred, with dents covering much of its plating. From the slight mismatched colours of the armour, he was sure it had been repaired many times, in stark contrast to the *Galactar* which he remembered as being almost pristine. From what Recker had learned, the *Hexidine* had faced the Kilvar, while the *Galactar* had been left with the easier task of cleaning up the last few Meklon planets and sucking the life energy from their inhabitants.

The crew on that ship know how to fight, Recker warned himself.

There again, however clean their hull, the crew on the *Galactar* had known how to fight as well. The Lavorix were opponents only a fool would underestimate.

"We lost the *Vengeance* and our escort during that mode 3 transit, sir," said Burner.

"No surprise there, Lieutenant," said Recker.

The *Aeklu* had emerged stationary from its mode 3 transit and Recker pushed the engines straight to one hundred percent output before switching them into an overstressed state. Expecting the noise to be dramatic, he was not prepared for the bestial roar that filled the bridge. The sound was akin to nothing he'd heard from a spaceship before, like the *Aeklu* had transcended its creators and become a god rather than a mere construction of alloy and ternium.

Recker heard many of the soldiers – their presence forgotten in the circumstances – swear profusely and he didn't blame them. The hairs all over his body wanted to stand on end, only the constriction of his spacesuit preventing them from doing so, while the stale scent of Lavorix was washed away by a sharp tang of metal coming through the bridge vents. Recker breathed it in, savouring the heady odour of straining technology.

"We've got another three mode 3 activations available, sir," said Eastwood. "Then the control hardware goes on recharge for ten minutes."

"Weapons locked," yelled Aston, her own eyes wide. "Starboard side clusters one through thirty, forwards one through thirty, uppers one through thirty, all fired. Gauss countermeasures set to track and destroy. Failures on eighty-five launch tubes. Checking."

Deep within the *Aeklu*, Recker heard nothing of the discharge. Normally, he craved the visceral thunder of a spaceship's weapons systems. Here on the *Aeklu*, the propulsion note had hold of him and it was all he wanted. The *Aeklu* accelerated into the vacuum, pulling away from the *Hexidine* at a phenomenal rate. Meanwhile, the orange propulsions of almost a thousand missiles flashed across the intervening space.

The enemy were quick to react and they launched missiles of their own, though only five hundred. A faint drone – perhaps real, perhaps imagined - came to Recker as the *Aeklu*'s mighty array of gauss turrets fired at the incoming warheads.

"Our shield recharge has slowed right down, sir," warned Eastwood. "With the engines at full output, the ternium has less spare for the other systems."

"I hear you, Lieutenant," said Recker. He backed off the controls a fraction and banked to portside, intending to bring the rest of the loaded missile tubes to bear.

"*Aeklu* missiles: impact imminent," said Aston.

A moment before detonation, Recker suddenly realised he was about to be sucker punched. Sure enough, the *Hexidine* entered mode 3, breaking missile lock and appearing five thousand kilometres ahead of the *Aeklu* and with its loaded missile clusters pointing directly towards Recker's ship.

"Missile launch detected," said Aston. "Five hundred coming our way. They're not committing to a full launch, so they've always got some missiles ready to fire."

The previously launched missiles from the enemy ship had enormous propulsion sections and they flew unerringly across the tactical. Recker glanced at the velocity gauge and discovered that the *Aeklu* had gone past six thousand kilometres per second, yet still the missiles closed the gap.

"Hit them with a partial launch," Recker said.

"Portside clusters one through fifteen launched."

Recker touched an area of the tactical closer to Trinus-XN and the mode 3 button on his controls lit up. "Entering mode 3."

The in-out transition felt worse than the previous one and Recker's head thumped painfully. He cursed under his breath, wondering if fate were rolling a six-sided die to determine how bad the outcome would be for each transit.

Rolled a one, there Carl. You're gonna wish it came up a six.

The sensors cleared in moments, though Recker already had the *Aeklu*'s propulsion at maximum. Dead ahead, Trinus-XN was crumbling faster than before and its outline was becoming indistinct because of the dust particles drifting from its surface.

"Sensor lock on the *Hexidine*," said Burner.

Sure enough, the enemy warship had followed through lightspeed and emerged only a few hundred kilometres off the *Aeklu*'s stern.

"Enemy missile launch detected," said Aston. "*Aeklu* rear clusters one through fifteen launched. Our gauss repeaters are still set to track and destroy."

Several of the *Hexidine*'s missiles evaded the *Aeklu*'s countermeasures and the energy shield activated.

"Estimated twelve hits on our shield," said Eastwood. "Hardly moved the gauge."

"They're waiting for us to enter mode 3 again," said Recker.

This was a new kind of engagement with an additional set of rules and his mind tried to predict the course of the battle. The *Hexidine* fired another hundred missiles and accelerated diagonally away from the *Aeklu*.

"Fifteen of our missiles detonated against their shield," said Aston. "A scratch."

A nagging feeling that something was wrong wormed its way into Recker's brain. The *Aeklu*'s main armament was likely potent enough to give the *Hexidine*'s crew something to worry about, but their ship appeared to lack anything devastating that would trouble the *Aeklu*'s shield gauge in return. Recker doubted the Lavorix had ever foreseen a time when these two Laws of Ancidium would be duking it out, but he felt sure the opposing ship was holding something back and he didn't want to find out what it was.

Maybe the Extractor and the Tenixite Converter are enough.

Recker found out soon enough.

"I'm reading a series of power spikes on the enemy ship's hull, in an area just behind the nose, sir," said Eastwood.

"What are they up to?" asked Recker.

"I don't know, sir."

The *Aeklu*'s subverted battle computer spat out the answer without being asked and placed it on Recker's main screen in big, glowing letters.

> *Aeklu Target: Halo. Source: Hexidine.*

"What the hell?" Recker had no idea what the Halo weapon would do to his ship and he quickly selected a random location for the next mode 3 transit. Before he could press the activation button, another Extractor attack came and within a split-second Recker could tell this was going to be the worst one yet.

Unconsciousness or death beckoned; he didn't know which. The Frenziol and his will fought against both. A sound came from his mouth – pain and anger in combination. He tried to press the mode 3 activation button, only to find his hands had slipped from the controls. Recker sank towards darkness and desperately pulled himself back, already knowing even if he won this personal battle against the Extractor, the *Hexidine* would fire its Halo and the *Aeklu* would surely be destroyed.

The *Hexidine* launched another salvo of missiles and somehow Aston fired in response. Bright, flickering patterns of gauss repeaters cut vivid marks against the endless depths of space, while Trinus-XN's expanding core burned nearby, like a dark-rimmed star. Despite the agony crushing every nerve in his body, Recker thought he'd never seen anything so beautiful.

An even greater wonder appeared.

From out of nowhere, three colossal detonations blossomed on the *Hexidine*'s flank behind its energy shield and, a moment later, a fourth struck the Lavorix warship on the nose. Each blast created an enormous crater and hurled plates of armour into space. Without warning, the enemy ship vanished into lightspeed.

Before Recker's eyes, a third vision materialised. Corporal Hendrix, her expression filled with concern, stabbed him hard with a Frenziol injector. He felt nothing.

The Extractor won and Recker blacked out.

CHAPTER THIRTEEN

"I THINK HE'S AWAKE."

"Yes, Corporal Montero, I'm awake," said Recker. He was curiously free of pain, though his body felt detached, as if his mind were inhabiting a borrowed skin.

"You're full of painkillers, Frenziol and whatever other crap Corporal Hendrix's med-box thought you could handle," said Private Drawl cheerfully. "Sir," he added belatedly.

"Those are medical substances developed by the HPA's research labs, Private, and administered by a trained professional," said Hendrix from elsewhere. She didn't sound angry. "Not *crap*."

"The Captain's woken up," said Enfield, repeating what everyone who was conscious already knew.

Recker opened his eyes, expecting a pent-up wall of nausea and agony to be waiting for him. It didn't come.

"Someone's trying to reach us on the comms, sir," said Sergeant Vance. "It's Captain Vazox from the *Langinstol*."

Unsure how much time had elapsed since the *Hexidine*'s departure, and equally unsure when or if it would come back, Recker forced himself to alertness.

"Commander Aston?" he asked, his eyes jumping from the sensors to the tactical. Three green dots were close to the *Aeklu* and travelling in slow circles around it.

"I'm awake, sir."

"We've got to move," said Recker. "The *Hexidine* will probably come back and we can't face it like this."

"Lieutenant Larson ready for duty, sir." Larson didn't sound ready, but at least she was conscious and talking.

"Speak to the officers on the *Langinstol*, the *Incendus* and the *Pulveriser*," said Recker. "Whatever insight or information they have, I want to hear it." He turned to check the state of the personnel on the bridge. Most of the Daklan soldiers were out of it and the technicians likewise. Lieutenant Burner showed signs he was rousing and he mumbled nonsense.

"Corporal Hendrix, what's the status of my crew and soldiers?"

Hendrix rose from her crouch next to Ipanvir, clutching a handful of differently coloured injectors. "I've given your crew shots of four separate drugs from the medical box. They'll keep you conscious and pain free, but you're going to need some downtime eventually."

"What about the Daklan?"

"They're alive, sir, but I can't risk giving them any more Frenziol and I don't know how they'll react to the painkillers. It might be best if the Daklan remained unconscious."

"The Lavorix are adapting the Extractor," said Recker.

"Sooner or later, there'll be no drugs that will keep us alive."

"Yes, sir. Technically we've all taken a significant overdose of the Frenziol already. I'll have to keep monitoring everyone for signs of heart failure."

"We've reached a definite limit on the boosters?" asked Recker.

"I guess we'll do what we have to do, sir. In normal circumstances, I'd recommend letting the existing doses wear off, followed by three or four days in bed." She half-smiled. "Which isn't going to happen any time soon."

"Not likely, Corporal," Recker agreed.

"Sir, I've spoken to Captain Vazox," said Larson, waving to catch his attention while he was turned. "They managed to reprogram the *Langinstol*'s lightspeed missiles to bypass the enemy's shield and that's what drove away the *Hexidine*. Unfortunately, the guidance systems can only target a stationary warship and they haven't yet figured out a way around that limitation. Captain Vazox reports his ship and the others are scanning for the *Hexidine*. He recommends we leave this solar system as quickly as possible and await further instructions from our superiors."

Recker didn't commit to a response on that last recommendation. "Pass on my thanks for their assistance," he said. "How many missiles are the *Langinstol* and *Incendus* carrying?"

"Five on the annihilator and two on the desolator, sir. Their stocks are almost depleted and with Ivisto gone, they have no immediate way to rearm."

"Did any other members of the local fleet survive?"

"No, sir."

"The *Verumol*?"

"No, sir. It didn't get off the ground."

The fog in Recker's brain was gradually lifting and he paused for a moment in thought. Events at Ivisto had ended up somewhere between a disaster and a catastrophe, with the *Aeklu*'s escape being the only notable positive. He supposed as positives went, it wasn't a bad example.

"Where's the *Vengeance*?" he asked.

"I've located it, sir," said Burner, his words slurred like he was at the end of an eighteen-hour drinking session. "Back where we activated the first mode 3 after lift-off."

Recker furrowed his brow at the state of the man's speech and caught Corporal Hendrix's eye. She got the message and went over with her med-box to check Burner out.

By this point, Lieutenant Eastwood was also awake, though judging by the oaths spilling liberally from his mouth, he'd have preferred unconsciousness. "Our shield has recharged, sir, and we have no new status alerts."

"We're in a bad situation, folks," said Recker to his crew. "And that situation will only improve once we're in full control of the *Aeklu*."

"Awaiting orders, sir," said Larson.

Aston nodded. "Me too."

"Lieutenant Eastwood?"

"Give me five minutes and I'll bench press two hundred kilos for you, sir."

"What about you, Lieutenant Burner?"

"I *did* feel like total crap, sir, until Corporal Hendrix

jabbed me with a fat needle. Now I only feel like plain old normal crap."

"I need you, Lieutenant. Are you ready?"

"I'm getting better every passing moment, sir."

As far as answers went, it noticeably failed to address the original question, but Recker let it slide. "We don't know where the *Hexidine* went," he said. "Our brief experience suggests it'll come back."

"The enemy crew are cautious, sir," said Aston. "Four direct hits from lightspeed missiles is probably enough to convince them the Daklan overcame the technical problems with the guidance systems."

"You think the *Hexidine* will go elsewhere?"

Aston shrugged and pursed her lips. "We don't know how it located Ivisto in the first place. It's possible the enemy have secondary targets. After all, we know of two other Laws of Ancidium that we haven't encountered yet. Why would the *Hexidine*'s crew take the risk of further damage when backup may be on the way?"

"Commander Aston makes a good point, sir," said Eastwood. "The *Aeklu* and *Verumol* were fitted with Gateway hardware and it's certain the *Galactar* was too. That means the Laws of Ancidium can travel more or less anywhere they please and in practically zero time."

"The limitation could be comms travel time, sir," said Burner, his voice sounding much stronger than it had a couple of minutes ago. "As far as we're aware, the Lavorix can't send a comms message instantly, which means the *Hexidine* would be required to return to home territory by Gateway in order to call in reinforcements. At least that would be the fastest way to accomplish the task."

Recker tapped his knuckles on the console. "That's assuming the other Laws of Ancidium are free to respond. If the Kilvar are applying pressure, they may be assigned elsewhere."

"Which makes me wonder how much leeway the *Hexidine* has in its own mission," said Aston. "If it's here for a quick life energy grab to refuel the Ancidium, then I doubt its crew will allow it to suffer extensive damage."

"Or be delayed in an extended campaign against the *Aeklu*," mused Recker.

"Maybe. The Daklan lightspeed missiles hurt the enemy, sir. It's possible the Lavorix priorities have changed now."

The more Recker thought about it, the more the idea made sense. While he was certain the Lavorix would not abandon the captured *Aeklu*, they surely had other objectives - which made Recker ask another question.

"Assuming the *Hexidine* will come back for another attempt to recapture or destroy the *Aeklu*, how will they find us?"

"That's a good question, sir," said Eastwood.

"Maybe we can find them first, Lieutenant. Do you have access to a facility that allows you to locate and follow a lightspeed tunnel?" asked Recker.

Eastwood grimaced. "We've been working on the *Aeklu* for months but we know so little about how it works. The problem is, we've tied in our own control system, but our software doesn't know anything about lightspeed tunnels – it knows how to operate the tech in an HPA warship and nothing else."

"When was the software due to be reprogrammed to recognize the extra capabilities of the *Aeklu*?"

Lead Technician Roy was awake and slumped in the corner. She made no effort to answer, and Recker was glad that Eastwood – who wasn't officially part of the *Aeklu's* repair team – had kept his ear to the ground.

"The reprogramming was due to take place concurrently with the final stages of testing, sir," said Eastwood.

"Why not sooner?"

"It was thought the *Aeklu* would need to be in a fully operational state before we'd get any value from the effort, sir."

Decisions like this weren't taken without due consideration, so Recker accepted that a competent team of individuals had come to what they believed was the right decision. Given how events had unfolded, those individuals had made the wrong choice but it was far too late to do anything about it.

"Can you make it so our hardware speaks to the Lavorix hardware, Lieutenant?"

"I guessed that would be your next question, sir," said Eastwood. "The short answer is *yes, probably*. That's with the assistance of the technicians we have onboard. The long answer is *don't expect results any time soon*. This stage of the project was estimated to take between one and two weeks, and that's with the full resources of Ivisto available."

"I'm sure I don't need to tell you we don't have that long," said Recker. "If the *Hexidine* is on its way to one of our planets, we could lose billions of people. I have a feeling their Extractor doesn't require much more fine tuning before it'll kill humans and Daklan, with or without the Frenziol."

"All I can do is get started, sir," said Eastwood. He pointed towards the comms team. "Remember that everything in the navigational system is picked up by the sensors first."

Recker nodded. "The raw data." He let the words hang.

"Yes, sir," said Larson, stepping in obligingly. "The navigational system pulls out a specific data stream from the sensors and that's what Lieutenant Eastwood checks for output spikes, ternium waves and everything else he needs to tell you about. The other data streams can be interpreted into a visual format and that's what I deal with, alongside Lieutenant Burner."

"Since our control software isn't fully configured to handle the Lavorix navigational hardware, maybe there's something in the other sensor data you can extract that tells us where the *Hexidine* is going?"

Larson's face indicated she was considering the matter. "I can access the raw data no problem and I'm sure I can identify the stream intended for the navigational system..."

"I detect a *but* coming, Lieutenant."

"You do, sir. These sensor and comms stations lack the ability to process and interpret that particular data stream."

"Anything we can do to get around that? Like sit you next to Lieutenant Eastwood and let the two of you figure it out?"

"No, sir. The interpretation is done using a dedicated

hardware module in the console. If that module isn't tied in to the *Aeklu*'s navigational system, we'll have to manually read through the raw data. That won't be a quick process."

"How long?"

"I don't know, sir. We have no idea how a lightspeed tunnel shows up in that data, so I'll have to search for the parts I don't recognize and see if I can make sense of them. On top of that, the *Aeklu*'s sensors may well have detected dozens or maybe hundreds of different lightspeed tunnels from the other spaceships that came to and from Ivisto in the last days or weeks. I can't guarantee I could pick the *Hexidine* out of the other traffic."

"Just like when we confused the *Galactar* by sending all those transports into lightspeed back in Meklon space," said Eastwood.

"I don't appreciate the parallels, Lieutenant," said Recker without humour. He sat back in his seat, trying to ignore the sudden pounding in his head. "It's been too long – the *Hexidine* isn't coming back for us," he said. "That means it's gone elsewhere and we're flying the only spaceship that can meet it head on." Recker closed his eyes and the pounding receded. "I will not sit here and wait for the FTL comms reports telling me that another human or Daklan planet has been destroyed."

"We may not have a choice, sir," said Aston quietly.

Having survived the inferno on Trinus-XN and the planet's destruction, Recker couldn't accept the escape of his enemy. Worse, a voice inside told him that his ass had been comprehensively kicked during his short engagement with the *Hexidine* and that if he didn't learn fast, next time his ship and his crew might not be so lucky.

"Sir? I think I've found something," said Burner.

The barely concealed edge of excitement in the other man's voice was enough to plant a seed of hope within Recker.

"What have you got for me, Lieutenant?"

Burner told him.

CHAPTER FOURTEEN

"IT'S THE COMMS SYSTEM, SIR." The excitement was no longer contained and Burner talked fast. "I've located numerous FTL comms pings from the *Hexidine*. Not just the *Hexidine*."

"Handshakes?" asked Recker.

"No, sir, much more than handshakes. These are like the big data packets sent between warships on the same battle network. The *Aeklu* started receiving them when you entered your command codes back on Trinus-XN, but I didn't find out it was happening until now."

Recker knew at once this was enormously significant. "The other packets are from different Laws of Ancidium?"

"Yes, sir. We're receiving data from the *Gorgadar* and the *Ixidar* as well. I can open the packets but the contents don't make any sense. I'm confident that with Lieutenant Larson's help, I can figure out what they contain. And it won't take weeks."

"This is all well and good, Lieutenant, but I've spotted an obvious problem," said Recker.

"We're transmitting our own data packets as well, sir," Burner confirmed. "If the *Hexidine* hadn't already found out we'd captured the *Aeklu* and *Verumol*, I imagine our renewed transmissions would have come as a surprise to the Lavorix."

"Now they know what happened, why not cut the *Aeklu* off the network?" asked Eastwood.

"They want to find us again," said Burner. "And they're likely taking a gamble we won't discover the existence of their ship-to-ship comms."

"A gamble they've already lost," said Aston.

"That's right, Commander." Burner replied.

"Is an FTL battle network even worth a shit over such enormous distances?" asked Eastwood.

"Any comms is better than no comms," said Larson. "We don't even know what kind of amplification the Lavorix have achieved with their transmissions. If they're ahead of the new tech we've been testing in the HPA, then it's possible the Laws of Ancidium can speak to each other with only a short delay. Besides, we're talking about warships which can destroy empires. It's not like they need to call for backup every couple of days. They're designed to operate independently for months or years, so these comms are enough to keep the other members of the network informed."

Recker wanted clarification. "Does this mean we can track not only the *Hexidine* but the last two Laws of Ancidium as well?"

"Potentially, sir." Burner smiled apologetically.

"Assuming these comms packets contain the data I think they contain."

"I'm checking them now," said Larson. "Whoa! Coordinates!"

"Coordinates for where?" asked Recker.

"I haven't found out yet, sir. Since we didn't manage to hack into the Lavorix star charts, the *Aeklu* is carrying the HPA and Daklan equivalents on one of our own data arrays and these coordinates don't tie in with anything we have."

"So how can you find the *Hexidine?*"

Larson grinned and tapped the side of her head. "I recognize the format of the coordinates, sir. The Lavorix are using Meklon data – no doubt stolen – to navigate. We have the same Meklon charts on the *Vengeance*. I'll link to its data arrays and find out where the *Hexidine* was going."

"Will it take long?"

"I realize I made it sound easy, sir. There's a possibility it won't be so straightforward – I'll let you know as soon as I can."

Recker stared at Larson in admiration. "That is some excellent work, Lieutenant. Thank you."

"No worries, sir."

Nervous energy coursed through Recker, eradicating the vestiges of Extractor pain and reminding him what it felt like to experience normal emotions that weren't modified or dictated by a permanent drip feed of Frenziol. He jumped to his feet, intending to pace across the bridge. Remembering that it was far too dangerous a situation for him to leave his post, he sat again.

"Sir, what about the *Gorgadar* and the *Ixidar*?" asked Burner.

"Forget them for the moment, Lieutenant." Recker halted himself. "If you can learn something about those two ships without delaying your search for the *Hexidine*, then do it."

"Yes, sir," said Burner.

"Lieutenant Larson has given us a real boost," Recker continued, "But if you require assistance from either Commander Aston or from the comms teams on our escort ships, let me know at once."

"It won't harm to send the received data to the other comms teams, sir," said Burner. "With your permission, I'll provide the Daklan with a copy of the *Vengeance*'s star chart data as well."

"Do it."

"Yes, sir." Burner glanced at his console and then back at Recker. "The data packets from the *Gorgadar* are stamped *Prime*."

"Is that important, or does it just mean the *Gorgadar* created the initial battle network?"

"I think it means the *Gorgadar* is the command vessel amongst the Laws of Ancidium, sir. The head honcho."

"A bigger threat than the others?" asked Recker.

"I can't tell you that, sir." Burner took in a deep breath. "Particularly since the *Ixidar*'s response packets are stamped *Destroyer*. Maybe once time allows, I'll see if there're any clues in the comms records to explain the meaning behind the names."

"I think we can guess well enough, Lieutenant. Anyway, the time for digging isn't now," Recker confirmed. He clenched and unclenched his fists. His fingers were desperate to start punching buttons on the console – to take part in the search through the comms data – but this was something he was better sitting out.

With his comms team occupied, Recker opened channels to the other three warships in turn. Captain Vazox exuded the type of earned confidence that only came from extensive frontline experience, while Captain Vakh of the desolator *Incendus* – who sounded like he chewed a mouthful of wood splinters three times a day - seemed no less capable. Having witnessed both in action, Recker was confident he was accompanied by the best.

The lone HPA warship – the heavy cruiser *Pulveriser* – was commanded by Captain Lola Bowen. Bowen was softly spoken, yet Recker had seen her combat record and knew she could be relied on. Out of the entire allied fleet at Trinus-XN, these were the survivors and that truth spoke loudest of all.

"They're pretty beat up," said Aston, switching between the sensor feeds. "The *Langinstol* more than the others and that's the one carrying the most lightspeed missiles."

Aston wasn't exaggerating. The annihilator was a mess of varying-sized craters and on one flank, its ternium modules were exposed through a splayed-out section of the armour. While not in such a bad way, the *Incendus* and *Pulveriser* both required urgent repair yard attention. Such was the price of facing the Laws of Ancidium.

"Captain Vazox says he's coming with us and I won't tell him otherwise, Commander. We need those light-speed missiles," said Recker.

"Next time we should try our main armament, huh?" Aston replied. "The Toll. I wonder why the Lavorix chose that name."

"I don't care what they called it or why, as long as it fires straight," said Recker. "Next time we meet the *Hexidine*, I won't be so timid."

"You made the right call holding back on the Toll, sir," said Aston. "And you know I'll say it if I think you screwed up."

"I know, Commander. We got taught a lesson by the *Hexidine*, but I learned from it - I learned that missiles won't be enough. The enemy shield – and ours – recharge too quickly and the mode 3 transits make escape too easy. Those Lavorix know how their ship works and we could empty our magazines at them without bringing their defences down."

"Nobody needs a gun that big," said Aston, recalling her own words from back on Lustre, the first time the *Aeklu* had shown up at the planet. "Except now we do."

"It's strange how the universe works, Commander."

"And I don't think I'll ever tire of it, sir. Except for the wars and the mass murder."

"When this is over – not the entire war, just this part of it we're in the middle of – I'll recommend you for your own command. If that's what you want."

"I want my own ship, sir," said Aston, her expression peculiarly sad. "Not yet." She gestured around the bridge. "What we've got here...it's in my head that if we break the team, then everything will come tumbling down."

"I didn't know you were superstitious, Commander."

"I'm not, sir. Not normally." She shrugged. "You feel it

too, I can see it. You were scared to offer me the recommendation in case my leaving broke whatever blessing is keeping us alive and keeping the HPA away from extinction." Again, the sadness. "But you're too good a man to keep it inside."

"I'd hate to lose what we've got," Recker admitted, his chest thumping with an emotion he couldn't put a name to.

"The team stays together until the Lavorix are gone, sir." Aston gave him a surprise wink. "After that, who knows?"

"Let's get there first," said Recker, smiling despite the circumstances.

The lingering effects of the Extractor were gone, though the cocktail of drugs in his system hadn't nearly dispersed. Recker's body still seemed alien to him, but his thoughts were clear and he felt in control of himself. Each time he remembered the pain, he felt anger more than fear and a single word kept jumping into his head.

Revenge.

This was the first time Recker could remember craving retribution just for the sake of it and he felt no shame. He'd defeat the *Hexidine* and after that he'd volunteer to go looking for the *Gorgadar* and the *Ixidar*, though he expected to be the first name on Telar's list regardless.

"Got it!" said Larson. "Oh shit."

"I don't want to hear *oh shit*, Lieutenant. I want to know where the *Hexidine* is going."

"Lustre, sir. That's where they're going."

"And that's where we're heading as well," said Recker.

"I've entered the destination coordinates into the navigational system," said Eastwood. "I've requested the highest available lightspeed multiplier, but the software won't generate a predicted journey duration."

"Any idea why that is?"

"Because the *Aeklu* wasn't ready for combat duty, sir. The HPA control systems haven't been programmed to interpret the output from the Lavorix hardware." Eastwood looked pained. "And I don't think our software knows how to deal with the capabilities of the *Aeklu*'s ternium drive either. The easiest way to explain it is that the numbers are too big – they exceed numerous expected thresholds so the software assumes there's an error."

"This won't stop us entering lightspeed?"

"No, sir."

Recker drummed his fingers. Time was getting on and the *Hexidine* had a twenty-five-minute head start. "We can't wait any longer. Do we have a ballpark figure of the journey time for an HPA or Daklan warship?"

"The comms team on the *Langinstol* have a predicted travel time of five days to Lustre, sir," said Burner.

"Does that figure allow us to make any predictions based on what we learned from our experience with the *Galactar*?" asked Recker.

"Ten hours for the *Hexidine* to reach Lustre, sir," said Burner. "That's if they didn't mode 3 to the far end of the solar system and then open a Gateway."

If the enemy had travelled by Gateway, whatever Recker decided would be too late anyway. That left him to work on the assumption the *Hexidine* was using conventional lightspeed travel. With that in mind, he didn't ask Burner for confirmation on the accuracy of his ten-hour estimate, since he knew he'd get none. He directed his gaze towards Lieutenant Eastwood. "If we use ten hours as a prediction..."

"Can I just stop you there, sir?" said Eastwood quickly. "You're about to ask me to calculate the *Hexidine*'s potential lightspeed multiplier based on a mass comparison with the *Aeklu*. Well, there are too many variables, such as degree of propulsion overstress, percentage of mass as ternium and the drag."

It had always seemed strange to Recker to consider *drag* as a variable in lightspeed travel. However, the available lightspeed multiplier wasn't perfectly related to the output of a ternium drive, so the unknown variable was widely referred to as drag. Experimentation with warship design had yet to find a link between a vessel's shape and size, and their effect on this drag. Assuming they had any effect at all.

"I don't like launch and hope," said Recker.

"Maybe it's all we have, sir."

"Find out if we have enough tenixite for a Gateway transit to Lustre."

"I checked the moment Lieutenant Burner said the enemy's destination, sir. We're short on what we need."

"How short?"

"The readout doesn't give specifics – just that we don't have enough. There're only scraps in the storage bay – less than a million tons. I'd guess we need several times that amount."

Recker pursed his lips and checked the clock on his console again. Each second he wasted was a second he couldn't recover, but this was a time when acting in haste might guarantee a worse outcome later.

"If we head off in pursuit using the conventional light-speed drive, we'll leave these other warships behind," he said. "I'd prefer to have them with us."

"I've sent comms messages to base, apprising them of the situation sir," said Burner. "The Daklan have done likewise."

"We don't have a planet close enough to Lustre that our fleet will be able to send reinforcements in time," said Recker. "In truth, any ship without lightspeed missiles isn't going to be anything other than target practice for the *Hexidine*." He lowered his head in thought.

"An update for you, sir," said Burner. "I've checked the last coordinates we received from the *Gorgadar* and the *Ixidar*. The former is on the extreme edge of Meklon territory and the latter is showing unrecognized coordinates. Neither of them is anywhere nearby, though distance isn't such a barrier when you can pick a destination and open a Gateway."

"Thank you, Lieutenant. Keep me informed."

"Yes, sir."

Recker drummed his fingers a few more times and an idea came. "Lieutenant Eastwood, how does the *Aeklu*'s Gateway generator work?"

"We send an instruction to the hardware and the generator module targets the storage bay. Once the Gateway receives a launch command, it converts the tenixite into energy and the Gateway appears. Our hardware is tied in and the front-end method isn't much different to sending the *Aeklu* into lightspeed."

"What if you instructed the generator to target one of our ternium propulsion modules?"

Eastwood looked like he wanted to object and then thought better of it. "I'll take a look and see if that's possible, sir." He huffed and puffed for a full minute. "The converter can target a limited area outside the storage bay. Only one of the propulsion modules is within range, and it's tight. If I overrode the fail-safes, the converter could probably shave a small section off that ternium block."

"Will it work, Lieutenant? Will it be enough to activate the Gateway?"

"I can't predict the outcome, sir. Ternium contains a lot more potential energy than its ore, so maybe the generator would receive more than it needs and something would go wrong."

"Or it might work and send us to Lustre ahead of the *Hexidine*," said Recker.

"It might. Or the *Aeklu* might blow up."

"Is it so vital that we arrive first, sir?" said Aston. "I know a few million people were too stubborn to leave and I don't want to pretend they're unimportant, but they made the choice. We have other planets to consider first and if we disabled the *Aeklu* because something critical failed as a result of our actions, the end result for the HPA could be far worse."

"I don't want to pretend those people are unimportant either, Commander, but my primary aim here is to surprise the *Hexidine*. Every time we encounter the Laws of Ancidium, they make the opening move. This time, I'd prefer to be the one waiting for them. Not only that – the Gateway will allow us to take the *Langinstol*, the *Incendus* and the *Vengeance* to Lustre. With surprise, we might inflict some damage upon our enemy before they realise the danger."

"And we get a chance to save those people anyway," said Aston. She nodded. "Let's do it."

"Lieutenant Eastwood, it's time to put things in motion."

"I've been looking into it while you were talking to Commander Aston, sir. I reckon it'll take me thirty minutes to alter some of the configuration settings and override what I need to. Then we can give it a try."

"Go ahead, Lieutenant."

Recker settled himself in for a wait, though he was unable to relax given the possibility the *Hexidine* might surprise them all by returning to Trinus-XN for another shot at the *Aeklu*. He used the available time to take remote control of the *Vengeance* and he flew it onto the top plating near the stern. Meanwhile, Captain Vazox and Captain Vakh flew their warships close by, so they'd also be taken to Lustre when the Gateway opened.

With reluctance, Captain Bowen agreed to fly the *Pulveriser* directly to the closest HPA base capable of enacting repairs, that being the planet Basalt, four days travel time from Ivisto. What Bowen refused was the opportunity to leave before the *Aeklu* and she insisted on staying nearby to scan for the *Hexidine*'s return.

The delay was also enough for Corporal Hendrix and her forest of needles to get all the Daklan soldiers back on their feet. None of them looked healthy and even Sergeant Shadar appeared to be struggling with the aftereffects, though he declared himself ready to fight.

"I'd like to promise bed rest for everyone, but it's not within my power," said Recker.

Everyone knew the reality and he guessed they'd all forgotten what a good night's sleep felt like. Survival from day to day and hour to hour was what remained, along with a hundred inflamed needle holes in thighs and ass cheeks.

"I'm nearly done, sir," said Eastwood eventually. "Another five minutes."

"We've had nothing from Fleet Admiral Telar, sir," said Burner. "I wouldn't expect anything in the next five minutes either. The Ivisto comms hubs could speak to Earth without much delay, but the *Aeklu*'s comms can't amplify an FTL transmission to the same degree." He cleared his throat. "Well, they probably can, but I haven't figured out how to do it. I don't think our consoles can access all the available capabilities of the Lavorix comms systems."

"Look into it when you get the chance," said Recker. With the discovery of each new limitation, he was beginning to learn exactly how far short of combat readiness the *Aeklu* had been when the *Hexidine* arrived at Trinus-XN.

"Yes, sir."

"Still, some guidance would be nice," Recker muttered, putting the comms issue to one side. "We're acting blind to the wider activities of the HPA and Daklan."

That guidance didn't come. Thirty-two minutes after he started reconfiguring the navigational software, Lieutenant Eastwood declared his work complete.

The platoon didn't need reminding that Gateway

travel was rough and Recker did the courtesy of informing the technicians what they were about to suffer, assuming everything went to plan.

With that done and the other warships ready, he gave Eastwood the instruction. "Activate the Gateway, Lieutenant."

"Yes, sir. It'll take a few minutes for the Gateway to appear once I've entered the command."

"Do it."

Several minutes later, during which Recker heard no indication the *Aeklu*'s hardware was building to anything significant, an immense sphere of darkness expanded from an origin point deep inside the hull. The sensors registered zero input for a split second and then the four warships were carried elsewhere.

CHAPTER FIFTEEN

THE EXPECTED PAIN came and went, and Recker scarcely registered its passing, as if his body had become so accustomed to the torture that it had adapted in order to protect his mind from insanity.

"Status reports!" yelled Recker. He resisted the urge to push the *Aeklu* into high acceleration and relied on the energy shield to absorb any unexpected attacks.

"We didn't break up," said Eastwood, his voice registering mild surprise. "I've got an alert on the propulsion module I targeted with the Gateway hardware. Other than that, we're in good shape."

"Sensors online," said Larson. "The scan and lock on these arrays is damn fast. There's the *Langinstol* and the *Incendus*!" she said. "And the *Vengeance*!"

"And Lustre, sir," said Burner. "On the screen and at a hundred thousand klicks. I'm continuing my search for the *Hexidine*."

"We arrived dead on the nose," said Aston.

The planet appeared on one of the bulkhead screens and the level of detail obtained by the sensors was incredible – it was as if the Lavorix hardware could ignore both distance and atmospheric conditions and the feed appeared almost too real.

"We're on the Adamantine side," said Recker, peering at the grey rectangle of the base.

"It's no wonder we had such a job escaping from the *Galactar*," said Larson. "This sensor hardware is amazing."

"I'm more concerned about the *Hexidine*, Lieutenant," Recker reminded her.

"I'm looking, sir. I'm also scanning the surface broadcasts."

"There should be no military transmissions," said Recker.

"I've located one, sir. It's a transport ship called *Summit* and it's currently in low orbit not far from Adamantine."

"Fleet Admiral Telar must have left it there in case anyone changed their minds about staying. Does the *Summit*'s crew know we're here?"

"No, sir."

"Make them aware."

"On it."

"I haven't located any sign of the *Hexidine*," said Burner. "They could be blind side of the planet, or, if they're being cagey, they might be hiding behind the moon or one of the nearby planets."

"They're not being cagey, Lieutenant," said Recker. "If they were here, they'd have already fired their

Extractor at something and more than likely destroyed the *Summit* at the same time."

"The surface broadcasts indicate no alarm, sir," said Larson.

The calm was enough to give Recker a degree of reassurance. "Keep watching and listening. I'll fly us around the planet so we can scan the blind side and obtain a better viewing angle of the moon."

"I've sent a transmission to Earth - am I letting anyone on Lustre know we're here?" asked Burner.

"Only the *Summit*'s crew. Also alert them to the anticipated arrival of the *Hexidine* and suggest they request permission from base to hightail it out of here. They'll make an easy target and I'm sure the enemy won't care that it's only a transport."

"Lieutenant Bert Howell is in charge of the vessel, sir," said Burner. "He is not pleased to hear from us."

"I didn't think he would be," said Recker. He'd done his part and forgot about the transport. "Put a trajectory line on the tactical for me," he ordered.

"What about our escort ships, sir?" asked Larson.

"I've sent a synch code to the *Vengeance*," said Recker. "It'll match our vector and maintain a constant fifty-klick distance." He hesitated. So far, the Daklan had allowed him to take the lead, but he couldn't keep making that assumption.

"Get me a channel to Captain Vazox and Captain Vakh," he ordered. "Bridge speakers." Recker looked towards the ceiling. "If we have any."

"We do have bridge speakers, sir," Burner confirmed. "And a lot of guests on the bridge."

"I'm not about to convey any military secrets, Lieutenant."

"Yes, sir. I have both Daklan officers in the open channel."

"Gentlemen," said Recker, relying on the translation module to choose a suitable equivalent in the Daklan tongue. "We are working towards a single purpose and so far, we have escaped death."

"I know what you will ask, Captain Recker, and I agree," said Captain Vazox. "You command the *Aeklu* and I will follow your lead."

"As will I," said Captain Vakh. "Until I receive contrary instructions from my superiors."

And that was that. The Daklan went even further up in Recker's estimation and he thanked both for their determination to maximise the chance of this mission's success.

"Is there a plan, Captain Recker?" asked Vazox.

"First, we complete a blind side scan of Lustre."

"And after that?" asked Vakh.

"If we locate the *Hexidine*, we'll shoot it with the *Aeklu*'s main armament. I'll also look for a way to bring it to a standstill so you can hit it with lightspeed missiles."

One or both Daklan – Recker couldn't be sure which – broke into raucous laughter which lasted for several seconds.

"The plan is lacking in detail, Captain Recker!" said Vazox.

Recker detected no mockery in the words and he laughed as well. "The best ones always are."

The Daklan didn't stick around to chat and they exited the channel. During the short conversation, Burner had put a red line on the tactical, which indicated the most efficient course that would allow a scan of the moon and Lustre's blind side.

"I've got Fleet Admiral Telar holding on the comms, sir," said Larson. "He's routing through the Adamantine comms hub, so there isn't much travel time delay."

"Holding? How long has he been waiting?"

"I told him you were engaged in a vital tactical discussion with our Daklan allies."

"That I was," Recker said. "Bring him in. Open channel again."

"Captain Recker?" said Telar.

"Yes, sir." Seeing no reason to delay the mission while he talked, Recker unleashed the power of the engines and the *Aeklu* accelerated with the same bestial noise as before.

Aston waved to get his attention. "The escort, sir," she mouthed, thumbing over her shoulder.

Recker nodded and held the *Aeklu* at sixteen hundred kilometres per second, which was the usual maximum velocity of a desolator. All three ships kept pace.

"I have reports of what happened at Ivisto," Telar continued. "They do not fill me with joy."

"With good reason, sir," said Recker. He provided Telar with an outline of what had occurred and then described the current situation.

Telar was a good listener when he wasn't being fed evasive crap by underperforming officers, and he sat quietly while Recker talked.

"Can you defeat the *Hexidine?*" he asked when Recker was done.

"There're a whole lot of ifs and maybes, sir. It depends on whether the Toll – the *Aeklu*'s main armament – fires and it also depends on the Daklan lightspeed missiles."

"Once, I cursed the existence of those missiles," said Telar. "Now, I wish our allies had more of them in their arsenal."

"The *Langinstol* and the *Incendus* are carrying a total of seven between them, sir. Are we able to call on a few more annihilators and desolators? The *Hexidine* is already damaged and if its shield is negated, I'm sure we can bring the enemy ship down or drive it away."

"Assuming it arrives at Lustre as you expect, we want it to stay there, Captain Recker. If it departs, its next destination could be Ravel or Bronze. Or Earth. You say you can follow the *Hexidine*, but what if the Lavorix evade your pursuit? Better to finish them at Lustre." Telar paused for a half second. "Or die trying."

"What about those reinforcements, sir?"

"In forty-eight hours I could have one annihilator and three desolators at Lustre. In ninety-six hours you could add another six annihilators and nine desolators to the total."

"That's too long," said Recker. The glimmering of an idea appeared, though he needed to ask a few more questions first.

"Where is the shield breaker, sir? And is it ready for operational use?"

"The shield breaker underwent testing and I personally signed it off for deployment."

Recker detected the unspoken words. "Is it ready, sir?"

"The test routines were accelerated. The gun will

fire," said Telar. "As for where it is, the weapon is currently in the hold of the heavy lifter *Maximus* and in transit to a planet called Tronstal in the RETI-11 system."

"When will it arrive?"

"The *Maximus* and its escort are due to re-enter local space in thirty-six hours, and the deployment is estimated to take a further six hours."

"Is the *Maximus* due a mid-point re-entry to local space in case of updated orders?" asked Recker. A warship at lightspeed couldn't send or receive comms.

"No, Carl. The *Maximus* will not enter local space before it arrives at its destination."

Recker gritted his teeth at the news. "I could have used that gun," he said.

"Even if the *Maximus* broke lightspeed, it wouldn't reach Lustre in nine hours and it certainly couldn't finish the deployment."

"I need access to the tenixite processing facility here on Lustre, sir," said Recker. "If I can fill the *Aeklu*'s tanks, I'll be able to Gateway out to wherever those annihilators and desolators are stationed and then Gateway back to Lustre."

"And you'd hoped to do the same with the shield breaker," said Telar in understanding.

"Yes, sir."

"We took the ore with us when we evacuated the planet, Captain Recker. It was too valuable to leave behind." Telar sighed. "We had three lightspeed missiles in one of the Adamantine bunkers as well, along with a dedicated shuttle the Daklan use to load the warheads. Those are now on Earth."

Recker felt like putting his head in his hands. "In that case, I'll wait for the *Hexidine* to come and I'll do what I can, sir."

"I'm sorry, Carl. If I think of anything, I'll get back to you. Should I request the Daklan send their warships?"

"No, sir. How close are they to Tronstal?"

"I can't give you the specifics off the top of my head, but most are closer to Tronstal than they are to Lustre."

Recker didn't know what suggest and he needed more time to think. "Don't make any requests of those ships, sir. Not yet."

"If the *Aeklu* is destroyed, I will have to recall the shield breaker anyway, Carl. We have a second nearing the end of its production, but it will be many months before we have enough to install them on each of our planets. Even then, the Lavorix will be able to approach from our blind side and fire their Extractors without fear of a response. Blanket coverage of our worlds will take years."

"The shield breakers only perform a single function, sir. Once the shield is down, the warship behind it still needs to be destroyed and that's much easier said than done."

"You haven't forgotten our discussion from when you were on Ivisto, Captain Recker? If we prove too big a mouthful, the Lavorix may simply back off and hunt for softer prey. Withdrawal and consolidation do not work if you continue suffering losses."

Recker didn't want to be drawn into the speculation. Usually, it was something he enjoyed, but now he felt sure the Lavorix would never give up. They had no more

Meklon to hunt and they needed the life energies of humanity and the Daklan.

"I don't think the Lavorix have anywhere else to go, sir," he said. "I think we're all they have."

"You may be right, Carl," said Telar. "Part of me thinks it's better to fight now than have it hanging over us forever. Who is to say that in ten years the Lavorix won't come back, only this time with six new Laws of Ancidium?"

Thinking about it was depressing and Recker thought it time to end the conversation. "Sir, I must attend to my ship."

"Of course. Go. We'll speak soon."

"Yes, sir."

The channel went dead and Recker saw from the tactical that he'd travelled far enough for the blind side scan to commence. He slowed the *Aeklu* to a crawl and within two minutes, Burner was able to declare himself confident that the *Hexidine* was not in this part of the QS-9 system.

"Now, we wait," said Eastwood. "Nine hours."

"And no chance of a break," said Burner glumly.

"I can personally guarantee that you won't be sleeping any time this week, Lieutenant," said Corporal Hendrix. "Not with those drugs."

"He doesn't usually sleep anyway," said Larson. "Lieutenant Burner is nine parts caffeine, one part cheeseburger."

"It doesn't look like they installed a replicator on the *Aeklu* yet anyway," said Burner, not at all offended. "No coffee for me. And I bet the sleeping quarters are ten klicks from here."

"There's a Lavorix replicator down the steps and along the corridor outside," said LT Roy. "You don't want to know what comes out of it. The HPA replicators were due to be brought onboard and fitted tomorrow."

"Another reason to hate the Lavorix," said Burner. "They arrived at Ivisto a day too soon."

"We didn't clean the sleeping quarters either," Roy continued. "I'd recommend you stay away."

Burner's face indicated his curiosity and he looked as if he were about to ask for details. He thought better of it and kept his mouth closed.

Expecting the hands of the clock to drag interminably, Recker tried to bring himself into a state of calm, or at least into a state where he didn't feel the need to punch the nearest inanimate object. Forcing himself to breathe deeply, he concentrated his mind.

We've got the tools to come out on top, so why am I feeling pessimistic about the outcome?

It was a question he was determined to answer and he closed his eyes to see if it would help him think.

"We've got the lightspeed missiles, but the Toll is the only game changer," he said after a minute. Recker opened his eyes and found Aston was looking at him with her eyes narrowed. "Going into battle with an untested weapon is never a good idea," he finished.

"If it doesn't work as expected, it's better to know about it now," Aston nodded.

"And since we're not going to break the *Hexidine*'s shield without the Toll, it doesn't matter so much if the test ends up wrecking the *Aeklu*," Recker said. "Without that gun, we'll lose."

"Planet twelve in the QS-9 system: Ebos," said Aston. "Or we could just fire out into space and see what happens."

"I prefer a solid target, Commander," said Recker, feeling the need to take out his anger on something that wouldn't fire back.

The promise of action – even if it was just test firing an enormous gun – filled Recker with a sense of purpose. "Here's the plan, folks," he said. "We're taking a mode 3 flight to Ebos and we're going to put a big hole in its surface."

Reaching for the controls, Recker felt a childlike excitement and not for a moment did he allow himself to consider what might go wrong.

CHAPTER SIXTEEN

HAVING INFORMED the escort ships about his intention, Recker didn't delay. He cancelled the synch code keeping the *Vengeance* and *Aeklu* locked together. Then, he entered the mode 3 destination by tapping on the zoomed-out tactical display and finished by pressing the activation button on the control bar. Nausea came and went, but Recker hardly noticed. In moments, the sensor feeds appeared and the local area scans were finished.

"Ebos," he said, watching the feed. "I can see why there're no tourists." The planet was rocky and barren, with grey mountain peaks forming a ring around most of its circumference.

"Another ball of rock, like a million we've seen before," said Larson. "Diameter: three thousand klicks. Current distance from QS-9 is four billion klicks."

"And we are one million klicks from its surface," said Burner.

"That's a good combat range," said Aston.

Recker cast his mind back to his encounter with the *Aeklu* when it had been under Lavorix control - how the massive projectiles from the Toll had wrought havoc upon everything they struck and how a direct hit had drained two mesh deflector charges from the *Indarox*'s shield. And that had still not been enough to stop the projectile.

"Target the planet and fire the Toll, Commander," said Recker.

"Can't miss from a million klicks," laughed Eastwood.

"Let's hope the calibration didn't get screwed up when the Dark Bomb exploded," said Aston.

She leaned closer to her console in the way she always did when concentrating. It was a sign of both nerves and readiness which Recker had come to recognize.

"Target set. Firing the Toll."

Recker's eyes went to the topside sensor feeds and he saw the two-thousand-metre barrel jump so far back into the turret that it vanished completely before emerging again.

The sound of the discharge was peculiar, like a fog-muffled, doleful bell. The turret was several thousand metres above the bridge, but somehow it felt as if the source of the noise was just beyond the walls and its effects upon Recker were more than just physical, as if it somehow reverberated within his soul, dragging out unwanted emotions and making him feel like he was at the mass funeral of everyone he'd ever known.

Four seconds later, a crater, hundreds of kilometres in diameter, appeared on the surface of Ebos and a shock-wave rippled outwards at tremendous speed, making it seem as if the rocks had been turned to liquid. Before the shockwaves had completed their first circuit of the planet, the *Aeklu*'s sensors picked out countless ejected boulders thrown up by the impact and escaping into orbit.

"Extensive seismic trauma detected," said Larson. A grumbling and thumping of reload motors started and she had to raise her voice to be heard, but the cracking in her voice indicated she'd been affected by same feelings as Recker. "The surface plates surrounding the impact crater are breaking up. The sensors calculate the impact velocity at 289,000 klicks per second."

"Damn, that made me feel like I was dying," said Eastwood. "That's why they called it the Toll."

Recker blinked rapidly and took another deep breath. "I'm more interested in how the turret and barrel came through the discharge, Lieutenant."

"Sorry, sir – I'd have said right away if there'd been a problem. There are no changes to the status on the turret, the barrel or the loading mechanisms."

Recker didn't take his eyes from the feed. "How was the accuracy, Commander Aston?"

"Impact was sixty kilometres from target, sir." Her face was ashen, like she'd seen a vision of her own death.

"A large enough error to miss the *Hexidine* across a similar distance."

"Yes, sir. I hate to say it, but I recommend a second shot to help gauge the variation."

"Do I need to reposition the *Aeklu* for the sensors to detect the impact point?"

"I would recommend it, sir," said Larson, her voice steady now. "There's too much airborne debris around the first crater. Even with the *Aeklu*'s sensors, the reading might be off."

Maintaining the same distance from Ebos, Recker piloted the *Aeklu* a quarter of the way clockwise around the planet. From this new position, the dividing line between night and day cut a sharp line from north to south, while the original crater remained in sight. A smear of fast-moving dust, kicked up by the first impact, was spreading rapidly and would likely soon encompass the entire planet.

"Is this far enough?" asked Recker.

"Yes, sir," Larson confirmed.

"What are you waiting for, Commander?"

"You know what I'm waiting for, sir." Aston glanced his way then back to her console. "Here goes." Her fingertip delicately touched the activation panel and the Toll fired again.

Recker braced himself for the effects. The sound came for a second time, the same as it had before, only this time it was only sound, as if the initial experience was a unique insight into despair – a glimpse and a promise that would forever remain a memory.

A second impact crater appeared, as large as the first. A new series of shockwaves encircled the planet, while more debris was thrown up and another huge cloud of dust was formed. Larson zoomed in the sensors and hundreds of snaking cracks were apparent, some extending as far as the first crater.

"Fifty kilometres from target that time," said Aston, the colour returned to her face.

"Have you learned enough from the second shot, Commander?"

"Yes, sir. Either the barrel is too short or the rifling isn't perfect - the projectiles aren't spinning fast enough when they emerge from the muzzle and they have a slight wobble."

"We're shooting into a vacuum," said Burner in puzzlement. "How can the projectiles have a wobble without any atmospheric resistance?"

"The slugs are mostly ternium, Lieutenant, and that ternium is what increases the velocity both in and out of the barrel." said Eastwood patiently. "If the projectiles don't emerge precisely as intended, the acceleration in conjunction with a lopsided spin will shift them off course and then..."

"I'll take your word for it," said Burner.

"Quiet please," said Recker. "Commander Aston, can you compensate for the inaccuracy?"

"We can perform further testing, sir, but I suspect we could fire all nine of our remaining projectiles and still be unable to predict exactly how the tenth will fly."

"And from this I conclude that any discharge of the Toll should be from a closer range than one million klicks."

"Yes, sir. I'd suggest no more than a quarter of a million klicks, assuming a stationary target. If the *Hexidine* is in motion, you'll have to lead the shot as necessary."

"Not the outcome I'd hoped for," said Recker. "Damnit."

"Maybe we should return to Lustre, sir," said Aston. "In case we completely underestimated the *Hexidine*'s travel time."

Recker placed his hands on the controls and then was struck by a thought. "Lieutenant Eastwood, you said those Toll projectiles are mostly ternium in composition."

"Yes, sir. They contain a hardened alloy core, with a thick cladding of ternium - similar to the projectiles fired by the Tri-Cannon."

"And would I be right to think that the *Aeklu*'s ternium store is self-loading?"

"Yes, sir. The storage bay is just behind the underside armour plating. It's fitted with gravity scoops which are designed to suck in tenixite powder from a thousand metres – the *Aeklu* doesn't even need to land."

"Would those scoops work with larger objects? Like a ternium slug from the Toll?"

Eastwood stared straight ahead and Recker could have sworn he heard the cogs turning. "I don't think so, sir. Besides, we have no way to eject a slug from the magazine without shipyard facilities."

"I wasn't thinking about ejecting an unspent projectile, Lieutenant. We've fired two perfectly good shots into Ebos. We could recover those and use them as fuel for our Gateway generator and tenixite converter."

Again, Eastwood stared.

"He's thinking about collision elasticity," said Burner. "I can see it in his face."

"That is what I'm thinking about," Eastwood admitted. "And I believe the spent slugs will have been compressed into disks, but not broken into pieces. Therefore, they won't fit into our storage bay."

"Unless we subjected them to an extended burst of gauss fire," said Recker.

"Yes, that would do the trick."

Recker smiled. "Can you confirm the auto-loading system is functioning, Lieutenant Eastwood? Before we waste any ammunition."

"I haven't inspected the hardware personally, sir, but the lights are green."

"That's good enough. Let's travel a little closer to Ebos before we start firing."

"I've located what might be the second projectile, sir," said Larson.

"That dark orange smudge?" asked Recker, peering at the zoomed feed.

"That's it, sir. It's hot from impact."

Recker pushed the control bars forwards and the *Aeklu* sped towards the impact crater. Already, the clouds of dust from the twin impacts had obscured much of the surface and the feeds were becoming grainy. When it approached the planet, the *Aeklu*'s shield was struck by dozens of rocks, the largest being a hundred metres in diameter and travelling at high velocity. Not one of the impacts significantly affected the gauge.

Having such incredible defences at his disposal made Recker grudgingly impressed that the Lavorix had not taken their near invulnerability for granted and had treated the Laws of Ancidium as precious objects, not to be risked. That caution explained why these warships had been able to terrorise the Meklon for so long, without being destroyed in battle.

"That's definitely the ternium slug, sir," said Larson.

Recker guided the *Aeklu* through the dust. A few ejected rocks which hadn't escaped into orbit rained down in numbers too few to give any concern. The crater was vastly bigger than the *Aeklu* and Recker was left in awe that a single shot from a gun was capable of such a feat.

"I've taken manual control over one of the underside repeaters, sir," said Aston, once the warship was stationary over the crater.

"Be my guest," said Recker.

Aston used the backup controls to target the gauss gun and she directed a stream of bullets into the ternium slug. The orange metal turned white in patches and the disk split into pieces. For long seconds, Aston continued and the slug broke into progressively smaller parts.

"Is that enough?" she asked, taking her hands off the controls.

"I don't know," said Eastwood. "I've never operated the self-loading systems before."

"Give it some more," said Recker. "Better to spend a few extra seconds on it now."

Ten seconds later, Aston relented and sat back with a smile. "There was something satisfying about doing that."

"All that shooting mixed lots of rock in with the ternium," said Larson. "Along with pieces of alloy from the projectile's core."

"Which won't be a problem," said Eastwood. "The depleted ternium is turned into powder anyway and ejected from the *Aeklu* via a chute. Any impurities in the bay will get the same treatment."

"Let's go get our fuel," said Recker.

He brought the *Aeklu* steadily lower and the dust became thicker. In the background, he could hear Lieutenant Burner marvelling at the capabilities of the Lavorix sensors and, indeed, Recker had no problem with visibility.

The curvature at the bottom of the crater, in combination with the *Aeklu*'s twenty-eight-thousand-metre length, made it hard to bring the gravity scoops into their thousand-metre collection range. For a time, Recker thought he might have to instruct Aston to shoot a few of the larger ternium pieces up the side of the crater, like a fairground game played on a massively larger scale and where the prize was saving a few million people from Extractor death instead of an oversized and shoddy stuffed toy.

In the end, that game wasn't played. Following some careful positioning that saw the nose and stern come within a few metres of the rocky sides of the crater, Lieutenant Eastwood declared he had a green activation light on the scoops.

"Hold it right here, sir," he said. "We're playing with metres, and there's no wiggle room."

"I know, Lieutenant," said Recker through gritted teeth. "I just flew us down here and I'm aware of the margins."

Eastwood grinned and Recker knew he'd been done. "This won't take long, sir."

The crew, the mostly forgotten soldiers and the completely forgotten technicians watched the operation on the underside feed. A hatch in the *Aeklu*'s armour slid open, revealing a dark shaft. The gravity scoops weren't visible, but they began sucking up pieces from the surface immediately. Chunks of the ternium slug rose from the ground and disappeared into the opening.

"The scoops are selectively grabbing the ternium and

leaving the rocks behind!" said Eastwood in excitement. "We should have plenty in the tank when we're done."

Recker didn't have any firm plans for either the Gateway or the tenixite converter, but he felt nevertheless relieved that both would soon be available should they be needed. Given the tremendous possibilities offered by these technologies, he was certain it wouldn't be long before a suitable use became apparent.

Vacuuming the ternium from Ebos didn't take longer than ten minutes and towards the end, Recker was becoming fidgety at having to keep the *Aeklu* in one place for so long. The moment Eastwood declared the operation complete and the underside hatch closed, Recker piloted the warship away from the planet at maximum acceleration.

Those ten minutes had also given him some time to think and he had the beginnings of an idea. Before he revealed the details – scant as they were – he activated a mode 3 transit to Lustre, where his sensor team performed a rapid local area scan. Those scans were no more than a formality - the *Langinstol*, the *Incendus* and the *Vengeance* were in the same place as before, half a million kilometres from Lustre and directly above the deserted Adamantine base.

With the *Aeklu* back among the other warships, Recker turned the idea around in his mind.

"We need someone on the *Vengeance*," he said at last.

Aston was usually alert to Recker's ideas, but from the expression she wore, she couldn't guess what he intended.

"Why?" she asked.

"I said before that our only options against the *Hexi-*

dine are the lightspeed missiles and the *Aeklu*'s main armament," he said. "I was wrong. The *Vengeance* already created a big hole inside the enemy ship and we saw how it took off when we fired those missiles into the same place. That makes me wonder if we were close to hitting something critical. Like the shield generator."

Various emotions passed across Aston's face and Recker fully expected she'd talk through his plan before she voiced her main objections. He guessed right.

"Another mode 3 behind the *Hexidine*'s shield and a second Executor strike?" she said. "If the enemy shield went down, we'd have a good chance of destroying them. Even if they broke off the engagement, without that shield they'd be vulnerable to attacks from our fleet wherever they showed up next."

"Or if the Executor took out their life support module, they'd be stranded here at Lustre," said Recker. "That wouldn't be a positive outcome for the people who stayed behind, but it would prevent the *Hexidine* from troubling any of our other planets. It would effectively be out of the war."

"Alternatively, the Executor might not hit anything and the *Vengeance* would be destroyed," said Eastwood. "I'm sure you're about to tell me it's a worthwhile risk." He nodded. "And I'd agree with you."

"Thank you for the input, Lieutenant," said Recker dryly. "Now, Commander Aston, it looks as if you have something to say."

"The *Aeklu* is our most important warship. I can fly the *Vengeance*," she said.

"You can and you will be doing so," said Recker.

"You made it seems like..." Aston started.

He smiled. "I know what I made it seem like, Commander."

"We'll be spread thinly," she answered, recovering quickly.

"You'll take Corporal Montero for comms and sensors."

Montero had an aptitude for flight and planned to request a transfer to warship duties when the opportunity arose. Having made the jump himself and knowing the difficulties, Recker had allowed Montero to sit in with him and his crew during routine patrols over Trinus-XN. She was a fast learner and capable of operating both Meklon and HPA hardware.

"Sink or swim time for Corporal Montero," said Aston.

"It's got to happen for her some time. When the shooting starts, you'll need to keep the *Vengeance* out of trouble until the time comes to mode 3 behind the enemy's shield. Then, you fire the Executor." Recker smiled again and this time it was harder to make it seem genuine. "In truth, I'd prefer to go myself. That part you guessed right."

"You think it's a bigger risk being on the *Vengeance*," she said in a private channel.

"I don't know one way or another, Commander. It's the feeling I get."

Aston didn't normally sigh. Now she did. "Lieutenant Larson knows the weapons console, sir. How she'll handle it in real combat I couldn't tell you."

Montero wasn't the only one with ambitions and Aston had spent many hours with Lieutenant Larson, training her in new skills that would help her progress from comms lieutenant to warship commander. The ten months at Ivisto hadn't been entirely spent chewing the fat in front of the replicator.

"She'll cope the same way we all did on our first time," said Recker.

"She's good."

"I know."

"We're still too few to effectively manage two warships, sir. You could request assistance from the Daklan."

"Their crews know Daklan hardware. They don't know the Meklon or HPA kit. Besides, I had a different idea in mind. We have fuel for the Gateway – I'm going to take the *Aeklu* to Earth and pick up some extra crew. Enough for both ships." He pointed at the door. "I'd like you and Corporal Montero on the *Vengeance* before we leave. It'll make me feel better knowing we're prepared for the unexpected."

"How am I getting there, sir?"

"The same way you came in."

"Topside plating?"

"Yes. I'll remote land the *Vengeance* nearby."

"Don't accelerate while we're up there, sir."

"I'll try my best," said Recker. "If the *Hexidine* comes early and I have to take off, I'll be sure to give you a wave."

"As Corporal Montero and I go tumbling off into the void."

"Come to think of it, you'll more likely be killed when you impact the Toll turret at fifty klicks per second."

Aston stood. "If you need to clean any stains off, make sure you use Adam's toothbrush."

"Will do. Good luck, Commander. I'll give you further instructions once you're over there."

"Yes, sir."

"And look after that ship."

"Always."

Having picked up her gauss rifle, Aston beckoned for Corporal Montero to follow. Montero asked a couple of questions on the way through the still-open blast door, but didn't object to her new orders.

When they were gone, Recker called Lead Technician Roy across. With everything happening it seemed like she'd decided it was best to sit quietly in one corner with the other members of her team. Recker had different plans.

"While the interior scans indicate none of the Lavorix came onboard at Ivisto, I'd really like you to fix that damn door," he said mildly. In case Roy had forgotten exactly which door, he thumbed over his shoulder.

Bobbing her head in agreement, Roy got on with it and Recker turned back to his console.

CHAPTER SEVENTEEN

WHILE RECKER PILOTED the *Vengeance* remotely towards the *Aeklu*, Larson took the seat next to him. She looked nervous and was trying to hide it.

"We all started somewhere, Lieutenant. Now it's your turn."

Larson gathered herself and signed into the weapons console. "Yes, sir."

"Lieutenant Burner, please get in touch with Fleet Admiral Telar on Earth and tell him of our requirements for additional crew. We'll benefit from having a few dozen extra soldiers and a fully equipped medical team as well."

"I'm speaking to him right this moment, sir."

"Don't let me interrupt you," said Recker, watching Larson from the corner of his eye.

"I won't need assistance, sir," she said, noticing his attention.

"I know you won't, Lieutenant. If I thought you did, you wouldn't be sitting there."

"I finished hundreds of simulator runs when I was on Ivisto, sir. I know they're no replacement for the real thing, but I've got the muscle memory now." She patted the side of her head without taking her eyes from her console. "Once you've got the muscle memory, the limitation is up here, and I've been through enough to know I'll cope."

When she first came aboard the *Axiom* heavy cruiser, many months ago, Larson had been happy to accept a junior role to Lieutenant Burner. Gradually as time went by, she'd developed into an equal partner instead of a subordinate. Recker didn't think she'd ever have the same almost supernatural ability to glean snippets of vital information from raw sensor data as Burner, but she had the talent to advance through the ranks. Burner, on the other hand, had found his level and he was happy there.

The *Vengeance* was directly over the top of the *Aeklu* and Recker made some final adjustments. "This is your time and your chance, Lieutenant. I know you won't waste it."

"I'll be replaced in about twenty minutes," she said. "Once we pick up the new crew."

"That doesn't matter. You're here now and there's nobody else."

"Thank you, sir."

"We've got our crew!" called Burner. "We're invited to land at the Lancer base on Earth and pick them up."

"Did you hear that, Lieutenant Eastwood? Enter the coordinates into the navigational system and ready the Gateway. The moment Commander Aston and Corporal Montero are onboard, you can begin the warmup."

"Yes, sir."

"Now we've got enough tenixite for the Gateway, are you still intending to pick up some additional Daklan warships and bring them here to Lustre, sir?" asked Larson.

"Thank you for the reminder," said Recker. He set the *Vengeance* down on the upper plating and activated the autopilot so it would stay there. "Lieutenant Burner, put in the request with Fleet Admiral Telar. If we bring a few annihilators here to Lustre, they might turn the battle."

"Yes, sir."

"What's your progress, Commander Aston?" asked Recker on the comms.

"We only just left the bridge, sir."

"That was a full five minutes ago."

"I'll let you know when we're nearing the topside hatch, sir."

"Don't get lost."

Aston laughed and closed the channel. With a few minutes available, Recker spoke to Captains Vazox and Vakh on the comms, to ensure they were fully informed. Once finished, he called over Corporal Hendrix. She arrived at his seat and her expression was as flat as it always was these last months. Once, he felt the two of them had a connection, now he felt nothing and it tore him up inside.

Pull yourself together, Carl. You didn't even go on a date. Didn't even kiss. You were drawn together in battle and when peace came, you had nothing.

He offered a smile and the one Hendrix returned was polite.

"How's the platoon?" he asked.

"The human members are fine, sir, though that'll change when the drugs start wearing off in a few hours."

"What about the Daklan?"

"They aren't recovering nearly as quickly from the last Extractor and I don't know how many more drugs I can give them. If we had access to medical facilities, I'd suggest they each receive a complete system flush."

Another, much larger, figure appeared at Recker's shoulder. "We can fight, Captain Recker," said Sergeant Shadar.

Recker twisted so he could see the Daklan's face. "I'm sure you can, Sergeant." He didn't mention the sallowness which had crept into the dusky redness of Shadar's skin, nor the faded lustre in the alien's green eyes.

"You intend for us to leave the *Aeklu* once we return to your planet."

"Having heard Corporal Hendrix's evaluation, it would be for the best, Sergeant."

The Daklan slowly shook his head. "You would shame us, Captain Recker."

"You've more than played your part," said Recker. "There would be no shame."

"You do not understand."

"No, I probably don't," said Recker. "What I do understand is that I'd rather you were alive for the next mission, instead of dead to an Extractor attack."

"Please. Reconsider."

Recker didn't think he'd been given an opportunity to consider, let alone reconsider, since Shadar had interrupted his conversation with Corporal Hendrix. Still, effective command was about making snap decisions when necessary.

"The Daklan members of the platoon will disembark once we reach Earth," said Recker. "I will not have you dying to stubborn pride."

Shadar's features betrayed a range of emotions which Recker was beginning to recognize, having fought alongside these Daklan so often. Aside from anger and dismay, he thought that just perhaps, he detected a hint of relief in Shadar's face.

"Should you die, I want to look Vie-Rekh in the eye and tell her you were taken doing your duty, not helplessly killed by a piece of Lavorix tech fired from a million klicks," said Recker, his eyes locked with Shadar's.

A raucous laugh escaped the alien's throat and he grinned. "You would not survive such an encounter with my wife." The Daklan nodded. "Very well, I will order my squad to leave this ship once we arrive at Earth."

"Thank you."

Shadar re-joined the others, leaving Hendrix standing at Recker's side.

"Anything else I need to be aware of, Corporal?"

"No, sir."

Recker exhaled. "Thank you."

Hendrix returned to the platoon and Recker stared for long moments at nothing, until the faint earpiece crackle of an opening comms channel snatched him from his reverie.

"We're topside, sir," said Aston.

"That was quick."

"Just following orders, sir. We're doing a zero-gravity walk to the *Vengeance*'s forward ramp."

Recker didn't see the need to distract Burner, so he accessed the nearest sensor array himself and watched the two figures making their way awkwardly across the upper plating, using the gravity fields in their boots to stop themselves drifting into space.

"Maybe I should have landed at Adamantine," he said.

"We'll be onboard soon enough, sir. I'm glad I had some top-up practice with zero-grav when we were escaping the *Indarox*."

Recker could have occupied himself with any one of a dozen minor tasks. Instead, he watched Aston and Montero cross the *Aeklu*'s topside plating, tiny figures in the forest of towering alloy weaponry and even smaller in comparison to the *Vengeance*.

"Up we go," said Aston, climbing the steps leading to the warship's airlock.

"I'll order Lieutenant Eastwood to begin the Gateway warmup," said Recker.

"Yes, sir. We'll be on the bridge in good time."

"Get away from the *Aeklu* as quickly as possible so you don't accidentally come with us."

"We're on the case, sir."

"I'll stop micromanaging."

"That would be super."

Smiling, Recker cut the channel, though he kept the sensor focused on the *Vengeance*.

"Lieutenant Eastwood, we're going to Earth."

"Yes, sir. Uhh..."

"What's wrong?" said Recker.

"A particle wave appeared on the far side of Lustre, sir. The readings are similar to those we've obtained from the *Galactar* before."

"The *Hexidine*," said Recker. "Shit, they came by Gateway after all."

"Yes, sir – looks like it."

"Make the other ships aware," snapped Recker. He reopened the channel to Aston. "The *Hexidine* is here. Are you on the bridge?"

"Not yet, sir."

"We can't wait for you."

"No, sir. We'll hold on tight."

Recker closed the channel and raised his voice. "We're meeting those bastards head-on - before they can turn their Extractor on Lustre and before they recover from their Gateway transit."

He slammed the control bars forward and to the side. The propulsion gauge jumped straight to one hundred percent and the *Aeklu* surged into high acceleration, banking at the same time. On the sensor feed, Recker watched the *Vengeance* slide off the topside plating, missing the huge turret by a few hundred metres. The life support module on the smaller ship would keep the interior stable and he had no concerns about Aston's and Montero's safety.

"The *Langinstol* and the *Incendus* are with us, sir," said Burner. "I'm linked in with the Lustre satellite network and have located the enemy warship. We are still sending and receiving to the Lavorix battle network."

A red circle appeared on the tactical, far side of the planet and two million klicks beyond. The *Hexidine* wasn't moving, though Recker didn't expect that situation to last. His mind turned over the possibilities and came up with an idea.

"Hit those bastards with lightspeed missiles while they're at a standstill," he ordered. "Fire straight through the planet."

"The Daklan are planning to do just that, sir," said Burner. He cursed. "I've got some bad news. The most recent battle network comms packet from the *Ixidar* indicates a significant change in location. It's now in the Excon-1 solar system."

"Shit," said Recker. "What about the *Gorgadar*?"

"It hasn't moved from its original position, sir."

One Law of Ancidium was too much of an opponent and Recker wasn't pleased at the possibility he might soon be facing two. The thought made him determined to get this battle with the *Hexidine* over as quickly as possible, in case the *Ixidar*'s next jump took it here to the QS-9 system.

Gritting his teeth, Recker switched the *Aeklu*'s propulsion into overstress. The roar of pressurized air filled the bridge and the warship raced away from its escort. Ahead, the planet Lustre, and beyond that, an opponent Recker knew would take him to the limit.

CHAPTER EIGHTEEN

"THE DAKLAN HAVE FIRED their lightspeed missiles, sir," said Burner. "And now the *Hexidine* is on the move – it's heading straight for Lustre."

"As soon as you're confident of the shot, hit the enemy ship with the Toll, Lieutenant Larson," said Recker.

The *Aeklu*'s incredible velocity had closed the distance to Lustre in only a few seconds and Recker intended to skim across the planet's atmosphere to reduce travel time to a minimum. With the needle showing seven thousand kilometres per second, the warship sped past Lustre and the few scattered atmospheric particles were enough to trigger the energy shield, wrapping the *Aeklu* in the palest of blues.

As if sensing the approach, the enemy vessel shifted onto a new course which would intercept the *Aeklu*.

"They're on our battle network, sir, which means they can find us wherever we are," said Burner. "Want me to cut them off?"

"Don't bother, Lieutenant. The longer this fight goes on, the greater the chance those people on Lustre become casualties. We don't want this engagement turning into a game of hide and seek."

"They'll probably infiltrate the satellite network as well, sir."

"Keep an eye on it."

"We've reached the bridge of the *Vengeance*, sir," said Aston on the comms. "We'll head in pursuit of the *Aeklu* and wait for our opportunity."

Recker wanted to spell out his own idea of what that opportunity would be, so Aston would understand. It was hard to keep his mouth shut.

She knows. She'll do the right thing.

"The *Aeklu* leads," Recker said. "And we're going to blow the crap out of these bastards."

"Yes, sir."

"We'll have a sensor lock on the *Hexidine* any moment," said Burner. "There!"

Up it came on the bulkhead screen, a thirty-five-thousand-metre destroyer of planets and fleets alike. Not that it was undamaged. From its approach angle, the ripped-out armour from the Executor attack on Ivisto was visible and three separate areas glowed white from the most recent lightspeed missile detonations.

"Distance to target: one million klicks," said Larson. "They're making a slight course adjustment every second or two."

"They know what the Toll will do to their shield," said Recker. "Let's take this as a positive sign."

"The Daklan are holding their missile launches while

the enemy ship is moving, sir," said Burner. "Captain Vazox intends to remain behind Lustre and fire again when the opportunity arises."

"Targeting the enemy warship with our main armament," said Larson.

"Hold until we're closer," said Recker, glancing at the distance to target reading.

Seven hundred thousand klicks.

"Depletion burst locked and available," said Larson. "Missiles and gauss repeaters outside of lock range."

"Hit it with a full-strength depletion burst. Fire missiles when available."

Recker wasn't sure what physically debilitating outcome would result from the tenixite converter's activation. He didn't find out.

"Negative discharge on the tenixite converter, sir. All lights are green, so I don't know the cause of failure."

"I'm getting the same power spikes from their hull as last time, sir," said Eastwood. "They're readying the Halo."

"Half a million klicks to target."

"Fire the Toll."

"Toll fired."

Recker didn't wait to see the result. As quickly as he could, he touched an area of the tactical farther away from Lustre, and then activated a mode 3 transit. The propulsion thunder peaked louder than before and was joined by the clanging of the main armament and the thudding of the weapon's reload mechanisms. Clenching his jaw against the aftereffects of the transit, Recker gave the *Aeklu* full acceleration again.

"Sensors back online, hunting for the enemy," said Burner.

"Come on, come on," muttered Recker. He'd aimed directly beyond the opposing warship and he waited for Burner to obtain a sensor lock.

"There they are!" said Burner. "A million klicks off our portside and coming about for another shot at us. No indication they've suffered additional damage."

"The Toll shot missed, sir," said Larson. "Ten klicks wide, judging from the readings as the projectile left the barrel."

"Next time you'll be dead centre, Lieutenant."

"Yes, sir, I will."

Up for the challenge, Recker aimed directly for the *Hexidine*, feeling like a mediaeval jouster staring at the end of a lance.

"Twenty seconds on the Toll reload, sir," said Larson.

"They're readying the Halo again," said Eastwood. "I have no idea of its range."

Recker's eyes darted to the tactical. The *Langinstol* and the *Incendus* were completely hidden by Lustre but communicating their positions on the battle network. Elsewhere, the *Vengeance* was low to the planet's surface and near the cusp. Aston was keeping the warship just out of sight, while maintaining readiness to attack. With the *Hexidine* travelling so quickly, any attempt to mode 3 in for a second Executor shot was doomed to failure.

"We've got to draw them into a mode 3 jump of their own," said Recker. "They'll emerge from it at a near standstill and that'll be our opening."

"Yes, sir – the other commanding officers are aware," said Burner.

"Still out of missile range," said Larson.

"The power spikes from their hull have levelled off, sir," said Eastwood. "I think they're about to fire the Halo."

"Let's break their target lock," said Recker. He touched the tactical and activated mode 3 for a second time. The moment the transit was finished, he slammed the controls forward.

"There's the *Hexidine*!" said Burner, loudly over the renewed sound of the propulsion. "A quarter of a million klicks starboard."

"Missiles locked!" said Larson.

"Give them everything, Lieutenant. We want them to get scared and jump out of range," said Recker, banking to aim the Toll at the enemy warship. The turret could only adjust within a narrow arc and most of the targeting was accomplished by pointing the *Aeklu*'s nose in the right direction.

"Starboard clusters one through thirty: fired. Uppers one through fifteen: fired. Forwards one through fifteen: fired," said Larson. "Gauss countermeasures set to track and destroy. Enemy missile launch detected. 1080 missiles coming our way."

"Those will take a big chunk out of our shield reserves, sir," said Eastwood. "I'd recommend we don't soak them. I'm reading the Halo power spikes again."

Recker wasn't sure on the precise maximum range of the Extractor, but as the gap between the ships fell below two hundred thousand kilometres, he knew he was cutting it fine. Part of him hoped the enemy – having fired the

Extractor numerous times and leaving the *Aeklu* still operational – wouldn't fire it again. The cynic in him was sure the Lavorix would simply appreciate the opportunity to fine-tune the weapon in preparation for a total extraction of Lustre.

I'm scared of that weapon. Not for those people on Lustre, but for me and the people with me. For the pain it brings.

"I won't let it affect me," he snarled under his breath.

Holding focus, Recker brought the Toll into line with the *Hexidine*. The enemy ship was aware of the danger and it zig-zagged with physics-defying agility, making it hard for Larson to aim the shot. With a combination of intuition, experience and fast reactions, Recker kept the Toll barrel following the *Hexidine* and he could sense Larson's hesitation.

"If you overthink it, you'll miss your chance," said Recker.

Missiles covered the tactical in red and green. The *Aeklu*'s gauss repeaters started up, firing in a cacophony of perfectly machined alloy. Tracer lines stabbed into the vacuum, coming from both Laws of Ancidium, while orange trails of propellant from the boosters of two thousand missiles wove a twisting pattern that defied the eye and the brain. A gentle breeze from the bridge vents was laden with pungent odours of burned metal and ozone. For a fleeting moment, Recker felt pure exaltation, like this was everything he was meant to be.

"Halo power spikes levelling off!" shouted Eastwood.

"Firing the Toll," said Larson.

The *Hexidine* vanished into mode 3. Expecting it to

happen, Recker did the same with the *Aeklu*, a moment before the incoming missiles could crash into the shield. The in-out transition was worse than the others and he could feel the Frenziol holding back his body's urge to vomit.

"Find that damned ship!" yelled Recker, angrily.

"Scanning!"

"You can use mode 3 once more before the ten-minute cooldown kicks in, sir," said Eastwood. "If the *Hexidine* has the same capabilities as we do, they can activate three more."

Recker heard and understood the words, but most of his attention was on the tactical and the sensors. He hoped Aston and the two Daklan officers had been fast enough to grab this chance to hurt the enemy ship, but if the *Vengeance* was inside the *Hexidine*'s shield, it wouldn't survive long without assistance.

"Got them! They jumped right on top of Lustre!" said Burner. "Almost a million klicks from our position and accelerating for the blind side."

"What about the Toll? Did we hit them?" demanded Recker.

"No, sir – they entered lightspeed before the projectile could impact."

Cursing the fractions of seconds which separated success and failure, Recker brought the *Aeklu* around and aimed it straight at the planet. If luck were on his side, maybe the enemy would require a few seconds to obtain a sensor lock, though he wasn't pinning his hopes on that happening.

"The *Langinstol* targeted and launched a single lightspeed missile, sir, and Captain Vazox reports a successful detonation. The *Incendus* has no more lightspeed missiles to fire." said Burner. "Commander Aston did not active mode 3 on the *Vengeance*."

"Give me a course projection overlay for the *Hexidine*."

"Course projection overlay added to your tactical, sir," said Burner.

Holding the *Aeklu* steady, Recker checked the overlay. If the *Hexidine* continued on its current heading and at its current velocity, it would come within direct sensor sight of the *Langinstol* and the *Incendus* in twenty seconds. Aware of the danger, the annihilator and the desolator were accelerating in the opposite direction.

"We're on the enemy's battle network, so they know our position," said Larson. "What are they playing at?"

"The Lavorix have had enough of the lightspeed missiles," guessed Recker. "They've decided to go hunting for the source."

"I have communicated your insight to the Daklan, sir," said Burner. "We'll have sensor sight on the *Langinstol* and the *Incendus* in less than fifteen seconds," he continued. "Commander Aston is hugging the surface and taking the *Vengeance* north towards the pole. The *Hexidine* should pass straight by without obtaining line of sight."

"Do the Lavorix have the benefit of our sensor satellites?" asked Recker.

"They did have for a couple of minutes, sir, but not anymore," said Burner. "I've just diverted the data feed from one of the terrestrial TV channels into the satellite network. As of this moment, the Lavorix are watching *Casablanca*."

"How long before they regain access to the sensors?"

"I don't know, sir," Burner admitted. "A minute at the most."

"That'll have to be enough."

"Enough for what?" asked Larson.

"A plan. I'll let you know as soon as I think it's got a chance. Lieutenant Burner, can you put a hold on our battle network pings to the *Hexidine*?"

"Yes, sir, but they'll realise we're up to something."

"We only need a few seconds. Wait for my command."

"Yes, sir."

The *Aeklu*'s velocity gauge sped to seven thousand kilometres per second and Recker suddenly banked it so that it was heading away from the planet as if he'd decided to run from the engagement. He held it on course and watched the *Hexidine*, the *Langinstol* and the *Incendus* as they sped around Lustre.

"Ten seconds and we'll have sensor sight on the *Langinstol*. Five after that and we'll see the *Hexidine*. The enemy ship is less than ten klicks from the surface, sir. The atmospheric friction will be draining their shield."

"Not nearly enough," said Recker.

He chose his location – a place on the northern tip of the Sonlund continent and within five hundred kilometres of the *Vengeance*. There wasn't enough time to communicate his intent and he was relying on fast reactions from everyone.

"Here come the *Langinstol* and the *Incendus*."

"Hold the battle network packets, Lieutenant Burner."

"Done."

Recker activated the last available mode 3 charge and the *Aeklu* sped more than half a million kilometres in almost zero time. It emerged a hundred kilometres above the bleak northern Sonlund coastline, where the white foam of breakers created an uneven line separating hard stone from the dark sea.

Across the distant horizon, the *Langinstol* and the *Incendus* were burning pinpricks of white, and the smoke trails they left behind stretched for thousands of kilometres. After them came the *Hexidine*. Surrounded by its energy shield, the Lavorix ship left no trail, but the sensors tracked it anyway, four hundred kilometres south and low to the planet in its pursuit of the Daklan.

"Main armament targeted."

"Make the shot, Lieutenant."

With a delicate touch of her finger, Larson discharged the Toll.

CHAPTER NINETEEN

THE DISTANCE between the two warships was so insignificant that the projectile's travel time was only a split second. The *Aeklu*'s sensors registered a blur of motion and then the Toll slug impacted with the *Hexidine*'s shield. The faint ovoid surrounding the enemy ship turned to the deepest of blues and the huge warship immediately broke off its pursuit of the Daklan.

"Forward clusters one through thirty: fired. Upper clusters one through fifteen: fired. Underside clusters one through fifteen: fired. Gauss repeaters set to track and destroy."

The enemy pilot demonstrated his reactions and twisted the huge warship quickly enough in the air that the *Aeklu*'s upper and underside missiles flew wide, while all 360 warheads from the forward thirty clusters detonated against its energy shield. The blue deepened further.

"Enemy missile launch detected," said Larson.

"Halo charging," said Eastwood. "And I reckon the enemy are burning through their tenixite stores to keep the shield up."

"If their shield doesn't collapse soon, we're going to be in the crap," said Recker.

Accelerating from stationary left the *Aeklu* an easy target and despite his best efforts to avoid them, almost a thousand warheads from the *Hexidine* detonated successfully, causing the gauge to drop significantly.

The enemy pilot could have forced a collision, but instead the Lavorix warship banked in a tight curve, ejecting missiles from its rear tubes and spraying the *Aeklu*'s shield with gauss fire. Recker struggled to recover and knew he'd put too much faith in the main armament. His ship gathered speed and he tried to bring the Toll into line for a second shot. The clunking of the reload was enough reminder that the gun wouldn't be ready for many seconds yet.

If they fire the Extractor, it's game over.

Having watched the *Hexidine* empty its rear clusters, Recker anticipated the enemy would bank one way or the other to bring its loaded portside or starboard tubes into play. It went left, cutting through the thin, high atmosphere and heading for the planet's north pole.

Aware that he was dancing to his enemy's tune, Recker gave chase, listening for the Toll reload to complete and hoping it would happen before the inevitable Extractor or Halo discharge.

"Five seconds on the main armament," said Larson.

"The power spikes on their hull are levelling off, sir," said Eastwood. "I think they're about to discharge."

Having used the *Aeklu*'s last mode 3 charge getting here, Recker didn't have much choice other than to find out what was coming his way. A close-range missile launch from the *Hexidine* wrapped the *Aeklu*'s shield in plasma and the reserve gauge dropped again.

"Firing the main gun," said Larson.

The Toll discharged a moment before the Halo, and Recker saw the *Hexidine*'s shield turn even darker as it absorbed the impact - now it was more ternium in colour than it was blue. Then, a crackling black web of tightly woven, undulating energy tendrils appeared around the *Aeklu*'s shield. In an instant, the reserve gauge fell from sixty-five percent to zero.

"Shield down!" yelled Eastwood.

"Get it back," growled Recker.

"I'm trying, sir."

Recker scanned the console, hunting for something to nullify the Halo attack. Maybe he could channel the energy elsewhere or perhaps the Lavorix had built in a defence that would only become available under these specific circumstances. He found nothing – in fact, the other onboard systems were also affected and several of the minor ones had already gone offline.

They Lavorix still want their ship back. They're going to bring us down and recover the Aeklu.

Instead of leaving themselves open to another Toll shot from the failing *Aeklu*, the *Hexidine* decelerated suddenly. The *Aeklu*'s response to the controls was already blunted and Recker couldn't prevent his spaceship from overshooting.

"Everything's failing, sir," said Eastwood. "I'm doing

what I can to divert power to the critical systems, but all I'm doing is shuffling chairs on the deck."

The *Aeklu* wasn't travelling at anything like maximum velocity and on a downward trajectory which Recker guessed would see it hit the surface in the next couple of minutes, with the most probable landing place being one of Lustre's extensive oceans. Less than a hundred kilometres behind, the *Hexidine*, which had slowed dramatically, began accelerating in pursuit, doubtless intending to keep pace and soak the *Aeklu*'s conventional attacks until it crashed down.

"We're going to lose the weapons systems in a few seconds, sir," said Larson. "I can't figure out a way to prevent it happening."

"Commander Aston is on the open channel, sir!" yelled Burner.

Aston kept it short and sweet. "Wish me luck."

The channel went dead and Recker's eyes jumped to the rear feed, where he spotted a tiny, grey shape appear within the *Hexidine*'s shield.

"Come on!" he shouted. "Do it!"

The explosion from the *Vengeance*'s Executor discharge came so deep within the opening created by the earlier shot, that the dark edge of the blast sphere only just peeked out. Following the blast, an immense flash of plasma indicated Aston had sent a bunch of missiles into the guts of the *Hexidine* for good measure.

Recker's first reaction was disappointment – the ovoid shield protecting the Lavorix ship remained in place and their pursuit continued. Realisation came.

"They didn't mode 3 out of here," he said.

"I'm scanning the *Hexidine*'s hull output," said Eastwood. "Something's wrong."

"Find out what it is!" Recker's initial disappointment was replaced by a tentative excitement, though he didn't want to get his hopes up yet, especially with the enemy shield being operational. "And find out what happened to the *Vengeance!*"

"Commander Aston has taken shelter in the Executor hole, sir," said Burner.

"Rear missile tubes reloaded. Clusters one through thirty: fired," said Larson. "Uppers one through fifteen: fired. Lowers one through fifteen: fired."

At the same time as the *Aeklu*'s missiles became visible on the rear feed, Recker spotted two vast explosions ripping into the *Hexidine*'s armour plating.

"Lightspeed missiles!" he said. "The enemy ship must have slowed down enough that the Daklan became confident they could target it accurately!"

As the *Aeklu*'s wave of missiles detonated, Eastwood came out with a bombshell.

"The enemy has lost their propulsion, sir!" he yelled, his voice a full octave higher than normal.

It was an electrifying, monumental change in fortune and Recker could scarcely believe his luck.

"What about the enemy shield?" he asked.

"Still holding, sir. Our own propulsion output is dropping like a stone."

The news brought Recker crashing down again. Even deprived of its ability to escape, the *Hexidine* was far from defenceless, while the *Aeklu* no longer had a shield to rely on and its own propulsion output was heading rapidly towards zero as the Halo brought the spaceship to the brink of complete failure.

"Enemy missile launch detected," said Larson.

Recker hauled the control bars to the side and the *Aeklu* responded sluggishly, more akin to a lifter shuttle than a warship. The gauss repeaters punched dozens of the inbound missiles into glittering shards, which sparkled against the rising sun. Those warheads which evaded the countermeasures plunged into the *Aeklu*'s stern plating and exploded with devastating effect and to Recker's eyes, it appeared as though the rear fifth of his warship was completely hidden in the immense series of blasts. A sprinkling of red lights appeared on his console and, given the number of impacts, he was surprised there weren't more.

"We need to get out of range, sir," said Larson.

"Easier said than done, Lieutenant."

The *Aeklu* was gradually pulling away from the now-drifting *Hexidine*, but Recker wasn't convinced they'd beat the enemy ship's reload. He pulled back on the controls and the *Aeklu* hardly gained any altitude, making him wonder if it would reach escape velocity. Even with most of the planet's population evacuated, there was a risk of enormous casualties if an object as large as the *Aeklu*, the *Hexidine* or both hit the surface without control.

"Two more lightspeed missiles hit the *Hexidine*, sir. Same place as last time," Burner reported. "The *Langin-stol* and the *Incendus* are coming to offer support."

"Recommend they hold back," said Recker sharply. "The enemy ship is far from helpless."

"I passed on the warning, sir."

Another flash, which the *Aeklu*'s sensors detected through the near opacity of the *Hexidine*'s shield, informed Recker that the *Vengeance* was operational and giving the Lavorix ship hell. Maybe those warheads would take out another piece of critical hardware, but Recker wasn't banking on it.

"We're losing altitude," he said. "The response to my input is minimal. There's no chance we're coming about for another Toll shot."

Slowly, the *Aeklu* fell towards the ground, its engines unable to defy gravity any longer. The warship didn't drop as rapidly as expected and Recker could still hear the propulsion as a spluttering on-off background grumble and he guessed the kickstarter modules were unaffected by the Halo and were trying to fire up the engines again. He wasn't sure if they'd be successful in time, but those kick-starters were allowing him a tiny amount of control over the *Aeklu*.

"Oh shit, the *Hexidine* is charging up for something else, sir," said Eastwood.

"Another Halo?" asked Recker. As soon as the words left his mouth, he knew that couldn't be right. The enemy had already disabled the *Aeklu*, giving them no reason to fire the weapon again.

"Their tenixite converter, sir," said Eastwood. "They could probably take us out and the planet at the same time, if they're carrying enough ore in their hold."

Thoughts flew through Recker's mind. The *Vengeance* was equipped with the Fracture and if Aston fired it from within the *Hexidine*'s shield, the huge warship would be turned to dust. But maybe the planet would be affected at the same time. They knew so little about how the Fracture worked.

Recker opened his mouth, unsure what he was going to say. The *Hexidine* fired another wave of missiles at the same time as Larson announced she was giving them the same in return.

We can't lose the planet, thought Recker desperately. Still the words wouldn't come and he knew that whatever he said, he could do nothing to alter the fate of Lustre.

While the *Aeklu*'s and *Hexidine*'s missiles were in flight, another flash appeared within the latter's hull and two more lightspeed missiles detonated in the same place as the previous impacts. Recker had no idea which of the two attacks brought about the result, but the shield protecting the Lavorix warship vanished, winking out like it had never existed.

"Impact!" shouted Larson.

Recker wasn't sure which impacts she was referring to. The *Aeklu* was struck by missiles at the same time as the *Hexidine*. A dozen new alerts appeared at once on his console and it didn't take an instinctive feel for space flight to understand that the accumulating damage had changed from heavy to catastrophic.

"We lost two thousand metres of our stern," said Eastwood. "And there goes another few billion tons."

The *Hexidine* had fared no better and a huge section of its nose plummeted towards the ocean far below. Yet more of the *Vengeance*'s missiles exploded within the vast cavern in the enemy warship's hull and wreckage spilled out in a nonstop rain.

"Commander Aston, get out of there," said Recker.

"We can't let them escape from this, sir," said Aston, determination in her voice.

"They won't get away with it. I'll destroy them with the *Aeklu*."

"One more salvo," said Aston, her tone indicating she wouldn't be persuaded otherwise.

"You're in command of the *Vengeance*," said Recker. "It's your call."

He cut the channel and resumed his efforts to keep the *Aeklu* in the sky. Its engines were coughing and Recker guessed the kickstart modules were nearly out of juice. The controls were only responding in the loosest sense and every critical system had a low power warning. Once the life support cut out, the *Aeklu*'s crew would be killed upon impact with Lustre. Doing his best with what he had available, Recker guided the spaceship through a layer of thin clouds high above the ocean.

"The *Hexidine* is going down fast, sir," said Burner.

Although the Lavorix ship had lost many of its forward clusters, it ejected warheads from several of its uppers. Meanwhile, Larson targeted and fired a similarly reduced quantity of missiles from the *Aeklu*, while gauss repeaters raked to and fro, destroying some warheads and missing others.

"Going to be tight," said Eastwood.

"Tighter than tight," said Recker.

His eyes kept jumping to the *Hexidine*, which was arcing straight for the same ocean as the *Aeklu*. The angle of its descent prevented him seeing the detonations from the *Vengeance*'s next wave of missiles and he hoped Aston wasn't about to misjudge the time to exit.

"The *Vengeance*!" shouted Burner.

A grey shape – tiny in comparison to the *Hexidine* – raced into sight, accelerating hard across the sky in the direction of the *Aeklu*. It was a good tactic, allowing the *Vengeance* to benefit from the *Aeklu*'s gauss countermeasures. Recker hoped it would be enough.

Suddenly, green dots flashed across the fading light of the tactical screen and a hundred or more new explosions appeared on the *Hexidine*'s flank and then came another thirty.

"Those missiles came from the *Langinstol* and the *Incendus*, sir," said Burner.

Yet more of the enemy ship's armour was ripped out and Recker knew it was finished. The only unanswered question was how much damage it could inflict to the allied ships on the way down.

On this occasion, the outcome was more positive than Recker could have hoped. The *Hexidine* launched a few dozen missiles, most of which were shot down by the *Aeklu*'s gauss repeaters. Larson fired dozens more in response, while the *Vengeance* and the Daklan warships added the weight of their own firepower.

"The *Hexidine* is about to crash," said Burner.

"So are we, Lieutenant," said Recker, doing his best to keep the *Aeklu* underside down.

The ocean filled many of the sensor feeds with an angry blue-grey and white foam spat from the tops of enormous waves.

"It's five klicks to the bottom," said Burner. "Deep, but we won't go under."

Recker wasn't sure if fate had a hand – as if it were

trying to send him a message he was unable to comprehend - or if the simultaneous crash landings of the *Aeklu* and *Hexidine* were nothing more than coincidence.

Both Laws of Ancidium struck the ocean, with the *Hexidine* only just visible over the planet's curvature. Keeping his focus on his own warship, Recker watched as a fountain of displaced water was thrown upwards and forwards by the *Aeklu*'s nose. The rest of the hull crashed into the surface a moment later displacing so much water that the ocean bed was revealed briefly, before the complex interactions of currents brought the water flooding back.

The moment those waters contacted the burning alloys of the stern, they frothed violently, creating a billowing cloud of rapidly expanding superhot steam. Having landed at a modest speed, the *Aeklu*'s forward momentum was soon spent, though not before it had gouged an immense furrow in the ocean floor and created a tsunami of calamitous proportions.

The last of the *Aeklu*'s main power ran out, but the lights remained on and Recker was glad to see that the backups were online to power the internal doors and lifts. Those backups also powered basic comms functionality, as well as allowing the sensors to provide a low-resolution feed. Far away, the horizon was lit up by plasma fire, created by missiles from the three active allied warships.

For a moment, Recker sat and stared at the blank screens before him, feeling a combination of so many emotions he didn't know which one was overriding. He stood.

"Well, folks, we're down. Now let's get the hell off this ship."

Recker picked up his rifle and headed for the door. At that moment, he had a thought which gave him pause. He slowed and stopped.

"Sergeant Vance, Sergeant Shadar, take your squads to the upper plating and bring these technicians," he said. "LT Roy, pass on the order to your other teams – make sure they go up and not down. If they're not topside in time, they'll have to wait for rescue."

"Yes, sir."

"What about you and the crew, sir?" asked Sergeant Vance.

"We'll catch up." Recker smiled grimly. "First, we've got something to do."

Vance looked mystified but he didn't ask any questions and simply followed the already-evacuating soldiers from the bridge.

Recker didn't return to his seat and instead he placed himself at Lieutenant Burner's shoulder.

"What's the plan, sir?"

"I might know a way to trap a fly," said Recker.

CHAPTER TWENTY

"ARE we still on the Laws of Ancidium battle network?" asked Recker. "If we aren't, then my idea is going to be a non-starter."

"Yes, sir, we're on the battle network," said Burner. "I only put a temporary hold on our transmissions." He brought up some lines of text on a screen and peered at them. "I haven't checked these for a few minutes, what with everything that was going on, but looking here, we've received several additional comms packets from both the *Gorgadar* and the *Ixidar*."

"Where are they?"

"The *Ixidar* has left Excon-1 and...oh shit...it's not far from one of the Daklan systems."

"What about the *Gorgadar*?"

"Same as before, sir." Burner furrowed his brow. "It hasn't moved at all."

It struck Recker as peculiar that the prime ship amongst the Laws of Ancidium would be idle for so long and he wondered briefly at the cause. "We'll check it out later if we can," he said. "Right now I want to know if there's any way we can modify the *Aeklu*'s outbound data packets."

"I don't see why not," said Burner, using one hand to call up a menu on a separate screen. "Why do we need to do that?"

"What if the *Gorgadar* and *Ixidar* thought we were heading to Tronstal?"

Burner's expression twisted in concentration. "If the Lavorix were made to think the planet was populated by eighty billion people, but well-defended, maybe they'd want to pay it a visit, to help the *Aeklu* extract all that juicy life energy."

"And even if they're aware the HPA is in control of the *Aeklu*, those other Laws of Ancidium would still want to head over to Tronstal in order to get their ship back. Or destroy it," said Recker.

"We've got to modify the battle network data in a way that doesn't allow the Lavorix to guess that we know they're tracking us," said Burner peering closely at his screen.

Recker nodded. "If we could insert data that indicates we've begun a conventional lightspeed journey to the RETI-11 system, arriving a short time after the expected installation of the shield breaker, the *Ixidar* and *Gorgadar* might show up and we can test out their shields with our new weapon."

"Permission to highlight the obvious flaw in the plan, sir?" asked Eastwood.

"Go ahead, Lieutenant."

"Even without their shields, the Laws of Ancidium are not exactly vulnerable. If the *Ixidar* and *Gorgadar* turned up and assuming the shield breaker works, we'd require a massive fleet of warships to take them down. We'd be committing to an all-or-nothing venture where the odds are completely uncertain."

"I accept everything you've said, Lieutenant. However, I think you're underestimating the importance of knowing where those enemy ships might be and when. Given their Gateway hardware and enormous lightspeed multipliers, they can turn up anywhere of their choosing, without us having a chance to respond. The best medium-term outcome for the HPA and the Daklan is a slow death in which our fleets are taken out piecemeal by an enemy that can initiate combat at any time and escape just as easily."

Eastwood shrugged. "I'm glad I'm not the one making the call, sir."

"I'm not making the call either, Lieutenant," said Recker. "Get me Fleet Admiral Telar on the comms."

Telar didn't keep them waiting and he entered the channel immediately.

"Give me the details, Captain Recker," he said at once.

Recker obliged and without embellishment. When he was done, Telar went silent as he considered what was a possibly the most vital decision the HPA military would ever make.

"I agree," he said at last, without sounding happy about it. "However, I can only agree for the HPA. I will require a similar commitment from my Daklan opposite number."

"Will that be a problem, sir?"

"No. I would like you to send the modified battle network packets to the *Gorgadar* and the *Ixidar*, then board the *Vengeance* and head to the RETI-11 system. I'll do you the courtesy of confirming if the mission is a go before you enter lightspeed. From the sounds of it, you require a few minutes to escape the *Aeklu.*"

"Yes, sir. Do you have any advance orders?"

"I'll let you know if I think of any. The *Vengeance* is equipped with a unique weapon – I'll ensure you are under nobody's command but your own and therefore free to decide if the Fracture is used, without the encumbrance of competing orders."

It was a statement of great confidence in Recker's ability. "I'll do the best I can."

"As always. Now go. If you don't hear from me soon, your destination is Tronstal."

The channel went dead and Recker urged his crew from their seats. He dashed for the – still unfixed – blast door with the others following. As he led the way to the airlifts, Recker spoke to Aston on the comms and received confirmation that the *Hexidine* was completely out of action.

"Their hull power output is at near-zero, sir. The *Langinstol* and the *Incendus* are maintaining their bombardment, but I've withdrawn the *Vengeance.* It seems wise to keep some ammunition spare."

"We're going to need it, Commander," said Recker, repeating what he'd discussed with Telar. He entered the airlift which would take him to the topside hatch and touched the access panel to close the door behind him.

"Sounds like it's about to get messy," Aston said once he'd finished talking.

"That it is," he confirmed. "I'm trying not to think about it just yet. Land the *Vengeance* on the *Aeklu*'s hull and be ready to pick up some passengers."

"Yes, sir, on my way."

The airlift ascended and, shortly after, Recker and his crew joined the platoon and the technicians on the upper plating. This area of the *Aeklu* had avoided missile damage, though the clouds of blistering steam, the faraway crashing of the ocean and the indistinct shapes of the external armaments made Recker feel as if he was standing in a strange and threatening landscape.

A hundred and fifty metres closer to the *Aeklu*'s nose, the *Vengeance* was setting down, its forward boarding ramp open and the light from its airlock diffuse like that of a beacon on a fog-shrouded coastline. Running hard, Recker felt relief when he arrived at the steps and he climbed rapidly, pausing once to check that his crew were with him.

"We're inside," he said on the comms when everyone was onboard.

"Copy that," said Aston. "I'm closing the ramp."

The ramp motors groaned beneath the airlock floor and Recker didn't hang around. He sprinted into the tight passages of the *Vengeance*, glad that none of the soldiers were lingering to block his way. Vance and Shadar kept things tight even outside of combat and Recker had a free run to the bridge.

Arriving with his breathing deep and his heart

thumping in his chest, Recker made his way to the command console.

"Excellent work, Commander Aston, but I'm afraid I'll have to relieve you."

"No problem, sir," said Aston. She was clearly invigorated by the recent experience and she offered Recker a broad smile.

He dropped into his seat and performed a cursory check of the instrumentation. "You're relieved as well, Corporal Montero. Time to return to the platoon."

"Yes, sir. Thank you for the opportunity."

Recker glanced in Aston's direction and raised an eyebrow questioningly. She nodded, the words unspoken.

Corporal Montero came through for us.

"Thank you for making the most of it, Corporal," said Recker. "I'm sure you'll have another chance in the future."

"I hope so, sir," said Montero, as she exited the bridge.

Recker turned to ensure his crew were at their stations. Everyone was looking his way.

"Lieutenant Burner, I know Fleet Admiral Telar said he'd speak to us if the mission was a non-starter, but I'd like you to open a channel and ask politely if we're wasting our time going to lightspeed."

"Yes, sir."

"Lieutenant Larson, contact Captains Vazox and Vakh. Tell them of my admiration for their performance in the recent engagement with the *Hexidine* and ensure they understand how vital their military's lightspeed missiles have been in our joint success."

"Yes, sir. Should I give them details of the next mission?"

"Corporal Montero has already done so," said Aston. "I don't believe either the *Langinstol* or the *Incendus* is equipped for another engagement - their magazines are depleted and their hulls are full of holes. The best place for them is the shipyard. Whether they're ordered back to base or not is another matter."

"They've more than done, their duty," said Recker. "I hope their commanding officer does not commit them to this mission."

"Sir, I have obtained confirmation from Fleet Admiral Telar that the mission is to go ahead. We're to make fastest speed for an area of empty space on the fringes of the RETI-11 system. There, we will rendezvous with the other members of our fleet and we will receive updated orders."

"Nothing complicated or convoluted," said Recker. "Just how I like it."

The *Vengeance* was ready to fly and he grabbed the control bars. While the *Aeklu* had been a warship without peer amongst the allied fleets, it had been tainted by its origins and Recker had not entirely enjoyed commanding the vessel. The *Vengeance* was something else and when he heard the familiar engine note and felt the usual vibration through his palms, he wanted to smile despite everything that had happened and everything that was to come.

Climbing vertically, the spaceship emerged from the undiminished clouds of steam and the sensors offered him a sight of the *Aeklu*, half-submerged and beaten ineffectually by the ocean's waves, its rear five thousand metres ragged and still burning with the heat of plasma explosions. Aside from its stern, the warship was hardly damaged, and Recker was sure that Telar would soon order the salvage crews onboard to find out if it could be recovered.

Higher the *Vengeance* climbed and the *Hexidine* became visible on the horizon. The enemy ship was ablaze from the intense bombardment it had suffered and dark smoke mingled with steam to produce a veil across the sky which extended fifty kilometres north to south. There were times Recker was left dumbfounded by the destructive potential of technology and this was one of those moments.

"We beat them," said Aston, watching his expression from the corner of her eye. "Don't forget that."

"Yes, we did, Commander. I'm trying my hardest not to think of it as a partial victory."

"Four out of six Laws of Ancidium are gone," said Eastwood. "If I were top dog in the Lavorix hierarchy I'd be mighty pissed about the situation."

"Those six warships were probably the only things keeping them in the game against the Kilvar," said Larson. She laughed unsympathetically. "Not anymore."

"None of it will matter if we can't finish the job," said Recker. "The *Gorgadar* and *Ixidar* will not be easy opponents."

Recker hated his growing inability to see the positives. He joked with himself that he was getting old, but at only thirty-eight, he knew he was making excuses for his changing outlook. Maybe it was a natural reaction to living on the edge for long – each time he beat the odds, he had to do it again and again. Eventually he'd stop beating them and he was fearful of the inevitability.

Same as always, he locked those fears into a far corner of his mind and returned himself to the present. The *Vengeance*'s ascent had taken it through the clouds and towards the upper edges of the atmosphere. Way below, the Laws of Ancidium were grey shapes against the water, and the smoke from the *Hexidine* was a slow-spreading charcoal smear.

More worrying were the huge ripples on the ocean's surface, caused by the spaceships coming down into the water. Soon those ripples would hit land and when that happened, they'd make the tsunami that washed through Oracon-1 look like a pebble splash in comparison.

Recker diverted his eyes and concentrated on the minutiae of piloting the *Vengeance*. Once it was free of the thin atmosphere, he gave the warship maximum acceleration and it tore through space. Switching the propulsion into overstress brought the usual note of serenity, which Recker let wash through him like it could cleanse his soul.

"We probably don't need to fly to the usual distance from Lustre before we fire up the lightspeed drive, sir," said Eastwood. "I've entered the coordinates and I'm ready to press go."

"Thank you, Lieutenant. The *Vengeance* has a higher lightspeed multiplier than everything else in the HPA and Daklan fleets. We've got some leeway."

"Yes, sir." Eastwood sucked in an audible breath. "It would be nice to get away from the planet. Before the waves hit the shores."

"I understand, Lieutenant – I think we're too late for that."

"Yeah."

Even so, Recker brought the *Vengeance* to a standstill. "Warm up the ternium drive, Lieutenant. Take us to RETI-11."

"Ternium drive warming up," Eastwood confirmed. "Six minutes and we're out of here. ETA is thirty-seven hours. We'll have time to watch the deployment crews taking the shield breaker down to Tronstal."

Recker fidgeted his way through the first two minutes, his mind turning. He was sure the Laws of Ancidium were granted a great deal of autonomy and could act more or less as their commanding officers decided. Maybe the *Ixidar* would head to Tronstal early, late or maybe it would receive a contradictory order from the Ancidium and go somewhere else entirely.

"Lieutenant Burner, can you link to the *Aeklu*'s comms system?"

"Yes, sir. Of course."

"What about the battle network comms packets? Can you view the contents?"

"I'll tell you in one moment, sir." Burner went quiet, but not for long. "Yes, sir. Those data packets are accessible from here."

"Give me the updates."

"The *Ixidar* has moved from its last reported position but is still near the same Daklan system."

"That can't be good," said Aston.

"It never is with the Lavorix, Commander," said Recker. The enemy ship hadn't set off for Tronstal yet and he hoped that was a good thing – the Laws of Ancidium had no trouble crossing vast distances, so it wasn't like this one had to get an early start. If the *Ixidar* arrived first, that would throw a spanner in the works. "What about the *Gorgadar*? Where is that?"

"Same place as last time, sir. It hasn't moved."

"Anyone else think the *Gorgadar* is going to sit out on the fringes of Meklon space before coming to RETI-11 by Gateway just when we don't want it to happen?" asked Eastwood.

"I was trying not to," said Larson. "But you just made me do it."

"Sorry," shrugged Eastwood. "I like to consider everything."

Recker listened, fully expecting Burner to stick his oar in. Instead, the man remained quiet as if he were lost in thought.

"Shut off the underside feeds until we get out of here," said Recker. "We don't need to see what happens on Lustre."

Two of the bulkhead screens went blank. Nobody spoke and then the ternium drive fired, sending the *Vengeance* into lightspeed, its destination a place where the HPA and the Daklan had a chance to knock out the final two Laws of Ancidium.

If the mission was successful, Recker had no idea what it would mean for the Lavorix. Perhaps they'd never be seen again. Or perhaps the remains of their forces would retreat and the enemy would rebuild, in preparation for another attack decades – or centuries – from now.

Of one thing Recker was certain – victory at Tronstal

was vital and even if that was accomplished, the HPA and Daklan fleets would still have the *Gorgadar* to deal with, assuming the primary Law of Ancidium didn't show up for the fight.

Despite everything, the future had never seemed so uncertain to Recker as it did now.

CHAPTER TWENTY-ONE

THIRTY-SEVEN HOURS WAS, in terms of HPA military averages, neither a long trip nor a short one and Recker would have normally used the time to ensure his crew had caught up on enough sleep to be battle-ready at the end. Having filled his veins with so many drugs, he worried that his body might not require sleep until arrival was too close to allow it.

Lieutenant Burner apparently had no such concerns and, not five minutes after the post-lightspeed status checks were completed, he vended himself a large cup of super-strength moffee from the bridge replicator.

"Ah, that's the good stuff," he declared, breathing in the rising steam.

"It tastes like shit," said Eastwood. "Just like everything from the Meklon replicators."

"You become accustomed to the taste. Now, I'm a connoisseur."

"I can think of a hundred more appropriate descriptions for what you are," said Eastwood. "Want to hear a few?"

Burner raised a hand and aimed his palm in Eastwood's direction. "Do not disturb me while I'm enjoying this fine cup of moffee."

A verbal exchange ensued, which lasted for several minutes. As usual, there was no rancour and Recker let them get on with it, noting how every time things were on the verge of dying down, Lieutenant Larson would say something that started it going again.

After a time, Recker climbed from his seat. "Watch the bridge, Commander."

Aston peered at him. "What's wrong?"

"There's nothing wrong. We need some medical advice."

"Want me to go?"

He smiled. "No need."

Exiting the bridge, Recker took an extended route through the *Vengeance*'s interior. The Frenziol-13 urged him to run, but he was content just to stretch his muscles. Another headache was developing and he wondered if it was an early sign of fatigue.

The *Vengeance*'s medical bay wasn't much to look at, though it had been fitted out with an HPA medical bot several months ago on Ivisto. Corporal Hendrix was here, as Recker knew she would be. When he arrived, she was sitting on one of the pristine white beds, staring at the walls like she was remembering her family lost when planet Fortune was taken out by one of the tenixite converters.

"I need advice, Corporal," said Recker.

For a moment, Hendrix didn't respond. Then, she sighed and slid off the bed. "Ask away, sir."

"We're heading for a showdown with another enemy warship. When we break lightspeed in not much over thirty hours, I want to be ready for a fight, not nodding off in my seat."

Hendrix didn't answer directly. Instead, she thumbed in the robot's direction. It was a spindly device, two metres tall, all arms and screens on top of a compact gravity drive. "This bot can sew up a wound so you'd never knew it existed. It can reattach limbs and repair damaged nerves and blood vessels. Whatever injuries you would normally expect to suffer on a battlefield, this thing can fix them."

"But it can't do a body flush," said Recker, guessing what Hendrix was leading to.

"Nope, it can't do a body flush, sir. For that it would require extra reservoirs for the fluids, increasing its volume by fifty percent. And then it wouldn't fit in the medical bay of a riot class." She gestured vaguely at the nearest wall. "Or this medical bay here on the *Vengeance*."

"So what's the answer?"

"It's impossible to accurately predict how quickly the human body will perform its own flush of the drugs, sir. And if we're going to face another Extractor, it might be best if we're all running on the edge." Hendrix met his gaze. "And we should avoid cold turkey until we're guaranteed more than thirty hours downtime."

Recker gritted his teeth. "We'll keep topping up," he said at last. "Do we have enough supplies of Frenziol?"

Hendrix approached one of the wall cabinets and opened the metal door guarding the contents. Inside,

Recker saw neat rows of Frenziol injectors, along with various other drugs whose labels he couldn't read from this distance.

"This is fifteen rows deep," said Hendrix, pointing at one of the shelves. "We've got enough."

The door behind opened.

"Hey babe, I..."

"Private Enfield," said Recker.

"Uh, sorry, sir," said Enfield backing out of the room. "I need to be somewhere else."

The door closed.

"It was never going to happen with us, Carl," said Hendrix softly.

"No, I guess not," said Recker, realizing it no longer mattered to him. "Stay safe, Corporal Hendrix."

"You too, sir." Hendrix smiled and she looked almost happy. "Besides, you've already got what you need, except you're too dumb to see it. Sir."

"What?" asked Recker, mystified.

"If you need me to spell it out, then you'll never get what you want."

Recker held her gaze and judged she wouldn't say anything more. He withdrew from the medical bay and returned to the bridge.

"What's the recommended treatment?" said Aston, once Recker was back at the controls.

"More Frenziol. We're going to ride the wave until the Lavorix are all dead."

"Are you shitting us, sir?" said Eastwood.

"I'm afraid not, Lieutenant. We'll keep injecting and if we ever return to a surface medical facility with some time on our hands, and with no risk of an Extractor attack, maybe we'll be given a body flush."

"Great," said Eastwood, his voice dripping. "I'll look forward to the day."

"I thought your wife would appreciate you coming home boosted, Ken," said Burner with a knowing nod. "It might help with that problem you have *down below*."

Larson made a choking noise and Aston's mouth fell open. Meanwhile, Eastwood delivered a verbal tirade, aimed squarely at Burner's parentage.

"I think we need to call time on this, gentlemen," said Recker. "Save it for later."

The two officers shut up at once and Recker wondered what had got into them. No doubt the constantly building pressure was to blame and eventually one of them would say the wrong thing and then the joking would turn into something serious. What everyone needed was time away from the military – a month spent with family and friends on an HPA world, where they could pretend none of this crap existed.

"Lieutenant Eastwood, Lieutenant Larson, Commander Aston. You've got eight hours off duty. Find something to do that isn't here on the bridge."

The three officers didn't wait to be asked twice and they exited the bridge, leaving Burner and Recker alone.

"Anything I need to look at, sir?" asked Burner.

"I'll let you know if I think of something."

"We've been on plenty of missions where we don't know what to expect. This beats most of them."

"I'm not disagreeing with you, but how come?"

"One, possibly two Laws of Ancidium. A big fleet of

HPA and Daklan warships heading out to face them. Stir everything together and the only prediction I can make is that people are going to die. Beyond that, I can't imagine how it'll work out for us."

"You think this mission is destined for failure?"

"The odds don't look good to me, sir. That's my honest opinion."

"Screw the odds," said Recker with feeling. "We're going to beat them this one last time."

"It's never the last time. There's always something on the horizon, gathering speed and loading its guns."

"There's none of us can change the future, Lieutenant."

"I never thought otherwise, sir. That doesn't mean I can't flip it the bird." With that, Burner lifted a hand so that it was visible over the top of his console screens. He elevated the middle finger and waved it in the general direction of nowhere and everywhere.

"Feel better for that?"

"Not really."

The conversation – such as it was – ended and the bridge went quiet again. Sensing that Burner's strange mood would make the next eight hours drag, Recker opened a comms channel.

"Corporal Montero, if you aren't otherwise occupied, get your ass to the bridge."

"On my way, sir. What's up?"

"Nothing's up. Maybe you can cheer up my comms man and in return, he can teach you a few things you missed during your flight with Commander Aston."

Montero arrived soon after and dropped into the seat

next to Lieutenant Burner, where she spent several hours keeping him occupied, which in turn allowed Recker time to work through a few scenarios in his head. Combat involving multiple warships always involved a degree of chaos, no matter how much effort went into controlling it. This time, Recker expected it to be worse than ever and he wasn't keen to find out what would happen when the Extractor attacks started.

When the eight hours were finished, the other members of the crew returned, allowing Recker and Burner some time away, while Corporal Montero returned to the squad.

Not in the mood for small talk in the mess area, Recker spent his time lying in his compact room with his eyes closed and music playing softly in the background. His body wanted sleep, that much was apparent, but the Frenziol wasn't going to let it happen. Still, the relaxation helped him clear his mind and he thought about his family on Earth. He tried to picture his parents' faces, yet the images were indistinct, like he was starting to forget. Rather than bringing anger, the realisation brought only determination that he'd be back to see them one day.

One day soon.

Recker's eight hours ended and he returned to the bridge, bringing a tray of edible Meklon pastes with him. He knew the replicators could create a wide variety of products, but whatever shape and form those products took, none of them were like the good, honest, HPA military swill he'd become accustomed to.

"Sludge?" said Aston when she saw what he was carrying. She arched an eyebrow in his direction.

"I like this sludge. It tastes good."

"It's green. With lumps."

Though Recker hadn't eaten in the past few hours, his mouth was dry and he didn't feel much in the way of hunger – another expected outcome from the Frenziol. He set the tray down on the floor and pushed it farther away with the side of his foot.

"When do we have to boost again?" said Aston. She pulled an injector from her leg pocket and studied it with distaste.

"I don't know. I'll ask Corporal Hendrix later."

Recker turned his attention to his console. All the lights were green and nothing required his attention.

"We're only halfway to our destination," he said.

Aston offered him a sympathetic smile. "Feels like it's a long trip, huh?"

"Usually we've got something to talk about. Even when the *Galactar* was in pursuit, we could speculate on its capabilities and discuss ways to escape. Now we're flying to Tronstal and we'll arrive, fight the Lavorix and, if we're alive at the end of it, we'll return home."

"I don't know what else you want from it, sir," said Aston.

"I don't want anything else, Commander, other than to be at our destination instead of spending another sixteen hours watching the clock."

Recker had long ago learned that time's passage was inevitable and so it was. Each hour went by as if it were ten, though their numbers fell one by one. He gave his crew more time away from the bridge and took some himself. Nobody slept.

At the time recommended by Corporal Hendrix, Recker pulled out one of his injectors. The cylinder gleamed and he wanted more than anything to drop it to the floor and grind it flat with the sole of his boot. Instead, he pressed it to his thigh and held it there while the Frenziol he didn't want was squirted into his muscle tissue.

A few minutes later, once the drugs had taken effect, Recker felt slightly less terrible than he had before. The tiredness was held at bay, though his headache was too stubbornly entrenched to let go. The thumping pain was manageable and he convinced himself it was a welcome reminder that he wasn't dead.

After what had turned into one of the longest – perception wise at least – and least pleasant lightspeed journeys in Recker's memory, Lieutenant Eastwood shouted his ten-minute warning.

"Next stop: RETI-11 system!"

"Commander Aston, give us a run down, for the benefit of those who weren't listening on the previous occasions," said Recker.

"Yes, sir. The RETI-11 system comprises one star and six planets. RETI-11 itself is about thirty times more massive than Earth's sun, not that we'll be getting anywhere too close. Tronstal is planet number five and it's your usual grey lump of rock. I don't know why Fleet Admiral Telar decided this was a good place to test an experimental weapon – Tronstal has zero moons, which means there's nothing to interfere with the shield breaker's line of sight, but a planet without moons isn't exactly unheard of. Other than that, RETI-11 is home to a gas giant and not much else of interest."

"Thank you, Commander. We'll be exiting lightspeed a short distance beyond the sixth planet, Kolaes, the description of which closely matches that of Tronstal, with the exception that Kolaes has two moons. According to the star charts, our rendezvous point is approximately one billion kilometres from Tronstal."

"Close enough for us to strike quickly, but far enough away to avoid easy detection," said Burner.

"That's right. I'm assuming the gathered warships will be instructed to fly to Tronstal once it's clear the *Ixidar* isn't waiting in ambush. This could all go wrong if the Lavorix arrive early and shoot down the *Maximus*."

"There's plenty that could go wrong, sir," said Eastwood. "We'll deal with whatever comes our way, the same as we always do."

"That we will, Lieutenant." Standing, Recker smiled at his crew. "The time comes." He'd planned to say more, but for some reason the well was dry. He sat.

"Short speech," said Burner.

"Short and sweet, Lieutenant."

The final few minutes passed quicker than those which had preceded them and, at the exact moment predicted by the navigational computer, the *Vengeance*'s ternium drive cut out and the warship was deposited into local space.

CHAPTER TWENTY-TWO

"GET ME THOSE SCAN RESULTS!" shouted Recker.

"Sensors coming online, sir."

"Commencing the local area sweep," said Larson.

"No hardware problems to report, sir," called East-wood. "Greens on everything, just how I like it."

The sensors powered up and their undirected feeds appeared on the bulkhead displays. Burner and Larson acted quickly and they scanned the area.

"I've located Kolaes," said Burner. "No, sorry, that's one of its moons. There's the planet."

"Not much to look at," said Recker, hardly glancing at the rocky sphere on his feed. He had a bigger concern. "Where's the local battle network?"

"I'm searching for the receptor, sir," said Larson.

"We should have joined the network automatically."

"Yes, sir, assuming the battle network was correctly set up."

"Any mistake like that would have been spotted imme-diately."

"I know, sir."

"So why is there no battle network? We should have arrived before the latecomers, but I'd expect forty or more warships to be here already."

Recker didn't like it one bit and his stomach clenched. He grabbed the controls and the *Vengeance* accelerated steadily from its arrival place, aiming for Kolaes which was currently a quarter of a million kilometres away, with only one of its moons visible from the approach trajectory.

Holding the *Vengeance* in a straight line was easy and Recker watched the changing sensor feeds as his two comms officers built a picture of what lay in this part of the solar system. Although the RETI-11 star was enormous, distance turned it into a gleaming pinpoint, beyond the planet's edge.

"Tell me what is going on!" Recker shouted, his pent-up frustration spilling out.

"There's no battle network, sir," said Burner. "I sent a transmission to base, but we're too far out to receive an instant response. All I can think of is that our fleets received updated orders after we entered lightspeed, and they've rendezvoused elsewhere. I checked the coordinates Fleet Admiral Telar provided and we're definitely in RETI-11 and Tronstal is definitely in this solar system."

"I don't believe there's a different rendezvous point," said Recker. "Some of our fleet would have already been at lightspeed when the *Vengeance* set off this way. Those warships would have also missed the updated orders."

"Which leaves only one possibility," said Aston.

Larson spoke before Recker could respond.

"Oh crap," she said. "Tronstal isn't here. At first, I thought maybe I'd misread its expected orbital track position, but I didn't. I've located a cloud of expanding particles right where it should be. We're a billion klicks away, but what I'm looking at is the same thing that happened to Trinus-XN."

"And Fortune," said Recker. He cursed bitterly. "The *Ixidar* got here first. It destroyed the planet and probably our fleet and the shield breaker at the same time."

"We're not dead," said Aston. "Not yet."

Her words were a cold reminder that the enemy ship might still be in the vicinity, watching for latecomers and destroying them as they emerged from lightspeed. So far, the *Vengeance* had seemingly escaped detection and the only reason Recker could imagine for that was because it had emerged from lightspeed behind Kolaes. The planet wasn't dense enough to completely mask the ternium wave, but it would certainly make it harder to detect.

"Let's get away from here." Recker switched the engines into overstress and the planet grew rapidly larger on the forward feed. Kolaes wasn't going to offer much cover if the enemy came this way, but it was better than no cover at all.

"Lieutenant Burner, send a query to the *Aeklu*'s battle network data. I know we won't receive an instant response, but I would prefer to know if we're facing one or both Laws of Ancidium."

"Yes, sir, that request is sent. The moment the response comes, I'll let you know."

"I'm reading a ternium wave half a million klicks off

our ass," said Eastwood. "From the size of it, we've got several warships inbound and the wave formation indicates they're Daklan."

"Add a marker on the tactical to show me their expected arrival place," said Recker.

"The marker is added, sir."

Zooming the tactical out to maximum, Recker calculated the position of the inbound warships in relation to Kolaes and Tronstal. He grimaced – the Daklan ternium wave would be visible to any warships in the vicinity of the destroyed planet.

"Get on the comms!" said Recker urgently. "Tell them of the danger!"

"Yes, sir," said Larson. "Their receivers will stay offline for a few seconds after re-entry to local space."

"Let's hope the warning doesn't come too late for them," said Recker. His mind was beginning to grasp the likely extent of this disaster and he was petrified about what it would mean for the HPA.

"One Daklan annihilator and two desolators have entered the RETI-11 system," said Larson. "I am attempting communication."

Recker shifted his gaze briefly to the rear feeds, on which three grey shapes had appeared, too far away for him to discern specifics. One was noticeably larger than the others, which made it the battleship. All three were accelerating.

"They're broadcasting their names as the *Reisilon*, the *Kildis* and the *Verdinak*," said Larson. "The *Reisilon* has opened a comms receptor. I've requested a channel."

"We've got a second inbound ternium wave about a million klicks from the last one," said Eastwood. "Multiple ships, HPA in origin."

This was my idea. Their deaths will be on my hands.

Recker tried to ignore the thought and told himself nothing was yet confirmed. He brought the *Vengeance* low to the surface of Kolaes and reduced velocity in order to keep in sight of the arriving warships. The underside feed was a picture of ruggedness, of mountains and fissures.

"I've spoken to the Daklan, sir," said Larson. "And warned them of our fears. They're coming to join us behind Kolaes while we figure out what's going on."

The three Daklan warships sped towards the planet. They hadn't covered a quarter of the distance when six HPA warships emerged from their lightspeed transits. A glance at the feed was enough for Recker to identify them as a battleship, two cruisers and three riots. What the hell those riots were meant to accomplish against the *Ixidar*, he couldn't imagine.

"Oh shit, there it is!" said Burner. "The *Ixidar*!"

Exiting from its short range lightspeed jump, the enemy ship hung motionless in space, a million kilometres from the *Vengeance*. Burner focused the sensors, allowing the crew a clear view of their opponent.

Recker's first thought was that the *Ixidar* resembled the Interrogator satellite he'd encountered in orbit around Pinvos. However, with edges measuring eighteen thousand metres, this enemy ship was of a vastly greater volume and mass.

On each of its six faces of near-black alloy, Recker

spotted enormous hexagonal housings and from these housings, single gun barrels protruded. He could only stare at the sensor overlay figures in disbelief – each of the barrels measured four thousand metres in length and the bores were almost eight hundred.

The Destroyer.

The enemy spaceship was not undamaged and Recker counted numerous heat-rimmed craters in its armour. Not only that, he thought maybe the gun barrel on one of the hidden faces was out of alignment, as if its housing had been struck by the same lightspeed missiles which had detonated elsewhere. He couldn't be sure and even if it were missing one gun, that left five others presumably operational.

Recker drew an imaginary line from the *Vengeance* to the *Ixidar*. On one side of the line, the Daklan were seven hundred thousand kilometres from the enemy, while the newly arrived HPA spaceships were on the other side of the line and within half a million kilometres.

"I don't think those are gauss guns, sir," said Eastwood. "The readings from the housings aren't the same. I don't know what they hell they fire."

"Let's hope we don't find out," growled Recker, knowing he was never going to get his wish.

"The Daklan warships plan to hold back and launch lightspeed missiles, sir," said Larson. "I don't think the sensors on the HPA ships are back online yet."

"Should I recommend a withdrawal, sir?" asked Burner.

"It's too late for that, Lieutenant. Maybe too late for all

of us." Recker bared his teeth. "And I'm damned if we'll be spectators."

He fed power into the engines and switched them into overstress. The *Vengeance* sliced through the planet's thin atmosphere, scarcely accumulating heat before it was once more in space.

"The HPA ships are fully back online, sir," said Larson. "I have advised them what to expect if they engage and what to expect if they don't."

Nobody said the word, but they were all thinking it. *Death*.

Having evidently reached the conclusion that it was better to die fighting, the HPA warships banked towards the *Ixidar*. Their weapons were out of lock range and would remain so for several minutes.

"Damn our ships are slow," said Eastwood.

Recker grunted in acknowledgement, remembering a time when he commanded a warship that topped out at eleven hundred kilometres per second. The *Vengeance* had already exceeded four thousand per second and was approaching its 4500 kilometre per second maximum.

Still the *Ixidar* hadn't moved from its arrival position and Recker wondered if the Lavorix had suffered a hardware problem or if they were simply scanning for nearby warships. He soon got his answer. A split second after two lightspeed missiles detonated against one face of the *Ixidar*, it began accelerating straight for the Daklan. The rate of velocity gain was incredible and, in a moment, the Lavorix ship had surpassed two thousand kilometres per second.

"It's rotating," said Larson.

Sure enough, the *Ixidar* had begun rotating steadily clockwise about its vertical axis. The gun which Recker had thought was damaged came into sight and he saw that had been nearly ripped out of its housing, leaving it useless.

"I'm reading power spikes on each of those gun housings, sir," said Eastwood. "They're readying a discharge."

The *Vengeance* achieved maximum velocity and Recker held it there, breathing in the cold, clean air from the bridge vents.

"We're going to hit it with the Fracture," he said. "Warn the other ships and advise them not to come too close."

"The Fracture won't work, sir," said Aston.

"We've only assumed the Fracture won't work, Commander. Now we'll perform a field test."

"It's got a half-million klick lock and discharge range, sir," said Aston.

Recker had one eye on the tactical. The *Ixidar's* trajectory cut directly across that of the *Vengeance* and he adjusted course to meet it. It was clear the Lavorix intended to neutralise the Daklan ships quickly, and Recker wasn't surprised, given the massive payloads of the lightspeed missiles. This was probably the first time the *Ixidar* had suffered damage and the Lavorix were doubtless pissed about it happening.

Unfortunately, the alien bastards had learned from the experience and, rather than flying in a straight line towards the Daklan, they shifted left, right, up and down erratically, varying their approach velocity by a fraction at the same time. Given how the lightspeed missiles functioned, Recker guessed these evasive manoeuvres were going to make it significantly harder to land a hit on the *Ixidar*.

"One of those guns fired," said Eastwood. "The power readings on the housing dropped to zero and now they're climbing again."

Recker saw the outcome on the sensors. The closest desolator – the *Kildis* – was hit by the discharge. A flash of dark energy, much larger than the heavy cruiser, appeared briefly and then vanished just as quickly. In that split-second, the desolator's armour had been completely stripped away, as if the entire ship had been left for a week in the most corrosive substance imaginable. With its plating gone, the ternium modules underneath were exposed and even those were crumbling.

"Another discharge," said Eastwood.

A second flash of dark energy hid the remains of the desolator and this time, the Daklan ship was reduced to an irregular lump of metal, a quarter of its original mass, and completely unrecognizable from what it had once been.

"Gone," said Burner.

"There's a third discharge," said Eastwood.

This time it was the *Verdinak* which was hit by the Lavorix energy cannon and the results were no less devastating. The Daklan crew retained a semblance of control and they banked from their original course. It wasn't going to save them.

Recker's eyes shifted to the sensor feed of the *Ixidar* and suddenly he understood why it was rotating. The enemy ship's main guns were fixed in position, with little or no available adjustment and the only way it could aim was by turning the entire hull. Since the energy shots from the guns had no discernible travel time, the method was far less clumsy that it first appeared and he was sure the enforced firing interval gave each weapon time to recharge.

"Fourth discharge," said Eastwood.

The shot produced no visible effect from the gun – no recoil and nothing from the muzzle - but the *Verdinak* went the same way as the *Kildis*, its corroded hull fragmenting and breaking into pieces.

And still the *Ixidar* rotated, bringing its next gun to bear on the single remaining Daklan ship – the annihilator *Reisilon*. Two more lightspeed missiles detonated against the Lavorix hull, missing the facing gun by a few thousand metres. From what he'd learned at Ivisto, Recker guessed the reprogramming of the missile guidance systems didn't allow perfect targeting. As if the *Ixidar* needed any more advantages.

The Lavorix ship discharged its facing energy cannon and the *Reisilon*'s plating crumbled into dust, which trailed like a glittering streamer in the battleship's wake. Out of options, the Daklan could do nothing other than wait for death.

It came, moments later. Unable to withstand a second shot from the enemy cannon, the *Reisilon* fell apart, its destruction taking away the last available launch platform for the lightspeed missiles.

"Six hundred thousand klicks to target," said Aston. "We'll have the Fracture ready soon."

The *Ixidar* surprised the crew. Instead of coming for

the *Vengeance*, it executed an impossibly tight 180-degree turn that took it on a direct course for the HPA warships.

Recker could only stare in frustration as the *Ixidar*'s punishing velocity carried it rapidly away from the *Vengeance* and he wondered what the hell he could do about it.

CHAPTER TWENTY-THREE

THE *IXIDAR'S* energy cannon had a tremendous range and one of the HPA cruisers was reduced to a decaying cloud of flaking alloy. The ease with which the Lavorix warship finished its opponents left Recker feeling numb and he fought against a sense of helplessness. At one time, he'd thought the *Vengeance* offered enough tools to deal with anything war threw his way. The *Ixidar* was giving him an in-the-face demonstration of exactly how wrong he was.

"Distance to target increasing," said Aston. "We won't get a Fracture shot on it before those HPA ships are destroyed."

Watching events unfold, Recker's helplessness turned to despair. In his heart, he knew the Fracture wasn't going to collapse the *Ixidar*'s energy shield – the Meklon had built several terminator class warships like the *Vengeance* and they hadn't succeeded in damaging the Laws of Ancidium, let alone destroying them.

Which left two options – attempt a mode 3 transit into the *Ixidar*'s energy shield or turn tail and run.

Given the erratic course alterations of the enemy ship, Recker couldn't imagine how a mode 3 jump could work. Perhaps, given time, Eastwood could generate a predictive algorithm to increase the chance of a transit landing within the shield. Time, of course, wasn't an available luxury.

One of the riot class spaceships vanished when it was hit by the energy cannon, leaving the remaining HPA ships to scatter in the hope they'd survive long enough to fire their missiles – missiles which had no hope of bringing down the Lavorix energy shield.

"The enemy have introduced a complication to their rotation, sir," said Larson. "They've started tumbling."

"I see it," said Recker. The *Ixidar* was no longer turning about its vertical axis and its new pattern was about all three axes. "Full attack mode," he guessed. "They can fire each gun the moment it recharges."

"And hit targets that aren't right in front of them," said Aston.

As she finished the words, a warning light flashed up on Recker's console and the *Vengeance*'s bright mesh deflector shield appeared, forming a protective barrier around the warship.

"We took a hit," said Aston. "There goes our single mesh deflector charge. Five minutes and we'll have it available again."

"Our battleship – it's the *Sledgehammer* – has also been hit by the *Ixidar*'s cannon, sir," said Burner. "And they don't have a shield."

"I recommend we retreat, sir," said Aston. "We can't affect what's about to happen."

Recker knew it was true, but that didn't make it easier. With its mesh deflector on recharge, the *Vengeance* would be destroyed by the next shot. On the sensor feed, he saw the extensive damage the *Sledgehammer* had suffered and there was no chance in hell it would hold together when the next energy burst came.

The stubborn part of Recker – the part that couldn't give up – calculated the charge intervals on the *Ixidar's* guns at the same time as searching for a flaw in the enemy ship's rotation that would allow an opponent to stay ahead of the loaded weapons. It was useless and he ground his teeth together in fury.

A second shot engulfed the *Sledgehammer* and the battleship broke up like a log of rotten wood.

"We're next," said Larson.

"I've entered coordinates for Kolaes, sir," said Eastwood. "You want to go anywhere else and it'll take me some extra time."

This battle is lost. My duty now is to protect my crew.

Recker activated mode 3. The sensors went blank and the nausea was so fleeting he hardly noticed it. Acting at once, he fed power into the engines and the *Vengeance* accelerated.

"I'd recommend you hold steady, sir," said Eastwood.

The reason for the warning became apparent when the *Vengeance* crunched into a solid object. Recker backed off the controls and held the warship in place.

"Where are we?" he asked.

"As close to the far side of Kolaes as I dared, sir. The

planet's got a ternium-rich crust and I'm hoping that's going to make it harder for the enemy to pick up our location."

"Sensors coming online," said Burner.

When the feeds stabilised a moment later, Recker was presented with a view of high peaks all around the *Vengeance*. The sheer cliff face directly ahead was in a state of partial collapse as a result of the warship's recent impact, and a heap of stones lay at the bottom of a canyon which ran between this mountain and the next.

"What now?" said Aston. She exhaled noisily and swore. "Damn this has all gone to shit."

"I know, Commander," said Recker.

Aston detected the note in his voice and she speared him with her gaze. "Not your fault, sir. You offered advice and Fleet Admiral Telar acted upon it. We did the right thing, but the enemy outguessed us."

Recker could have said plenty but knew it wouldn't do any good. This wasn't the time to wallow in guilt and that duty to protect his crew hadn't diminished.

"We can't face the *Ixidar*," he said. "The fleet before us failed and now the Lavorix have figured out a way to minimise the threat of the Daklan lightspeed missiles."

"What about the Fracture?" said Aston.

"You were right, Commander. It won't be enough, but it's all we have. If we must, I'll mode 3 into range of the *Ixidar* and try it out anyway."

"We can't mode 3 for a few minutes, sir," Eastwood reminded him. "And it'll be another couple of minutes for the mesh deflector to recharge."

"If we aren't going to attack the *Ixidar* again, does that

mean we're heading back to an HPA planet?" asked Burner.

"I don't know, Lieutenant. Certainly, we can't head straight for home, in case the Lavorix follow us."

"It's looking increasingly likely the enemy know exactly where our planets are located anyway, sir," said Aston. "If not all, then some."

Recker spent a few moments in thought. It was in no way certain the *Ixidar* wouldn't find the *Vengeance* hiding here behind the planet. Equally, it was possible that a few stragglers from the Daklan and HPA fleets might show up and give the Lavorix some extra target practice. Recker wasn't sure he could handle sitting back and watching it happen.

He closed his eyes, hating that he'd been forced into this position – where doing the right thing left him feeling like a coward. Staying here in RETI-11 meant thinking of a way to lure the *Ixidar* into a stationary position long enough that the *Vengeance* could mode 3 behind its shield and then hit it with the Fracture. Success would likely kill his crew at the same time, though Recker was sure it was a price they would willingly pay.

"We're not going to throw the *Vengeance* against the enemy shield," he said. "It makes me feel sick to my stomach, but we're pulling out, folks." Recker held his lips tightly together and then said the words. "Lieutenant Eastwood, warm up the ternium drive. Target a location six hours from here, in a direction of your choosing."

"Yes, sir."

At that moment, Recker was offered certainty that his plan to escape wasn't going to work. On one of the starboard feeds, he spotted a shape racing low across the eastern horizon. The *Ixidar* was momentarily hidden by the mountains and then it reappeared, this time north-east of the *Vengeance*.

"Hold that last order, Lieutenant Eastwood," said Recker.

He felt emotionally and physically drained, but even so, his hands rested themselves on the controls. Recker turned the *Vengeance* on the spot and reduced its altitude as much as he could. Once he had its nose pointing along the canyon, he accelerated, guiding the warship between the peaks.

"I've added a course overlay for the enemy ship onto the tactical, sir," said Burner. "At their detected velocity, they'll complete a full circuit of the planet in less than three minutes."

"They know we came this side of the planet," said Eastwood. "There's no way they're going to do circuits in the hope they stumble into us."

Recker knew it too and he increased the *Vengeance*'s speed. The *Ixidar* was too potent and its crew too experienced – they wouldn't circle the planet and rely on chance to bring the fleeing ship into sensor sight. Once again, despair threatened and a whispering voice told Recker he was only delaying the inevitable and that his defiance would do nothing more than prolong his agony.

Like hell.

As the *Vengeance* gathered speed, Recker lifted it to a greater altitude, above the highest of the peaks. This mountain range covered the planet's visible surface in all directions like a carpet of knives and Recker's eyes scanned the horizons for a place he might hide the *Vengeance*. Though he'd used this crudest of tactics in the past, this time Recker gave it up, sure that the *Ixidar's* sensor team wouldn't be fooled.

"Less than a minute on the mesh deflector," said Aston.

"A couple minutes longer and we'll have mode 3 functionality again," said Eastwood. "If we fire off into space, that might buy us some breathing room."

"I want more than breathing room," snarled Recker. The despair was suddenly gone, replaced by an absolute determination to spit in death's eye one more time. An idea came. "Commander Aston, you mentioned a gas giant in the RETI-11 system."

"Yes, sir. It's approximately two billion klicks from Kolaes. Diameter 120,000 klicks. Composition..."

"I don't care if it's got a core made from compressed horse shit, Commander," Recker interrupted. "Pass the coordinates to Lieutenant Eastwood."

"I take it that's our target, sir?"

"That it is, Lieutenant. Aim for the blind side and deep in the clouds."

"Yes, sir. Coordinates entered."

Recker nodded in acknowledgement but kept his gaze on the feeds. The *Vengeance* was travelling fast and even given the sparsity of atmospheric molecules, heat was beginning to accumulate on the nose. Soon, the warship would trail smoke and that would make it an easy spot for the enemy.

It turned out the Lavorix didn't need the assistance anyway.

"The *Ixidar*!" yelled Burner.

Far behind, the enemy warship became visible on the horizon's edge as a fast-moving shape against the planet's black sky. Instinctively, Recker sent the *Vengeance* lower, hoping to drop out of sight amongst the mountains and around the planet's curve.

Sensing imminent attack, he angled the *Vengeance* left around one of the larger peaks. A flash of darkness appeared on the rear sensors and then was gone, leaving the warship undamaged. For the mountains, it was different – the Lavorix energy cannon had created an eight-kilometre crater which went deep into the solid rock. Where once there had been proud summits, the weapon left behind only crumbling powder.

"Near miss," said Aston.

"Mode 3 is still not ready," said Eastwood. "It's got a long way to go."

Only a couple of minutes remained on the recharge timer, but Recker understood the sentiments. He banked again and fed extra power into the warship's engines. The nose temperature climbed as the *Vengeance* raced on, and wisps of faint smoke whipped into the sky.

"Any moment..." said Aston.

The second shot erupted so close to the *Vengeance*'s stern that it blocked the view from several of the portside and starboard arrays as well, and Recker watched in anticipation of the warning lights appearing on his console. The lights stayed green and he knew they'd escaped by the skin of their teeth. Behind lay another crater of similar magnitude to the first, and the *Ixidar* was made visible by the mountains it had destroyed. The

Lavorix ship had matched velocity and distance, and on it came.

"Why aren't they going high and fast?" wondered Larson. "They could guarantee a clean shot."

"They're enjoying the chase, Lieutenant. Those assholes will give us enough leash to think we're in with a chance and then they'll finish us."

Recker didn't know if he was correct – it was just a feeling he had. The crew of the *Ixidar* would remain in RETI-11 until they were sure no more Daklan or HPA ships were coming and then they'd go elsewhere. In the meantime, the *Vengeance* made good sport.

"The Lavorix must know we're equipped with a Fracture," said Aston.

"And they don't give a damn, Commander. I guess they've answered our question for us."

Aston gave a tight smile. "So no need to risk everything to get off a shot."

The mental countdown Recker was keeping of the *Ixidar*'s reload approached zero and he threw the *Vengeance* to one side. His effort was in vain and a third energy cannon shot caught the warship dead-centre, activating the mesh deflector a few seconds after its recharge was completed.

"This isn't working," said Recker angrily.

He jammed the controls to the end of their slots and they clacked against metal. A howl of overstressed propulsion hurled the *Vengeance* across the planet and the ground below turned into a blur of shapes and colours.

"The *Ixidar* is going high," said Larson.

Recker's heart jumped in hope. "They've misjudged," he said.

The blistering pace of the *Vengeance* had caught the enemy unawares and the steep ascent of the *Ixidar* gave Recker a chance to escape to the blind side of Kolaes. A temperature alert appeared for the nose plating and he ignored it. The warship's speed was climbing fast and the smoke trail thickened. This was a balancing act, Recker knew. If the *Vengeance* became too hot, the *Ixidar* could follow the trail. If Recker was too cautious, the enemy would turn his warship to dust before he made it out of sight.

"Ninety seconds on mode 3," said Eastwood.

"Too long," muttered Recker.

The *Vengeance* left the mountain range behind and entered an area of undulating stone. So high was its speed that the rolling plains looked more like an ocean of dark waves, and the spaceship a boat scudding across them.

"The enemy have altered heading and velocity," said Burner.

A course projection line appeared on the tactical, showing Recker that the *Ixidar* was arcing and accelerating at such a rate that it would soon have an easy shot directly onto the *Vengeance.*

"Shit, I misjudged, not them," swore Recker bitterly.

"We can't beat that warship, sir," said Aston. "It's like we're facing the *Galactar* again."

Fate and luck, which Recker sometimes maligned, came to his rescue, though in the manner of a double-edged sword dripping with the blood of sacrifice.

"Ternium wave!" shouted Eastwood. "One-point-five

million klicks on the far side of Kolaes! I estimate four more Daklan ships are inbound."

Recker knew what was coming. As if it had never existed, the *Ixidar* disappeared from the sensors.

"The Lavorix detected those warships and entered mode 3 to greet them as they enter local space," said Eastwood. "Damnit."

"Get on the comms," said Recker. "It'll be too late, but..."

He couldn't bring himself to finish the sentence and the muscles in his jaw tightened. Having been granted some time by the arrival of the Daklan, he reduced the *Vengeance*'s speed to give its nose a chance to cool. In the background, he could hear Lieutenant Larson's frantic efforts to reach the Daklan. Whatever she told them, it wouldn't have any bearing on the outcome.

"The Daklan are engaged with the *Ixidar*," she said at last.

"Our mode 3 is ready, sir," said Eastwood.

"Are the coordinates set?"

"Yes, sir."

Recker activated the *Vengeance*'s mode 3. The warship entered lightspeed for a split second and then exited into the maelstrom of RETI-11's gas giant. Every sensor feed became fuzzy with interference, though not so much that Recker was unable to discern the swirling clouds of toxic gases.

Not wishing to stay anywhere near the arrival point in case the *Ixidar* tracked the *Vengeance* to its destination, Recker guided the warship clockwise around the planet and deeper until the brown murk of gases was too much for the sensors to pierce.

"Let's hope that's enough, folks," he said.

Feeling lower than at any point he could remember, Recker tipped his head back and closed his eyes.

CHAPTER TWENTY-FOUR

MINUTES PASSED, during which Recker and his crew remained in their seats. The winds outside blew viciously against the *Vengeance*, without shifting it a fraction out of position. Burner and Larson made regular adjustments to the sensor arrays in the hope of obtaining a clear view into space. It was no use – the warship was too far below the gaseous surface for the Meklon technology to penetrate. Not only that, but interference had effectively cut off the comms, preventing inbound and outbound transmissions, except for the occasional corrupted data packet which somehow made it to the antennae.

So far, the *Vengeance* remained undiscovered, though nobody had any idea if the *Ixidar* was actively searching for the warship, or if it was still elsewhere in RETI-11, hunting members of the HPA and Daklan fleets.

"How long are we planning to wait, sir?" said Aston eventually.

"Longer than this," said Recker.

"We can activate the ternium drive safely from here, sir," said Eastwood.

"I know, but we don't know if the *Ixidar* will detect our lightspeed tunnel as it emerges from the planet's surface."

"That probably won't..."

"There's the word, Lieutenant. *Probably*. If we're going to run from trouble, we might as well make the best job of it." Recker's guilt and anger flared and he swallowed them down.

"Meaning we sit here for what? Days?" asked Eastwood. "This is not your fault, sir. You were presented with a situation where the only outcome was to lose, and that's what happened. It doesn't mean we give up."

"I haven't given up, Lieutenant."

"It sure seems that way, sir."

"We need you," said Aston softly. "You're the only one who sees the right path amongst the millions of others."

"Not this time, Commander."

"We can't stop trying. Please."

Recker knew he was standing on the brink and he also knew he was too stubborn to let himself go over the edge. That left him with no option other than to keep fighting. Wallowing in guilt wasn't helping anyone.

"Lieutenant Burner," he said. "Did we receive those data packets from the *Aeklu*'s battle network?"

"Yes, sir. One came in a moment before you activated mode 3 and I've had a scrambled version since then. The data in that last one isn't intact, but some of it is readable. The first packet confirms the presence of the *Ixidar* in RETI-11, but we already knew that. In the second packet, the data has been stirred around so I can't confirm the enemy's location."

"It's not the *Ixidar* I'm interested in, Lieutenant. What about the *Gorgadar*?"

"It hasn't moved, sir."

"That's a long time for a warship to stay in one place," said Recker, tapping his fingertips against his console.

"What if it's a space station?" asked Larson. "The Lavorix might have set the *Gorgadar* in planetary orbit and left it there."

"It's a possibility," Recker admitted.

"You don't believe it, though," said Aston.

Recker shook his head slowly. "I think the *Gorgadar* is a warship like all the other Laws of Ancidium."

"You think we should go check it out," said Aston.

"Yes."

"What's the reasoning, sir?" asked Eastwood.

"I want to see what we're up against."

"There's more," said Larson.

"Yes, there is, Lieutenant. I think something happened to the *Gorgadar* and I want to find out what." Recker climbed from his seat and faced his crew. "And I promise you one thing – this is not intended as a suicide run. Commander Aston, you told me I can see the right path and this is the one. If I'm wrong, the *Vengeance* will be destroyed and we'll die."

"We've had more than our share of escapes up to now, sir," said Burner. "I say we're due another."

"That's what I think too, Lieutenant." Recker looked at the others. "Anyone think this is a bad idea?"

"Permission to state that it's a terrible idea, but also agree to it anyway?" said Larson.

"Your opinion is noted." Recker smiled thinly. "Anyone else?"

"If I'm going to die, I might as well be one of the few living souls to have seen all six Laws of Ancidium when it happens," said Eastwood. He gave a snort of laughter. "Damn that's bad reasoning."

"Too late to back out now, Ken," said Aston.

Eastwood puffed out his chest. "I never backed out of anything and I'm not about to start now."

"We're leaving RETI-11," said Recker. "And we're leaving as soon as possible."

"What about the lightspeed tunnel you thought the *Ixidar* might follow?" asked Burner.

"That possibility was more of a concern when we were heading to HPA space, Lieutenant. Since we're heading in the opposite direction, I'm willing to take the risk."

"I suggest we drop lower into the planet, sir," said Eastwood. "Our ternium cloud will be the easiest thing to spot, so it makes sense if we can minimise the likelihood."

"I agree," said Recker, taking his seat again.

"What about Fleet Admiral Telar, sir?" asked Larson. "We won't be able to send a transmission to base."

"We'll do that once we arrive, Lieutenant."

Recker guided the warship deeper. Out of overstress, the *Vengeance*'s engines were a distant, grumbling thunder and the warship descended into the gloom. The pressure on the hull built steadily.

"The *Vengeance* is enormously resistant to pressure

since it's almost solid," said Eastwood. "However, the sensor arrays aren't so tough and they'll break soon."

"I hear you," said Recker. Just thinking about the hull being crushed made him imagine sounds of groaning and strain.

Far below the surface of the planet, he brought the *Vengeance* to a standstill. "What's the name of the place we're going?"

"It's not in the *Vengeance*'s star charts, sir," said Burner. "The *Gorgadar* is in a different sphere to where our ship was built. Our navigational system recognizes the coordinates and it'll take us to the right place."

"Pick a suitable destination - not too close – and provide those details to Lieutenant Eastwood."

"Yes, sir. From the looks of it, the *Gorgadar* is right on top of the local star."

"I've entered the coordinates," said Eastwood a moment later. "We've got a nine-day journey ahead of us."

"Shame the *Aeklu*'s going nowhere," said Burner. "We could have used its Gateway."

Nine days at lightspeed was longer than Recker wanted and he briefly considered a return to Lustre to find out of the *Aeklu* was still offline. He dismissed the idea – it was another long journey with no guarantee of success. Besides, Recker didn't want Fleet Admiral Telar giving him a contradictory order, which was a distinct possibility once the *Vengeance* came back on grid. This voyage to the *Gorgadar* was something Recker had to finish.

"Lieutenant Eastwood, warm up the ternium drive. Destination, as ordered."

"Ternium drive warming up, sir."

Six minutes later, the *Vengeance* entered lightspeed, leaving behind RETI-11 and the disastrous encounter with the *Ixidar*.

Waiting no longer, Recker set up a schedule for his crew so they could have time off the bridge. The latest dose of Frenziol-13 ensured sleep was not a possibility and there wasn't much else to do on the *Vengeance*, but nobody complained.

Recker fell into a new routine of twelve hours on, twelve hours off. He kept mostly to himself and only showed his face in the mess room at mealtimes. It seemed fair to keep the platoon informed of recent events, and the new destination. The soldiers accepted this new mission with shrugs and wisecracks, as Recker knew they would.

"What are you hoping to find, Captain Recker?" asked Sergeant Shadar on the third day. The mess room was full and Recker poked an unappetising heap of glutinous lumps around his metal tray.

Recker met his officer's eyes. The Daklan seemed older than before, as if the Extractor had done him lasting harm, though his gaze was unwavering and his voice strong.

"Death or salvation, Sergeant. One or the other awaits us, and nothing in between."

Shadar understood. Somehow, he always understood. "I choose salvation."

Sergeant Vance was also sitting at the table, his suit helmet and rifle next to his own tray. His expression showed uncertainty and a willingness to believe, even if he didn't know exactly what he was supposed to believe in.

He gave a short laugh. "I guess I choose salvation too."

Recker was grateful neither officer asked him to make promises or predictions and he wasn't sure what answers he would have given. His appetite hadn't returned and he took his leave, pausing only to push his tray of unfinished food into the disposal slot. On the nearby table, Corporal Hendrix, Private Enfield and a couple of the other soldiers laughed and joked like they were in a bar on the first night of a month's shore leave.

Halfway through the nine days, Recker managed a fitful sleep, from which fevered thoughts regularly brought him back to consciousness. Two days after that, he was sleeping as solidly as ever, though his guilt and sorrow had not entirely dissipated. Maybe they never would.

If I don't come to terms with the past, I might as well stop living. And I'm damned if I'm ready to lay down and die.

The same thought played in his mind so often it became a refrain. *I won't lay down and die.* Soon, every time the self-destructive part of his mind goaded him about his failings, those six words jumped to the forefront of his consciousness, drowning out everything else.

In the end, Recker knew he was coming to terms with what had happened and the familiar on-the-edge sense of agitation returned, like it always did when something critical was on the horizon.

By the end of the eighth day, everyone onboard had made good progress in recovering from not only the Extractor attacks, but also the drugs used to combat the effects of that same weapon. Even the Daklan were looking much improved and it gave Recker hope that they'd end up as healthy as before.

The only trouble was, he'd soon be asking everyone to take a double dose of Frenziol, while flying them towards another warship equipped with an Extractor. Nobody ever promised an easy life in the military.

When Lieutenant Eastwood called out his ten-minute warning, the *Vengeance*'s crew were at their stations and ready for whatever fate would bring. The two shots of boosters had left Recker with the feeling that he needed to vomit, while his mouth was parched.

"Maybe we'll get lucky," said Aston. "We're sure the Laws of Ancidium keep modifying their Extractors, but maybe they don't communicate those updates to each other."

"How would they even know if those modifications are working?" demanded Burner. "We either die or we don't."

"A discussion for later," warned Recker. "We're about to drop into hostile territory – a solar system we know nothing about - and I want you focused."

"Yes, sir."

The timer fell and Recker felt a cold sweat prickling. His heart thumped in his chest, something he put down to the boosters.

"Two minutes!" shouted Eastwood.

Recker nodded in response and didn't take his eyes off the timer. On an older HPA warship, the lightspeed calculations were usually a few seconds out, but the processing core on the *Vengeance* rarely made an error.

"Twenty seconds," said Recker.

The timer counted to zero and he felt the juddering of the ternium drive switching over, sending the *Vengeance* out of lightspeed and into local space.

CHAPTER TWENTY-FIVE

THE ARRIVAL PLACE chosen by Lieutenant Eastwood was a billion kilometres from the sun, which was an acceptable distance given the advanced detection capabilities exhibited by the Laws of Ancidium. Recker gave the *Vengeance* maximum acceleration and waited for his sensor officers to report.

"Local scan complete," said Larson. "There's nothing close by."

Recker didn't slow the warship and listened for the next update.

"Far scans underway," said Burner. "I've located the star and it's on the sensors. Not much to say about it – it's a hundred percent larger in diameter and three times the mass of Earth's sun. A star like others we've seen before."

Recker didn't spend much time looking at the fully zoomed feed. The star was little more than a bright, wavering disk on the screen.

"The *Gorgadar* is on the facing side," said Larson.

"We'll talk about the best way to find it once we've completed the rest of the scans."

"I know the routine, Lieutenant."

"Far scans complete," said Burner a short time later. "I've located a total of four planets, all of them farther from their sun than we are. Probability modelling suggests an exceptionally high likelihood of other planets, as-yet undetected."

"Keep searching," said Recker.

"Is it important we find other planets, sir?" asked Larson.

"Probably not, Lieutenant. Sometimes it's good to have a place to run. Lieutenant Burner, have you sent that transmission to Earth?"

"Yes, sir. It won't reach its destination for a long time."

"No chance we'll be recalled, then," said Aston.

Recker looked her way and she offered him a grin. He felt better knowing her good spirits had returned and he smiled in response.

"I've located a fifth and sixth planet," said Larson. "They're both heading blind side of the sun and I've added them to the local chart we're building of this solar system."

"Thank you, Lieutenant. Now stop what you're doing – it's time to concentrate on the star."

"There's not a chance in hell of detecting anything from this range, sir," protested Burner.

"I thought we had precise coordinates, Lieutenant?"

"I don't know how the Lavorix configure their battle networks, but I assume they're precise," said Burner. "That doesn't mean our sensors have suddenly learned how to ignore the radiation and other crap that spills from a star. If our information is accurate, the *Gorgadar* is on the edge of the corona."

"Five million klicks from the surface," said Recker.

"It's sixty-two hours from here to there at our maximum sub-light velocity," said Eastwood helpfully.

"Lieutenant Burner, you've informed me of the difficulties, but I'd like you to take a look before we start up the ternium drive," said Recker.

"Yes, sir," said Burner. "Just don't be disappointed at the results."

With nothing hostile in the vicinity, Recker slowed the *Vengeance* to a crawl, considered the matter further and then brought it to a standstill. Fixed sensors always gathered more data. "That should help."

Neither Burner nor Larson responded, though the former muttered quietly under his breath.

"Uh, I've located something," said Burner. "I should feel embarrassed because I said it would never happen, but instead I'm going to pat myself on the back."

"What have you found?" asked Recker.

"I don't know, sir. It's not a physical object – more of an energy reading." Burner made a *hmm* sound. "A distortion."

"What kind of distortion, Lieutenant?"

"I don't know, sir. It could even be coming from the star."

"You don't think so."

"No."

"Add it to the tactical."

"Done. The readings are coming from dead on the battle network coordinates."

"Shame we don't have a lightspeed missile to poke the hornet's nest," said Eastwood.

Recker stared at the red dot on the tactical. No additional insight came, but there again he'd already made up his mind.

"We're going closer," he said. "Lieutenant Eastwood – target a place five million klicks from the source of that reading. That's five million klicks farther out from the sun in case you hadn't realised."

"Thank you for spelling that out, sir. I have entered the destination. Six minutes on the timer."

"What aren't you telling us, sir?" said Aston. "It's like you've brought us here with more knowledge than you're letting on."

"I don't know anything, Commander. All I've got is a feeling." He sighed without knowing why. "When you started talking about roads and how I could see the right one amongst the others, it made me start thinking about the *Gorgadar* and what it's doing here in the back end of beyond instead of fighting the Kilvar or guarding the Ancidium."

"What conclusions did you reach?"

"The Lavorix won't have left a primary asset doing nothing. That much is obvious. So the *Gorgadar* either has a purpose being out here that we don't understand, or something else happened."

"What else?" said Aston.

"That's what we're here to find out."

"Death or salvation." She smiled.

"Where did you hear that?"

"The mess room. It's what the soldiers keep saying – that we're here for death or salvation."

Recker laughed and it was so long since he'd done so that the noise was strange in his ears. "And they'd be right, Commander."

Six minutes after the timer started, the *Vengeance* entered lightspeed in a quick in-out that made Recker's stomach lurch. Without waiting for the sensors, he requested maximum power from the engines and the warship sped away from its arrival place.

The sensors came online quickly and most of the feeds were of the local star, the light from which filled the bridge with a white-tinted yellow that made him squint. Once again, the sensor team scanned the locality and this time the tension was more palpable than before.

"Nothing on the near scan," said Larson. "I'm searching for the energy reading."

"Fars ongoing," said Burner.

"I've located the energy reading," said Larson. "The type is still unknown – maybe there's an interaction with the sun's radiation that's fooling the sensors."

"Fars clear, sir. And we're not dead yet."

"There's plenty of time for that to happen, Lieutenant."

"I've located an object, sir," said Larson.

Recker's heart thudded harder than before. "Tell me."

"It's stationary and made of alloy, with an active energy shield which has probably been triggered by proximity to the sun - the temperatures there are high enough to melt any known substance. I'd estimate its longest dimension at approximately twenty-nine thousand metres."

The agitation Recker was experiencing didn't go away. "Zoom and enhance, please."

"Working on it. Here."

"Definitely a spaceship," said Recker. "Can you enhance further?"

"That's the best we'll get from this range, sir."

"Maybe the *Gorgadar* is the oldest of the six," said Eastwood. "From its looks, anyway."

"Age doesn't explain what it's doing here."

The distant spaceship's flank was facing the *Vengeance*, giving Recker an idea of its shape despite the light and radiation interference affecting the sensors. If this was the *Gorgadar*, its profile more closely resembled an older model HPA battleship, with perhaps some extra bulk and twenty-five-thousand-metre landing skids instead of legs. There was something else – the intense light of the star was suppressed as it passed the warship, as if a sphere different to the energy shield surrounded the *Gorgadar*'s hull.

"What is that...*darkness*...around it?" asked Recker.

"I don't know, sir," said Burner. "But it's producing the same readings as I took from a billion klicks."

Recker stared and Aston mistook his silence for uncertainty. She offered a suggestion. "Our missiles won't lock from here, but they'll hit a stationary target with a bit of guidance reprogramming. We could fire a shot and see what happens."

"Hold the weapons, Commander. We're heading in."

The cold sweat from before had dried on Recker's skin

and his scalp itched. He took the *Vengeance* to maximum velocity and the tactical informed him the warship was eighteen minutes from target.

"Shouldn't we watch things from range for a while longer?" asked Burner.

"Scan for a receptor, Lieutenant," said Recker, not answering the question.

"No visible receptors, sir."

The distance between the two spaceships decreased and the outside temperature climbed. Soon, the first of the hull alerts appeared on Recker's console and, at two million kilometres from the target, he slowed once again to a standstill. From this distance, the suppression of the sun's light was much more apparent.

"That sphere has an eighty-klick radius, sir. The energy type is something I'm unfamiliar with and there's no match in the *Vengeance*'s databanks," said Burner. "I won't be able to tell you what it is."

Recker placed his finger on the mode 3 activation button. "Open up a comms receptor and start sending transmissions to that ship, Lieutenant."

"The miniscule chance they don't know we're here will then fall to zero, sir."

"Open the receptor, Lieutenant."

"Receptor open...bombarding unknown warship with comms transmissions."

The warship, which Recker deep down knew was the *Gorgadar*, didn't respond.

"I've seen enough," he said. "We're going to mode 3 into its shield. Lieutenant Eastwood, program the coordinates into the navigational system."

"Already, sir?" said Aston. "Perhaps we should continue our observation."

She was the second member of the crew to express doubts and Recker saw the concern in her face.

"I haven't gone mad, Commander. That's the *Gorgadar*, I'm sure of it. Fleet Admiral Telar believes the Lavorix are in retreat and I think it started when they lost that warship."

"They've lost four others, sir."

"I know, and I think the enemy have been acting in desperation since this happened." Recker lifted a hand and pointed at the spaceship on the feed.

"That sphere?" said Aston, struggling for comprehension.

"I think the Kilvar did something. Whatever it was, we're looking at the results."

"A dead ship," said Eastwood.

"If I'm right, we have an opportunity," said Recker. "If I'm wrong..."

"Death," said Larson. "Whatever happened to the Lavorix will happen to us."

"I'm willing to take the chance, Lieutenant. Are you?"

"I'd prefer a better idea of what effects that sphere might have on us."

"I'm not dictating anything, Lieutenant. I'd like agreement first."

"The sphere might be something emitted by the spaceship," said Larson. "If the *Gorgadar* was attacked, there's no reason to believe the effects have lingered."

"Except that the Lavorix haven't recovered their warship," said Recker.

"You're hoping that we're resistant to an unknown weapon in the same way we are to the Extractor," said Larson.

"I feel like we should have died in RETI-11, Lieutenant, yet here we are. The *Ixidar* will soon be on its way to HPA or Daklan territory and we have nothing that can stop it. We've been given a chance."

"Death or salvation." said Larson. She smiled at Recker. "Let's do it."

Recker didn't wait any longer and he pressed the mode 3 button on the control bar.

CHAPTER TWENTY-SIX

RECKER WAITED in anticipation of that death. It didn't come, though a strange tingling made his skin feel like he'd just stepped out of a hot bath and he experienced a vague feeling of detachment from his body which was different to that imparted by the Frenziol. None of it was pleasant but he could live with it, assuming it didn't get any worse.

"Sensors coming online," said Burner.

Recker didn't take his hands off the controls, but made no effort to use them. The sensors came up and the port-side arrays were full of spaceship, the *Vengeance* being too close for everything to be visible. The part Recker saw was an immense slab of alloy, which was curved rather than flat like he'd expected. On the opposite side arrays, he saw the same translucent effect caused by the energy shield as he'd seen in the Ivisto construction yard.

"We're not dead," said Eastwood. "But I don't feel right."

"Me either," said Larson.

Now that he had external visibility, Recker carefully turned the *Vengeance* to obtain a better view of the *Gorgadar*. From this close, it was impressive and while the general shape still bore a resemblance to an older HPA design, the curves added a sleekness that made it appear far in advance of anything humanity had constructed. Aside from that, the pointed nose and the long main structure were as classical as it came.

"I can only see conventional weaponry," said Burner. "Missiles and shit."

"This is the *Gorgadar*, Lieutenant. It has more than just missiles."

"Now that we're so near, I'm getting some clearer hull readings, sir," said Eastwood. "I wonder if that other energy was masking them." He swore loudly. "These hull readings are of another unknown type."

Recker glanced at the outside readings. Despite the *Gorgadar*'s proximity to the star, temperatures within its shield were far below zero. "Hold the analysis, Lieutenant Eastwood – we're going onboard."

"How?" said Aston.

"The same way we entered the *Aeklu* – through the topside hatch."

"What about the security?" asked Burner.

"The construction yard discovered only limited security systems on the *Aeklu*, Lieutenant. There was an access system, but you could touch almost any panel and the door would open. Almost as if it never occurred to the Lavorix that someone would try to break in. Most importantly, I have the command codes we extracted from the *Aeklu*'s control core."

"Which will definitely work on a different warship," said Eastwood.

"The generator software we extracted from the *Aeklu* created codes which were also recognized by the *Verumol*."

"I didn't know that," said Eastwood. He opened his mouth again, like he was about to launch into speculation on Lavorix security protocols.

Recker lifted a hand to stop him. "Later, please."

"The topside hatch it is, sir."

"Lieutenant Burner, order the platoon to the forward airlock."

"Yes, sir. Sergeant Shadar is already requesting a channel."

Recker frowned. "Speak to him."

"Unvak is dead, sir," said Burner a few seconds later. "He just dropped down when we exited the mode 3. Corporal Hendrix is attempting to revive him, but it doesn't sound like it's going to happen."

"Damn," said Recker. He lowered his head. "What about the others?"

"No casualties except Unvak, sir."

"We can't hold the mission," said Recker. He took a deep breath. "Order the squads to the forward airlock," he repeated.

"Sergeant Shadar acknowledges, sir."

The death of Unvak was a hard blow, coming as it did so unexpectedly. It also raised questions about the short- and longer-term effects of whatever aura it was that surrounded the *Gorgadar*.

Having come so far, Recker was not about to give up.

He guided the *Vengeance* up the sloping flank of the *Gorgadar* and then piloted it above the upper armour. From this vantage, the warship's broad beam was apparent, as was the gentle port-to-starboard curve of its topside. Towards the nose, the hull beam narrowed in two abrupt steps and the frontmost section of the plating was flat, unlike the rest of the spaceship.

No external weaponry broke the clean lines, though the spaceship still exuded a menace that went beyond any physical appearance. Recker wondered if the *Gorgadar's* creators had somehow imbued the vessel with their own cruelty in the same way as they had the *Aeklu*.

"Find me a hatch," he said.

"I'm scanning the midsection, six thousand metres from the nose, sir," said Burner. "Found something!"

"That's an entrance, right enough," said Aston. "The access panel is visible."

Recker dropped the *Vengeance* onto the *Gorgadar's* upper armour, at the top of the curve.

"We're all going," he said. "I've set the *Vengeance* on autopilot. If necessary, I can send it a return to base command and it'll fly back to Earth."

Picking up his gauss rifle, Recker patted his leg pocket unconsciously, to be sure it still contained spare booster needles. Then, he exited the bridge and dashed for the forward airlock along with his crew.

Fitting everyone into the airlock was a tight and Recker found himself pushed up against one of the side walls. When the inner door was closed, he ordered Sergeant Shadar to open the boarding ramp.

"Ramp opening," Shadar confirmed.

The air rushed out and the temperature fell rapidly. Too late, Recker wondered if the hull of the *Vengeance* had been protecting everyone from the worst effects of the energy which killed Unvak. No one died and the soldiers descended the ramp at speed. When it was his turn, Recker followed into another example of the universe's wonder.

Light from the nearby star was filtered by the *Gorgadar*'s energy shield and was even further muted by an intermingled fog of darkness which somehow coexisted with the sun's glare. Whenever Recker tried to focus on this darkness, it eluded him, remaining forever in his periphery.

Other business came first and Recker hurried towards the entrance hatch, using the gravity fields in his boots to keep him planted. The soldiers gathered nearby, leaving him room to approach.

"I'm sorry about Unvak," said Recker, crouching next to Shadar at the access panel.

"As am I, Captain Recker."

The grief in the Daklan's face was naked and it caught Recker unawares, though perhaps it shouldn't have done so.

"No one will be forgotten, Sergeant."

Recker touched the access panel and nothing happened. Prepared for that outcome, he ordered his suit computer to interface and then sent his command codes across the link. A slab of metal dropped soundlessly into the hull and steps emerged from the inner wall of the shaft.

"Just like the *Aeklu*," said Recker.

The need for progress spurred him on and he climbed to the platform below, where he located an airlift door. Without waiting, he summoned the car without being asked to enter any command codes. By the time the door opened, most of the soldiers were already on the platform with him.

The lift was in darkness and Recker turned on his helmet torch. "In," he ordered.

Nobody wanted to be left outside and the platoon squeezed into the car. Behind their visors, the expressions of the soldiers were uniformly severe – wide eyes and bared teeth.

"What's the plan, sir?" asked Private Raimi.

"This is the *Gorgadar* and we're going to steal it, Private."

"The Lavorix should have remembered to lock up, huh?"

The man's tone was light, but Recker wasn't fooled. Everyone was on edge, him included.

"What're we going to find when the lift door opens?" asked Private Gantry.

"Dead Lavorix," said Recker.

The lift stopped and the door opened into a dark corridor. Immediately, Recker noticed the background thrum of propulsion, different to anything he'd heard before. The air was a little above freezing and carried the same scents as the *Aeklu* – musty age, as well as something unpleasant and hard to identify.

A corpse lay outside, dressed in the near-black material of ultra-fine links worn by the Lavorix. Directing the beam of his torch around, Recker spotted other bodies. He stooped and, without sympathy, grabbed the helmet of the dead alien and turned it so he could see into its visor.

"Shit, look at that," said Corporal Montero.

The skin of the Lavorix had darkened from its usual pale green-white and had shrivelled tightly about the creature's skull, revealing its sunken cheekbones and narrow forehead. Sharp teeth had yellowed and the gums holding them had vanished completely.

"Come on," said Recker, rising and heading along the corridor. "I hope these bastards rot in hell."

The journey to the bridge was straightforward and Recker only took a single wrong turn when the interior layout of the *Gorgadar* varied from that of the *Aeklu*. Many Lavorix crowded the passages, all of them desiccated in the same way. Recker felt no sympathy for his enemy, though he couldn't revel in their deaths.

Located at the top of twenty steps, the bridge door was closed. Sergeant Vance wanted to take additional care, but Recker was in no mood for delays. He entered the command codes and the blast door opened onto the bridge.

"Just like the *Aeklu*'s," he said. "Except with the original hardware and the original crew still in place."

Recker ordered his own crew to find themselves a station so they could begin poking around.

"Sergeant Vance, I'd be grateful if you could remove these bodies. I don't care where you put them."

"Yes, sir," said Vance, motioning for the soldiers nearby to get started.

"We've been here before," Recker said to his crew. "Time to learn."

A Lavorix dressed like all the others faced the command console and Recker dragged it onto the floor. He felt like kicking the corpse and with an effort he refrained. Instead, he dropped into the seat, noticing that the covering – a material which might have once been leather – was cracked and split, like it had also been affected by whatever had killed the Lavorix.

The command console readily accepted Recker's codes and a prompt appeared on the central screen in Lavorix script. Recker's translation software had been updated using data from the *Vengeance*, allowing him to read the text.

Gorgadar>

After a few seconds of experimentation, he was able to give his other crew members sign-in access.

"It's been a long road to here, folks," he said. "And I don't know what lies ahead. One thing I'm sure of, is that I want this spaceship. We're going to find the *Ixidar* and we're going to destroy it."

"I'll check the battle network, sir," said Larson. "If we're lucky, we'll be able to track the enemy position." She went silent. "Oh crap."

Recker knew instinctively he was about to hear something terrible.

"The Ancidium is coming," she said.

"How?" asked Eastwood. "It's the Lavorix's home world, isn't it?"

"Apparently not, Lieutenant. Not if it's coming for us."

It felt to Recker as if everything had been building to this – that his every hard-fought victory had brought him to this moment. No despair came and no fear. Instead, he felt emptiness and that was worse than anything.

"The Lavorix started this and we're going to finish it," he said. "Whatever it takes."

As ever, the hardest person to fool was himself, but Recker knew he couldn't let the reality of this war grind him down. The *Gorgadar* was a tool and he was damn well going to figure out how to use it. When the Ancidium came, it would face the most powerful of its Laws.

Win or lose, Recker would fight.

––––––

Sign up to my mailing list here to be the first to find out about new releases, or follow me on Facebook @AnthonyJamesAuthor

OTHER SCIENCE FICTION BOOKS BY ANTHONY JAMES

Survival Wars (Seven Books) – Available in Ebook, Paperback and Audio.

1. Crimson Tempest
2. Bane of Worlds
3. Chains of Duty
4. Fires of Oblivion
5. Terminus Gate
6. Guns of the Valpian
7. Mission: Nemesis

Obsidiar Fleet (Six Books – set after the events in Survival Wars) – Available in Ebook and Paperback.

1. Negation Force
2. Inferno Sphere
3. God Ship
4. Earth's Fury

5. Suns of the Aranol
6. Mission: Eradicate

The Transcended (Seven Books – set after the events in Obsidiar Fleet) – Available in Ebook, Paperback and Audio

1. Augmented
2. Fleet Vanguard
3. Far Strike
4. Galaxy Bomb
5. Void Blade
6. Monolith
7. Mission: Destructor

Fire and Rust (Seven Books) – Available in Ebook, Paperback and Audio.

1. Iron Dogs
2. Alien Firestorm
3. Havoc Squad
4. Death Skies
5. Refuge 9
6. Nullifier
7. Scum of the Universe

Anomalies (Two Books) – Available in Ebook and Paperback.

1. Planet Wreckers
2. Assault Amplified